O9-CFU-392

PORTLAND, OR 97229

(503) 644-0043

WITHDRAWN

CEDAR MILL LIBRARY

Betsy and the Great World

CEDAR MILL COMM LIBRARY
12505 NW CORNELL RD.
PORTLAND OR 97229
(503) 644-0043
A HOLIDAY
CEDAR MILL LIBRARY

Books by Maude Hart Lovelace

Betsy-Tacy
Betsy-Tacy and Tib
Betsy and Tacy Go Over the Big Hill
Betsy and Tacy Go Downtown
Heaven to Betsy
Betsy in Spite of Herself
Betsy Was a Junior
Betsy and Joe
Emily of Deep Valley
Betsy and the Great World
Betsy's Wedding

Betsy and
the Great World

MAUD HART LOVELACE

Illustrated by Vera Neville

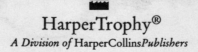

HarperTrophy®
A Division of HarperCollinsPublishers

Betsy and the Great World

Copyright 1952 by Maud Hart Lovelace

Copyright renewed 1980 by Merian L. Kirchner

All rights reserved. No part of this book may be used or
reproduced in any manner whatsoever without written permission
except in the case of brief quotations embodied in critical articles
and reviews. Printed in the United States of America.
For information address HarperCollins Children's Books,
a division of HarperCollins Publishers,
10 East 53rd Street, New York, NY 10022.

LC Number 52-8657

ISBN 0-06-440545-1 (pbk.)

First published by Thomas Y. Crowell Company in 1952

First Harper Trophy edition, 1996.

Harper Trophy® is a registered trademark
of HarperCollins Publishers Inc.

For ELIZABETH LESLIE

Contents

1. Traveling Alone 1
2. "Haply I May Remember" 14
3. "And Haply May Forget" 28
4. Enchanted Island......................................49
5. The Deluge..64
6. The Captain's Ball....................................80
7. The *Diner d'Adieu* 95
8. Travel Is Broadening.................................107
9. Miss Surprise's Surprise.............................123
10. Betsy Makes a Friend 139
11. Betsy Takes a Bath..................................155
12. Three's Not a Crowd 172
13. Dark Fairy Tale.....................................188
14. A Very Special Doll.................................202
15. A Short Stay in Heaven..............................217
16. Betsy Curls Her Hair...............................232
17. Forgetting Again 244
18. The Second Moon in Venice 258
19. Betsy Writes a Letter..............................274
20. The Roll of Drums 292
21. The Agony Column 309

1
TRAVELING ALONE

Down to Gehenna or up to the Throne,
He travels the fastest who travels alone.

Betsy was chanting it under her breath to give herself courage as, laden with camera, handbag, umbrella, and *Complete Pocket Guide to Europe*, she started up the gangplank to the deck of the *S.S. Columbic.*

Behind her was a barnlike structure, crowded with carriages, automobiles, baggage carts, and milling distracted passengers. Before her loomed the great bulk of the liner. Thirteen thousand tons of it, according to the advertisements over which she had pored—far, far back in Minnesota. It had layers of decks, a smokestack in the center, and tall masts flying flags. She could smell the waters of Boston Harbor—cold, salty, fishy—into which she would presently be sailing.

" 'Down to Gehenna or up to the Throne . . .' " Her teeth were almost chattering. Not from cold, for she wore furs over her long tight coat and carried a muff. Fur trimmed, too, was her hat. She shivered because she was shaky inside, fearful and bewildered.

" 'He travels the fastest who travels alone . . .' " She wasn't alone, exactly. A porter had seized her suitcases, and he strode beside her shoulder. But he was a stranger, like the throngs of people all around her. And they all seemed to be in groups—sociable, laughing, chattering groups.

Of course, Betsy, too, would be with someone else shortly. Her father and mother had seen to that. A bachelor professor and his unmarried sister, friends of Betsy's father's brother, had agreed to keep an eye on her during the voyage. But at her first meeting with them, this morning at the Parker House, she had managed to convey the impression that their chaperonage was extremely nominal. And when they had suggested that she join them for some travel later, she had been purposefully vague. It wasn't her idea to go through Europe with the Wilsons, kind as they were, and homesick as she already was.

"Tacy ought to be here," she thought forlornly.

She and Tacy had planned trips through all the long years of their friendship. They had planned to go around the world together, to see the Taj Mahal by moonlight, to go to the top of the Himalayas and up the Amazon, and above all to live in Paris . . . with ladies' maids.

Celeste and Hortense, they had christened their maids . . . imaginary ones, of course.

"Thank goodness I have Celeste, at least," Betsy muttered. For Tacy had faithlessly married. Julia was married too. Betsy had been her older sister's maid of honor in December.

It was January now, 1914.

"Julia settling down!" Betsy scoffed.

Julia wasn't, of course, settling down. A singer, she had married a flutist, and they planned to pursue their careers together. But Betsy was in no mood to be fair. The confusion on deck was more subtly terrifying even than the tumult below. The well-dressed men, the women with corsage bouquets blooming on their shoulders, seemed so assured, so gaily sufficient to themselves and one another, so completely indifferent to the great adventure of one Betsy Ray, aged twenty-one, from Minneapolis, Minnesota.

The porter turned her over to a uniformed steward.

She was taken below decks, along labyrinthine corridors, carpeted, smelling of the sea, to her stateroom, Number 52.

Number 52! They had selected it back in Minneapolis. She remembered the chart on the travel agent's desk and her family rejoicing because this stateroom had a porthole giving on the ocean.

There it was, the porthole! And the room was a small white affair with a washstand and two bunks, one above the other. Miss Wilson would have the lower one. Betsy's steamer trunk had already been placed in a corner. The steward put her bags on it, and she tipped him, trying to act casual.

Back on deck, she secured a steamer chair—Julia had told her that was the first thing to do. But what about her ticket? Shouldn't she give that to someone? She found the office of the purser.

He was very busy, besieged from all sides, but when she said with anxious dignity, "I'm Miss Elizabeth Ray," he turned quickly.

"And it's Miss Betsy Ray herself," he remarked surprisingly.

He spoke with an Irish inflection and he looked the Irishman, too . . . smooth black hair with a touch of gray at the temples, blue eyes with a light in them, a dimple in his chin.

Betsy felt her color rising. How maddening to blush before his gay assurance!

"I beg your pardon?" she said and remembered to sink into her debutante slouch.

This fashionable pose became her, for she was very slender. (Some girls had to wear special corsets to get the debutante slouch.) She was glad her fur boa was tossed lightly over her shoulder.

Mr. O'Farrell—that was the name above his window—continued to look at her.

"Faith, and I'm inter-r-r-ested to meet you!" He rolled his *r*'s in a fascinating way. "Letters to Miss Betsy Ray take up half that mountain of mail in the library yonder."

"Really?" Betsy forgot her pose. Her smile was a burst of sunshine.

A small space between her teeth in front gave her a look of candor. She had a friendly merry face with brown hair pushed over her cheeks in the soft disarray affected that season, and hazel eyes that glowed now into Mr. O'Farrell's.

Letters from home! Letters from that paradise lost, lying three long days behind her!

"Oh, how wonderful!" she cried.

"Telegrams, too," said Mr. O'Farrell teasingly. "And boxes! I believe there are even some blossoms. Are you traveling alone?"

"Yes . . . practically."

"Well, I'm going to give you a special place at table so you won't get lonely. You pick it up after we sail."

"But what about my ticket?"

"The steward will collect it in your cabin," he said.

Betsy pushed her way eagerly through crowded corridors to the paneled library, but the mail was not yet sorted.

"The flowers are though, Mum," a steward said. All the stewards sounded as English as Mr. O'Farrell did Irish. He looked over a line of green boxes and selected one for her.

Betsy opened it with joyful fingers. Bob Barhydt's card lay on top. Inside was a corsage bouquet of pink roses and lilies of the valley.

"Oh, how sweet of Bob!" she cried.

She pinned on the flowers at the nearest mirror, lifted her chin, and went out on deck less afraid of the surging indifferent people.

"That was really sweet of Bob," she thought again, and felt guilty because he and the University of Minnesota campus seemed suddenly so remote.

It was a bleak afternoon. The sky was overcast and the air had a damp bite. She found the Wilsons engaged with the deck steward.

Dr. Wilson was a thin erect little man with white mustaches and a pointed white beard. His complexion was as pretty as Betsy's. That came, perhaps, from his theories on diet which he had explained to her at breakfast. He scorned coffee and meat. Carrots, lettuce, apples, and whole-grain breads were his delight.

His sister, like himself, was white-haired, slender, and erect, but she liked a slice of pound cake now and then, she had admitted to Betsy with a twinkle.

Having greeted them, Betsy went to the rail and looked down on the chaos below.

Now long lines of Italians were filing into the steerage. Some were wrapped in red blankets. They carried tin dishes and piles of canned goods. Little dark-eyed children danced along in front, or crowded close to their parents, frightened and crying. Betsy wondered why they were going back to Italy.

A gong clanged commandingly.

"That means good-bye," said a woman in a large noisy group at Betsy's left. And suddenly all around her people were kissing and embracing. A line began to push down the gangplank.

Soon the windows of the building below were full of faces . . . people crying and laughing, waving handkerchieves and blowing kisses. The passengers leaning over the rail were likewise crying and laughing, waving handkerchieves and blowing kisses. The air was full of ejaculations. "Oh, *there* he is! Oh, *there* she is!"

"Don't forget you're married!" called the man who had left the group beside her.

Betsy noticed a sobbing Italian woman, gazing at the steerage passengers who were bound for her native land. At times she would forget to cry. She would catch her breath, like a child distracted by a toy; then she would

7

remember, and start to sob again.

Somewhere, someone was strumming a guitar. *"O sole mio . . ."* A lump swelled in Betsy's throat.

"I'd better get out of here," she thought.

Suddenly she couldn't imagine why she had wanted to go traveling. Her thoughts reached back yearningly to her family. How could she have left them!

Her darling father who worked so hard for them all, and was always so cheerful about it! Her pretty red-haired mother who had shopped so tirelessly buying these new clothes! Margaret, now sixteen, so sweet, and beginning to have beaux. And Julia, such a wonderful big sister, even though married!

Betsy sniffed.

She could see them all, and the gray stucco cottage out in Minneapolis with snow clinging to the bare vines and lying on the evergreens around the glassed-in porch. Inside, there would be a fire in the fireplace. They always had Sunday night lunch around that fire. Her father made the sandwiches.

Tears flooded Betsy's eyes.

Someone beside her called to someone else. "Did you know we had an author on board?"

An author? Betsy dashed away her tears. For a wild moment she thought they meant her, for she planned to be an author. That was one reason she was going abroad.

"Yes," came the answer, shrilling above her head.

"Some reporters were talking to her down in the library. They're taking pictures now, over there by the gangplank."

Betsy turned eagerly to look.

She saw a small stout woman with bright auburn hair under a purple veil and hat. Her purple coat was laden with flowers. Flashbulbs popped.

"Maybe they'll be doing that for me someday," thought Betsy.

Then the photographers shouldered their cameras and ran down the gangplank with reporters following—the last ones to leave the ship.

Betsy looked over the railing quickly. There was something familiar about one of the reporters. There was a swing to his shoulders . . . He had taken off his hat, and she saw that his hair was blond. Before she realized what she was doing Betsy leaned still farther and called out frantically, "Joe!"

But her voice was lost in the hubbub, for now the gangplanks were being pulled up and the engines began to tug and strain. Deep-throated horns were blowing. Screams and shouts of farewell rose in a frenzied babel.

Betsy's eyes searched the windows of the building below. And sure enough a blond head appeared. She recognized the pompadour haircut. But this young man had a mustache—a close-cropped blond mustache! Nevertheless he was, he was. Joe Willard!

He was scanning the rail, frowning. He didn't see

her. At least, she didn't think he did, and she didn't call again. She was glad he hadn't heard. He would never forgive her—probably he was never going to anyway—but he certainly never would if he knew she had come through Boston without letting him know.

Now he was frowning down at a paper of some kind.

The passenger list? Betsy had one in her pocket; she had seen her own name. He looked up sharply.

But the *S.S. Columbic* was moving. Slowly, inexorably, the horn still blowing, it edged out of the pier. A line of churned white foam appeared, and the space of cold green water widened. The barnlike building faded, and the shoreline came into view.

Betsy couldn't see it, for her tears were back again.

It wasn't surprising, she thought, as the steamer picked its way past a fringe of ships at anchor, and along a busy channel, it wasn't at all surprising that Joe was at the ship. She knew he worked part-time on the *Boston Transcript.*

"I wish I hadn't seen him," she thought. It would be harder to forget him now, and that was another reason she was going abroad . . . to forget Joe Willard. She wiped her eyes with grim determination.

" 'Haply I may remember and haply may forget,' " she quoted flippantly.

The woman standing next to her looked around, startled.

Then Betsy turned her back on the Hub of the Universe, which was rising along the horizon. She'd write a letter or two to go back with the pilot, she decided abruptly.

In the library she found a desk and scribbled a note to her family. She tried to sound ecstatic, and didn't mention Joe, although she longed to share the news of his mustache. She thanked Bob Barhydt for the flowers. Returning to her stateroom, she replaced her hat with a scarf, got out her steamer rug, and went above, hoping that good-byes were over. But the pilot was just leaving, waving, followed by cheers. His boat bobbed off into gathering fog.

The *Columbic* now had left all traffic far behind. They were in the open ocean. Betsy leaned against the rail and the wind tore at her unkindly. Looking out at the leaden waves, the joyless, circling gulls, she felt unutterably lonely. Seeing Joe had made her hurt inside. She didn't even want to read her mail.

The water grew rougher. Her body could feel the new movement, the climb up, the drop down. A poem she had learned one time began to toll in her head:

Up and down! Up and down!
From the base of the wave, to the billow's crown . . .

But suddenly there was too much up and down. Walking unsteadily, she found her deck chair and the steward tucked her in. He offered her tea, but she didn't want tea. Burrowing miserably into her rug, she watched the vessel rise and fall.

People were walking around the deck with incomprehensible zest. Presently she saw Dr. Wilson, walking briskly, smiling. He recognized her and paused.

"Would you care to walk, Miss Betsy?"

She shook her head. "I don't feel so good."

"Seasickness," he said, "can be controlled by diet." But he looked sympathetic. "My sister hasn't learned how either, and she believes in going to bed. She always goes to her bunk and stays there until she's accustomed to the motion."

"I think that's what I'll do," Betsy replied, struggling to her feet. He helped her to the passageway.

Miss Wilson was in bed and greeted her faintly. Betsy undressed too, although, above decks, the bugle was blowing merrily for dinner. Pinned to her innermost garments was a chamois bag containing money, some extra American Express checks, and a check signed in blank by her father—for emergencies. Betsy transferred this treasure to the bosom of her flannel nightgown. Then, without even stopping to wind her hair on curlers, she climbed to the upper bunk, pulled up the blankets, and lay flat.

She could see a patch of sea and sky through the porthole, but down here, too, it appeared and disappeared in menacing rhythm. She closed her eyes.

After a time the stewardess came in. She was a dainty little Englishwoman with an encouraging manner. She asked Miss Wilson and Betsy whether they wanted dinner. They both declined.

"I'd like to see my mail though," Betsy said feebly. Her letters, telegrams, and boxes had been sent to the cabin and made a tantalizing pile, far below on her trunk.

The stewardess handed them up, and although Betsy didn't feel able to read them, it was comforting to have them near. She found a fat letter from home. It would be a round robin—the Ray family was always writing round robins—and put it under her cheek.

An orchestra was playing now. For dinner, probably. It had said in the folder that there was music for dinner. People dressed up for it and it had sounded such fun.

> *It's a long way to Tipperary,*
> *It's a long way to go . . .*

Betsy had danced to that tune and she had always liked it, but it sounded dreary now. Tears dripped into the round robin.

She wasn't sick, exactly . . . not like Miss Wilson was. Miss Wilson occasionally jumped out of bed and was very sick indeed. But Betsy felt frightened and lonesome and forlorn.

She wondered just what she was doing here. Why should she be in the bowels of a ship ploughing through sullen, turbulent waters, going to a foreign continent alone? Why? Why?

She turned her thoughts backward and tried to pull all the reasons together.

2
"HAPLY I MAY REMEMBER"

She hadn't, Betsy confided to her pillow, done what she wanted to in college.

She had gotten off to a bad start because her freshman year was interrupted by appendicitis, and afterwards she had gone to California for a long convalescence in her grandmother's home. She had loved California. It seemed unbelievable to find rioting flowers and oranges on shiny green trees and warm fragrant air in the middle of winter. She had loved the peace of her grandmother's home. An actor uncle who grew grapes near San Diego had given her a typewriter, and she had sold her first story.

"I found myself out there," Betsy had declared more than once.

Yes, but back at the University she had lost herself again. Was life always like that? she wondered. A game of hide and seek in which you only occasionally found the person you wanted to be?

It had been discouraging, next fall, to be a year behind her old high school class. Everyone else was a sophomore while she was still a freshman. And it had seemed unjust to find Advanced Botany and Higher Algebra still lying in wait. Betsy loved English and French but she had always hated mathematics and science. Feeling herself almost a professional writer now (because she sometimes sold a story for ten or twelve dollars), she resented these unpleasant subjects even more.

Plunging zealously into activities, she became Woman's Editor of the college paper. (A tall well-dressed young man named Bob Barhydt was also on the staff.) She wrote stories which were accepted by the college magazine. One was better than the others. It was really good and Betsy didn't quite know why, for it was just a simple story laid in her Uncle Keith's vineyard. But the famous professor, Dr. Maria Sanford, had praised it. She had written Betsy a letter about it. This success made science and mathematics all the more arduous, and Betsy's grades had slipped.

Joe Willard, on the other hand, to whom she was almost—but not quite—engaged, had done very well at the U, although he was a part-time copy reader on the *Minneapolis Tribune*. Because of his outstanding work he was offered a scholarship to Harvard and went east at the beginning of his junior year.

Betsy was happy for him, and very proud, and he planned to come back the following summer, which made parting easier. Yet his going had hurt her, too. After he left she gave up all scholastic strivings. Her friends were juniors; she was only a humble sophomore.

"I'll be a success socially, at least," she decided flippantly and joined a sorority although she had never liked them.

It wasn't a good thing to do. She soon grew tired of pretending that her deepest interests were social. She made a few close friends in the group, but not many, and the exclusive Greek letter club separated her from congenial girls on the *Daily* and the *Mag*.

But after she became a sorority girl Bob Barhydt started to rush her. He was very much the fraternity man. (Joe had never joined a fraternity. He had no time or money or inclination for them.) Because of Bob, Betsy's sophomore year went in a gay whirl of parties.

She wasn't happy, though, in spite of her social success, her achievements on the *Daily* and the *Mag*, and her name on committees and the membership lists of many organizations. Betsy felt that she had failed herself. She hadn't meant to be sucked into the social current. She hadn't meant to flirt with Bob, or to settle down to any one man while Joe was away. She had meant to get an education. And she wasn't doing it.

It wasn't, she knew, the fault of the University. People all around her were getting excellent educations there. It wasn't even the fault of the sorority. Many of the outstanding girls on the campus belonged to these groups.

Betsy admitted to the night and the deep Atlantic that the fault had lain strictly with herself.

As spring came on she became more and more frivolous. The gossip column in the *Daily* was full of jokes about her and Bob. (A corner of the Oak Tree, the campus ice cream parlor, was called the B and B.) The Year Book showed kodak pictures of them riverbanking—the University phrase for strolling along the Mississippi.

Joe subscribed to the *Minnesota Daily* and he bought a copy of the Year Book. Suddenly his letters became as cold as ice.

Betsy was looking forward longingly to his promised visit. Her dissatisfaction with herself, her wasted year, the flirtation with Bob, couldn't be explained in letters. If she and Joe could talk, she could make him understand. But he didn't come back. He wrote that he had a good summer job on the *Boston Transcript*. He mentioned his roommate's pretty sister. Their letters grew farther and farther apart.

"I believe I like Bob better anyway," Betsy told Tacy, who knew that wasn't true. For something in Betsy had always reached out to Joe Willard—blond and stalwart with a proud swing in his shoulders, a deep contagious laugh, and a look of clear goodness in his eyes.

He was an orphan. He had earned his own way since his early teens, gallantly ignoring shabby clothes and lack of money. He had been her ideal since her freshman year in high school. And Betsy was tenacious in her affections.

Tacy, too, was tenacious in her affections, and when she completed her course in public school music that June, she had married Harry Kerr.

He was an aggressive young salesman whom she had met at the Rays' four years before. They had planned a festive wedding with her sister Katie as maid of honor and Betsy and Tib as bridesmaids. But early that spring Tacy's father died. Everyone agreed Tacy's marriage should not be postponed, but it was celebrated quietly with only Katie and Harry's brother present.

Before starting off for Niagara Falls on their honeymoon, Tacy and her husband had come for a few days to the Ray house. The Rays moved out for them. Mr. Ray took Mrs. Ray on a business trip. Betsy and Margaret moved over to Betsy's sorority house.

They couldn't have helped Tacy more. The Ray

house for many years had been a second home to her; and in Minneapolis as in Deep Valley it was always the same—a fire in the grate in winter, flowers in summer, the smell of good cooking in Anna's cheerful kitchen, and above all an atmosphere of happiness, of harmony, of love.

That atmosphere and her husband's tenderness helped to assuage Tacy's grief. It was a help, too, after she and Harry moved into their Minneapolis apartment, to have Betsy near. And Tacy's need of her helped Betsy.

That summer, Betsy made her bedroom into an office. She was still going on dates with Bob. They went dancing on the Radisson Roof, and canoeing on the Minneapolis lakes. They went to band concerts and the movies, and he came to Sunday night supper. But Betsy's really happy hours were spent at her desk.

She worked faithfully every morning on short stories and at last settled down to one she liked, trying to make it as good as the one Dr. Sanford had praised. Meanwhile, as she had done since she was in high school, she kept all her old stories on the go. Neatly typed, with return postage enclosed, they went from magazine to magazine.

Betsy had long ago worked out a system. When she finished a story she made a list of magazines to which she thought it might sell. As soon as it came back from one it was sent to the next. Many of her manuscripts had made twenty and thirty trips, and the record of their journeyings was kept in a small notebook which was now in Margaret's keeping. She had promised to send out the stories while Betsy was abroad.

September brought the beginning of the senior year for Joe. Betsy would be a disconsolate junior. More than once the pages of her story . . . underlined, crossed out, written in the margins . . . were damp with tears shed, not at the woes of her heroine, but at the prospect of beginning so miserable a year.

At last, in a desperate moment, she went to her father. She broached the idea that perhaps—for a girl who wished to be a writer—two years of college were enough.

He listened thoughtfully, sitting in his armchair with his legs crossed and his thumbs hooked in his vest. He looked at her with his kind, wise hazel eyes.

"I don't think so, Betsy," he said. "I have an idea that the more education a writer has, the better. It's a mistake, too, in this life, to start things and not finish them."

Betsy bent her head dejectedly. She had been sure that was what he would say.

Mr. Ray took a cigar out of his pocket. He clipped off the end and lighted it and began to puff slowly.

"Of course," he went on, "we all make mistakes. If you've made a mistake in getting so little out of college, why, you have . . . that's all. And it would be a pretty poor world if we couldn't sweep up our mistakes, now and then, and go ahead.

"You might make yourself finish college. But you

certainly wouldn't have much heart in it. And it seems too bad to throw away two years of your life just as a matter of discipline."

Betsy looked up quickly. This was encouraging. And the aromatic smell of his cigar, beginning to drift through the room, had something comforting about it. He always smoked when he was advising his children.

"Don't think," Mr. Ray continued, "that Mamma and I haven't seen which way the wind was blowing. You haven't been happy, Betsy, and we've known it."

Betsy didn't speak.

"You're going to be a writer," he proceeded thoughtfully. "No doubt about that! You've been writing all your life. And you've worked harder this summer at that story you're writing than you've worked for all your professors put together. What's the name of it, anyway?"

" 'Emma Middleton Cuts Cross Country,' " Betsy replied. "It's about a little dressmaker, like the one who made my Junior Ball dress. She gets disgusted with everything and walks out and makes a new start."

"Sounds good," said Mr. Ray, nodding sagely, although he never read stories, except Betsy's. "You certainly write like a whiz. Do you remember the letter Dr. Sanford wrote you about your story in the college magazine?"

Betsy nodded, moist-eyed.

"I was very proud of that letter," Mr. Ray said, which made her tears spill over for it seemed to her that she had given him very little reason to be proud of her lately. He put down his cigar.

"You're going to be a writer," he repeated, "and you need more education. That's plain. But college isn't the only place to get an education. I have a 'snoggestion.' " That was what Mr. Ray always called a particularly good suggestion. "I've sounded Mamma out and she approves. How would you like a year abroad?"

"But, Papa!" Betsy had thrown her arms around him, frankly crying now. "What a glo-glo-glorious snoggestion! I've always planned to go. But I never thought of you sending me. I thought I'd earn the money for myself someday."

"Oh, I don't think it would cost so much more than a year at the U!" said Mr. Ray. "You'd have to go in a modest way, of course. But Julia had two trips abroad. You're entitled to one, too. Maybe when Margaret goes, Mamma and I will go along."

"Would I . . . would I go to school over there?"

"You don't seem to be getting what you need out of a school. But judging by our experience with Julia, you learn a lot just from traveling in Europe . . . seeing the art galleries, learning the languages, and all that stuff. You could go on a guided tour, like Julia did."

"No, Papa!" Betsy knelt beside him, her hands on his knee. "Guided tours are all right for some people, but not for a writer. I ought to stay in just two or three places. Really live in them, learn them. Then if I want to mention

London, for example, in a story, I would know the names of the streets and how they run and the buildings and the atmosphere of the city. I could move a character around in London just as though it were Minneapolis. I don't want to hurry from place to place with a party the way Julia did."

Her father looked perplexed.

"But it doesn't seem safe, Betsy. You're only twenty-one. You know how much confidence Mamma and I have in you, but we wouldn't want you living in those big foreign cities all alone."

"Maybe we could pick out cities where I know someone . . . or you do, or Julia."

"Maybe. I'll talk it over with your mother."

So Betsy dashed off to Tacy's apartment and they talked, talked about the wonderful trip.

"I'm just going to travel around like Paragot," Betsy said, referring to a character in William J. Locke's novel, *The Beloved Vagabond*, a favorite with both of them.

She wrote Tib, still in college in Milwaukee. And Carney, who was now Mrs. Sam Hutchinson and lived at Murmuring Lake. She took a yellow streetcar over the Mississippi to the University and told her sorority sisters. It sounded so glamorous, "studying abroad."

She went downtown and collected travel folders. She bought a paper-bound *Italian Self-Taught* and dug out her German grammar. She had studied German for a year in high school. She was thankful for her college French.

"French is really all I need. French is the universal language," she told Tacy grandly.

"Of course, you'll see Joe while you're in the East," Tacy said. Red-haired Tacy was so happy in her own marriage that she was anxious for Betsy to get married, too.

Betsy shook her head. "Joe and I don't even correspond anymore."

As Tacy was silent Betsy burst out indignantly, "You know, Tacy, I don't usually quarrel with people. You and I have been friends since my fifth birthday party. I'm still friends with the high-school gang and the people I knew in college. Joe is just too touchy."

"You don't quarrel when you're together," Tacy answered. "He's so perfect for you, Betsy." She looked at Betsy with pleading tender eyes. "Maybe you'll just let him know about the trip."

But Betsy was stubborn. She didn't write her great news to Joe. And presently her attention was distracted by greater news. Julia, the coquette, had fallen in love, and this time, she wrote, it was for keeps!

She had met Paige in New York, where she was singing in the opera. Like Julia, he came from the Middle West, from Indiana, where he had attended the University before studying the flute in the East. Now he played with one of the orchestras there. He was, Betsy discovered later, a very attractive young man, tall, light haired, and ethereal looking.

24

Julia wanted to be married at Christmas time. Bettina must be maid of honor; Margaret must string ribbons.

"That's all I care about. You plan the rest of it," Julia wrote her mother.

And because of all this excitement Betsy didn't miss college at all. At Thanksgiving Julia came briefly to introduce her fiancé, and at Christmas they were married.

It wasn't a large wedding, but it was candle lit and flower scented. Margaret, straight and slender, her dark hair in coronet braids, carried ribbons down the aisle of the Episcopal Church. Betsy, wearing green chiffon over pink, was maid of honor.

Julia, in trailing bridal white, looked gravely lovely as she looked when she sang. An Indiana friend of Paige's came to be best man, and afterward there was a merry supper at the Ray house.

But through it all Betsy had felt an aching loneliness. What joy was there in a beautiful green dress, long and draped to the front, and an armful of pink roses, if Joe wasn't there to see?

Julia had insisted upon sending Joe an invitation. "He's my friend as well as yours, Betsy."

"All right," Betsy had conceded grudgingly, and for a few days she had felt a fluttering in her heart. If Joe was looking for a chance to make up, here it was! Maybe he would come!

But he didn't. He sent a silver serving spoon with a rhyme he had composed himself.

"Could Betsy do as well as this?" he scrawled across the bottom.

"Maybe he thinks I'll use that as an excuse for writing him. Well, I won't!" Betsy said.

While Mrs. Ray and Betsy were busy with the wedding, Mr. Ray had occupied himself with Betsy's trip. He had written his younger brother, a professor at the University of Chicago. Perhaps Steve knew some Europe-bound traveler who wouldn't mind keeping an eye on Betsy?

Steve did know just the person. Dr. Wilson and his sister, both on sabbatical leave, were sailing in January on the *S.S. Columbic* from Boston.

Boston! Betsy wouldn't have chosen that port. It was too near Harvard University. But she was far too proud to raise this objection. And the plan dovetailed beautifully with another which had already been worked out.

Julia had a friend studying singing in Munich. Miss Surprise wouldn't mind, she wrote, helping Betsy get settled there. Betsy had never thought of going to Munich. But it would do as a starting point. So her tickets were bought for the *S.S. Columbic*, which would take her to Genoa, where she could board a train for Munich.

A crowd of friends saw her off at the Minneapolis station one January night. The green baize curtains of her berth drawn tightly, she had looked out at a dark, ghostly world rushing past. She had changed trains at Chicago, sending back a shower of excited postcards, and for two days had journeyed eastward, leaving the lakes and the flat familiar Middle West behind, climbing snowy mountains and pausing at towns full of staid green-shuttered houses.

In Boston, she had made a patriotic pilgrimage . . . Faneuil Hall, the Cradle of Liberty, the State House, and the Old South Church.

"If I lived in Boston I'd wear red, white, and blue costumes and eagle headdresses," she wrote her family.

She went through the Public Library and inspected the Art Museum. She marveled at the narrow twisting streets and walked elatedly across The Common. But she didn't go out to Harvard. She did look up the telephone number of Joe's college house and stood for a long time with her hand on the receiver. But she took her hand down at last, and walked away.

Although lonely, the day had been exciting. It was fun to sleep in a hotel, and she had met the Wilsons at breakfast. Everything had gone according to plan.

It had seemed like a wonderful plan. But it didn't now, as she lay lonesomely in the upper berth of stateroom 52 listening to the dinner music being played above.

3
"AND HAPLY MAY FORGET"

Betsy wasn't seasick any more. Observing with sympathy and alarm the depths of Miss Wilson's anguish, she suspected next morning that her own miseries had sprung more from homesickness than from *mal de mer*.

Although Miss Wilson refused even coffee with a groan, Betsy ate breakfast in her bunk, charmed with the discovery that there was no salt in the butter and that hot milk was offered instead of cream. How continental! She lay down with the snowy blankets pulled up to her chin and her head on two fat pillows and reflected with astonishment on last night's despair. Travel was delightful. How could she ever have thought otherwise?

Later, she began on her steamer letters. Bob had sent one for each day of the voyage. So had Tacy. Tib, Carney, Cab, and Effie, her favorite sorority sister, had marked their letters "to be read when homesick" or "to be read when seasick" or "to be read when you need advice." Betsy didn't open many.

But she did open Tib's. (Tib Muller, next to Tacy, was her oldest friend.) And the letter was hilarious. She and Tacy had teased Betsy about picking up an American millionaire abroad, and Tib enclosed a sketch of Betsy strolling on deck in the moonlight with a man who was obviously a millionaire. He was dressed in a golfing suit, used a cigarette holder, and wore the dollar sign like a flower in his buttonhole.

Julia and Paige had sent a box with a small gift for each day. The first one was a leather-bound book titled in gold lettering, "My Trip Abroad." From other friends and relatives came a fountain pen, a lacy handkerchief, a collar and cuff set, a traveling clock, books. It was like Christmas morning in Betsy's upper bunk.

Presently the bath steward rapped. "Your bath is ready, Mum." And Betsy descended softly past the stricken Miss Wilson. She put on her cherry-red bathrobe, boudoir cap, and slippers, collected toothbrush, soap, and towels, and tiptoed down the swaying corridor.

The salt bath was exhilarating, and after she was dressed she regretted that she had not put her hair up on curlers last night. To offset its lamentable straightness, she tried to tie her scarf artfully.

"I wish Julia . . . or Tib . . . was here," she thought. They were good at coquetries like scarves. She squinted critically into a hand mirror. "Oh, well," she said, "Celeste does her best."

Miss Wilson was still sleeping. Donning coat and furs, Betsy picked up a pencil and one of the small notebooks she always liked to carry to catch random thoughts "that might work into a story." Her letters home were to be her diary.

But when she was settled in her steamer chair, wrapped in the rug, her head back and her feet up, she had no wish to write or read or even think. The waves rose and fell and broke into foam as far as her eye could see and she gazed in dreamy fascination.

She roused when two large ladies, rigidly corseted beneath their flopping coats and with elaborately waved coiffures under hats tied down by veils, settled into the chairs at her left. Two younger women helped them and ran errands patiently. At first Betsy thought these were merely devoted friends. Then she realized that one was called Taylor and the other Rosa (in kind but patronizing tones), and it dawned on her that they were ladies' maids.

Ladies' maids! She was always putting them in stories. What luck to see some in the flesh!

"I must write to Tacy," she thought gleefully. "I'll tell her that Celeste finds them most congenial."

She got out the passenger list and, sure enough, there they were! "Mrs. Sims and Maid. Mrs. Cheney and Maid." But it was too bad, Betsy thought, to say just "Maid" as though these pleasant women had no names! She resolved to study them a bit.

"And I want to get acquainted with that authoress. Maybe she can give me some hints . . ."

But Betsy caught herself short. The authoress might, she just might, comment on Joe. And he was already too painfully clear in Betsy's memory. She didn't want him brought further to life by a vivid phrase or anecdote.

She stretched back in her chair and watched the promenaders. There weren't many, for the water was increasingly rough. Dr. Wilson was out, and Betsy noticed a pretty girl making the rounds. Her clothes were sensible and dowdy and her heels flat but she had a handsome aquiline nose and long fair hair blowing like a veil behind. When she came to rest at last it was in a deck chair but one removed from Betsy's. Betsy smiled but she didn't respond.

Mrs. Sims and Mrs. Cheney, however, were extremely

31

affable. Betsy chatted with them over the mid-morning bouillon. They were sisters, Bostonians, and well accustomed to travel.

They went to the dining saloon for their lunch. (Saloon was what they called it, which seemed surprising to Betsy. A saloon, she had always thought, was a disreputable place where whisky was sold.) Betsy let the steward give her a tray on deck and she ate with appetite in the gray windy cold, watching the unremitting waves.

The afternoon went like the morning. No reading, no writing, just lazily watching the water. Betsy bestirred herself only to visit Miss Wilson, who waved her away with feeble moans.

At four o'clock the steward brought tea with fascinating little scones and cakes.

"And they do this every day! What bliss!" Betsy cried to Mrs. Sims and Mrs. Cheney, who smiled indulgently. "I love eating out of doors."

Over their trays she told them about the picnics she and Tacy had had since they were five. She told them about the Ray family picnics. Betsy was always a talker, but her loquacity today was partly the fault of her companions. They sustained it with questions—politely indirect, at first; then amused; then frankly startled. Was she going abroad . . . alone?

"Practically," Betsy answered as she had answered Mr. O'Farrell. "I want to be a writer, and my father thinks I ought to see the world. A writer has to *live*, you know," she explained, feeling dashing. She glanced toward the second chair at her right, but the pretty girl was engrossed in a magazine.

"*Comme elle est charmante!*" said Mrs. Sims.

"*Et excessivement naïve,*" replied her sister.

Betsy was annoyed to be thought naive but delighted to be found charming. She wondered whether honor compelled her to say that she understood French and decided that it didn't.

Returning from one of her fruitless calls on Miss Wilson, Betsy found it hard to keep her footing. Luckily she encountered Mr. O'Farrell, who removed his stiff cap, guided her safely back to her chair, folded her into her rug with solicitous care. When she thanked him he said, "It's a pleasur-r-re to me!" and smiled into her eyes.

"He's a charmer!" Betsy thought. Looking after the trim erect figure in nautical blue, she decided to go down for a nap and put her hair in curlers.

"Do we dress for dinner, Mrs. Sims?"

"Not formally, except for the Captain's Ball and the *Diner d'Adieu.* A dark silk will do."

Betsy was pleased that she had a dark silk. It was maroon, piped with old gold and trimmed with gold buttons. The skirt was long and fashionably tight. The sleeves, too, were long and tight with frills at the wrists. Betsy liked the frills for she knew her hands were pretty.

She knew all her good points—or thought she did. (She never included her smile, unaware that it was quick and very bright.) She valued highly her slender figure, pink and white skin, and red lips.

She was even more conscious of her defects—straight hair, irregular features, the space between her teeth in front. But she did not brood upon them as she had in her teens.

Like most girls she had worked out a technique for fascination. With Betsy it was thoroughly curled hair, perfume, bracelets, the color green, immaculate daintiness, and a languid enigmatic pose. This last was less successful than she realized. People were likely to think of her as full of fun, friendly, and responsive. And her friends knew that she was doggedly persistent—anything but languid.

Betsy was strong in her faith, however. Out in the corridor, after a cheerful good-bye to Miss Wilson, she paused to assume the debutante slouch. Then she sauntered, with the swaying gait required by a hobble skirt, up to the dining saloon.

"The Hungarian Rhapsody" came out to greet her. Cheeks flaming, she stood in the doorway and a steward beckoned to her. She found out then where Mr. O'Farrell had placed her. It was at his right.

"I thought since you were all, all alone, I'd have you where I could look after you," he said.

He looked very worldly in his dress uniform, with its debonair short jacket. Betsy wondered how old he was. Pretty old. Thirty-five or so.

"But I like older men. I wouldn't mind marrying an older man," she thought, wishing Joe could know what she was thinking. He and his mustache!

Dr. Wilson was at the same table, asking for raw carrots, and an English lady, and a pallid young Bostonian named Mr. Glenn. Betsy was confused by all the strange accents. The missing *r*'s and the long soft *a*'s. Even Dr. Wilson was a New Englander, although he taught in Chicago.

No one seemed to know much about the Middle West. The English lady had never even heard of Minneapolis. Mr. Glenn asked what state it was in, and Mr. O'Farrell questioned her about the Indians out there. But he, of course, was joking. He seemed to know everything.

"He's the most cosmopolitan person I ever met in my life," Betsy thought.

Speaking rapidly, his Irish brogue becoming more apparent as he warmed to the subject, he steered the conversation with easy skill so that everyone entered in.

"Maybe some night you'll tell us about those Indians," he teased, lighting a cigarette. Having secured the ladies' permission to smoke, he smoked continually.

"I could tell you about Minnehaha Falls."

To her surprise everyone looked up with interest.

"Really?" (It sounded like "rilly.") The English lady leaned forward. "Have you actually seen the Minnehaha Falls?"

"Of course. They're in Minneapolis."

"How extr'ordinary!" A faraway smile lighted her plain face. "Do you know, we used to study it in school.

> *Where the Falls of Minnehaha*
> *Flash and gleam among the oak-trees . . .*"

Mr. Glenn's face glowed. "That isn't the part I remember. It's . . .

> *"By the shores of Gitche Gumee,*
> *By the shining Big-Sea-Water . . ."*

"I remember something else entirely," Mr. O'Farrell said, his eyes laughing.

> *"In the land of the Dacotahs*
> *Lives the Arrow-maker's daughter*
> *Minnehaha, Laughing Water*
> *Handsomest of all the women . . .*

"Let's call Miss Ray, Minnehaha."

Betsy blushed.

The dinner was in a multitude of courses, and the orchestra played alluringly through it all. For dessert they had little steamed puddings with a sweet hot sauce. Afterward there was coffee in tiny cups, nuts and raisins, biscuits with cheese. Mr. O'Farrell asked (in French) for a special kind of cheese. He had a genial but masterly way with the waiter.

Betsy went down to her stateroom fairly dancing.

"What luck to meet such a fascinating man! And won't Tacy be pleased because he's Irish?"

She prepared for bed softly, not to disturb Miss

36

Wilson, but she put her hair up on curlers tonight, tucking them carefully under her boudoir cap. Settled in her bunk, she wrote her letter home, telling her family about Mrs. Sims and Mrs. Cheney, about Taylor and Rosa and the girl with the long hair who wouldn't speak. Lady Vere de Vere, Betsy dubbed her.

"And now . . . 'Hearts and Flowers,' please . . . our purser, Mr. O'Farrell, who looks like Chauncey Olcott."

Finishing her letter, she got out her Bible and Prayer Book. And finishing her prayers, she snuggled beneath the warm blankets. She looked at the porthole. It seemed cozy and not alarming tonight to think of the vast heaving blackness outside. She was so happy she could even think about Joe. Or rather, she could even *not* think about Joe.

" 'And haply may forget,' " she murmured, flouncing beneath the blankets.

For a day or two the sea was so rough that the decks were shut in by canvas. Betsy and Lady Vere de Vere were the only members of their sex at divine service on Sunday, and the weather made especially solemn the prayer For Persons Going to Sea.

"O Eternal God, who alone spreadest out the heavens, and rulest the raging of the sea . . ." Betsy resolved to read that to herself every night during the voyage.

Deck chairs were deserted, and dishes were clamped to the tables, but Betsy ate straight through the menu at every meal.

"Say you were ill and just came to keep me from being bored," Mr. O'Farrell implored her when she first appeared at breakfast.

"Why, I'm not a bit ill!" Betsy began but he interrupted, his eyes dancing.

"Oh, keep me in me fool's paradise!"

"I really must write Tacy about Mr. O'Farrell," Betsy often chuckled to herself.

She was thinking about him as she made her way to the bow on the fourth day out. The *Columbic* was still tossing, although buckets of sunshine seemed to have been thrown over the water, and the waves were merely frolicsome, not alarming, any more. She had paced the deck every day but had never gone this far front . . .

"Front!" she checked herself scornfully. "I mean forward, on the starboard side!"

Shocked by her inland ignorance, Mr. O'Farrell had been instructing her in nautical terms—bow and stern, port and starboard, forward, midships, aft. He had explained ship's bells and the changing time.

"The sun rises in the east and so, since we are going eastward, we gain time. Every noon the ship's clocks are set correctly and you should set your watch correctly."

"I'll remember, teacher."

"No frivolity, Miss! There's a difference of five hours between New York and London."

"And I have to add two hours for Minneapolis!" Betsy grumbled. "I can't even think what my family is doing without solving a problem in arithmetic first."

Mr. O'Farrell shook his handsome head. "You leave your family behind when you start out to travel," he told her.

Betsy was very happy. It was amazing, she thought, inching forward, how quickly one fell into this lazy routine: deck chairs, bouillon, promenading, luncheon, promenading, dressing for dinner, DINNER.

"I feel as though I'd been born on this old ship!" she thought, reaching the bow at last.

She clung to the railing in scared exhilaration and watched the *Columbic* plough its white furrow, until the spray drove her back. Presently the long-haired girl came up. Ignoring Betsy, she, too, looked out at the waves' wild seesaw. But one exuberant wave leaped the railing. It spilled over Lady Vere de Vere, and Betsy could not help laughing.

"I'm sorry," she apologized as the blonde girl ruefully stood on one sopping foot to shake the other. "But that was funny."

And Lady Vere de Vere laughed back, all her aloofness washed away.

"You'd better go right down and change," Betsy advised.

"Oh, there's no danger from saltwater drenchings!" This was a new accent. Canadian, Betsy suspected. English, Irish, Bostonian, and Canadian, so far!

"Then won't you sit down and dry off? My name's Betsy Ray."

"I'm Maida Bartlett from Toronto."

"You're a good sailor. You must have crossed before."

"Many times, to England."

They began eagerly to talk.

"I'm going to Europe to study," Betsy said.

"Alone? How frightfully jolly! Mother and I are going to Madeira for her health," Maida replied.

A junior officer came hurrying up. Mr. Chandler was good-looking, big-shouldered, with thick hair set in glistening waves and large white teeth. He showed his teeth in a wide smile now as he said chidingly, "You young ladies aren't supposed to be up here. The Captain sent me to fetch you."

He took them back, one on each arm, to their deck chairs, and sat down between them.

Betsy didn't care much for him, but Maida seemed to like him, and he certainly liked Maida. He waved her hair in his fingers to dry it. He called her a Christmas angel.

"Maybe you two will come to tea in my cabin. I've been saving my Christmas cake, and now I know why."

"How frightfully jolly!" Maida cried. Over his head, to Betsy's surprise, she winked.

After he left they sat talking about him with bursts of laughter. Betsy confided her admiration for the purser. They had tea, still talking, while Mrs. Sims and Mrs. Cheney looked on benevolently. The waves were growing calmer. And Miss Wilson, when Betsy went down to dress for dinner, was sitting up with her dinner tray on her knees.

Her plain bed jacket was impeccably neat. Her white hair was smoothly arranged and her eyeglasses perched on a straight, well-formed nose. She watched with interest as Betsy twisted her hair in intricate loops, and put on a peg-top skirt and her best lace blouse which had frills around both neck and wrists. Betsy added bracelets and sprayed perfume on her hair. She directed a spray at Miss Wilson's bed jacket.

"Mercy!" Miss Wilson cried, but she looked pleased.

"Tomorrow night you'll be coming up. And you're going to love our table. Mr. O'Farrell is perfectly fascinating. Last night we talked about South Africa. He served there with *distinction,* and he told about his adventures with an absolute flood of eloquence."

"Really?"

"He and I sat arguing afterward for ages. I sympathize with the Boers, you see. So does my father."

"Did he mind?" asked Miss Wilson. "The purser, I mean?"

"No. He likes to argue. But when we stopped, he said, 'Faith! Think of discussing such subjects with a woman!'" Betsy tried to imitate the Irish inflection and Miss Wilson laughed.

He had a way of looking at her, Betsy remembered, his head bent, a cigarette between his fingers, his eyes intent or gaily quizzical. She didn't try to imitate that.

Books came up for discussion that night. The rough sea of the day before caused Mr. O'Farrell to mention the storm in Joseph Conrad's *The Nigger of the Narcissus*. Betsy had never read it, but Joe Willard had.

"A friend of mine has told me about that description."

The English lady was reading *Jean Christophe*.

"My sister considers it simply magnificent," Betsy contributed.

Joe had read Ibsen and Julia had read Shaw. Betsy was increasingly grateful for these two inquiring minds. Betsy, too, was a reader, but she read Dickens, Thackeray, and Scott. She read Shakespeare and the poets. Shouldn't an author know the classics?

But people at dinner tables, she discovered, didn't talk about the classics much.

Fortunately she had one dear love among books that was not a classic. And Mr. O'Farrell mentioned it.

"*The Beloved Vagabond*? Why, I've read that over and over!" Betsy cried.

"I've read it more than once myself," said Mr. O'Farrell. "Every seaman has something of the vagabond in him, I suspect. And Paragot was partly Irish."

"Do you remember when he decided to go to Budapest, and just went, all of a sudden? That's the way I like to do things," Betsy declared.

The English lady knew Paragot, too. "But I wished he'd cut his nails," she remarked. "And I didn't like it when he put his hairbrush in the butter."

"Pooh!" said Betsy, smiling so she wouldn't sound

rude, and Mr. O'Farrell proclaimed, "Your attitude, Madame, seems to us effete. But I'm afraid Mr. Glenn agrees with you."

"I haven't read it," said Mr. Glenn seriously, "I don't like hairbrushes in butter, though." Which sent them all into laughter.

Their table was gayer even than the Captain's table, although Betsy knew that was supposed to be the smartest. It was really stuffy, according to Maida, who sat there. The lady author, whose name, Betsy had learned, was Mrs. Main-Whittaker, sat next to the Captain. She always dressed for dinner, complete with jewels and feathers. She was smoking. Betsy had never seen a woman smoke before except on a stage.

"I hope it isn't necessary to smoke in order to write. Papa and Mamma would never let me," she thought.

The evening air was almost balmy. For the first time the decks were more attractive, after dinner, than the lounge. Maida and Betsy stayed out in their chairs and were joined by Mr. Chandler, Mr. Glenn, and a Mr. Burton, middle-aged, with mustaches that drooped to his shoulders.

That night Betsy changed to a thin nightgown— pink silk, trimmed with lace.

"Well! I look more like it now!" she remarked as she tucked her curlers under a lacy cap before the mirror.

"More like what?" asked the mystified Miss Wilson.

"A young lady on a *romantic* Mediterranean cruise."

43

In the morning she put on her red blazer and a red and green cap. The cap was reversible—red on one side and green on the other and could be poked into jaunty shapes. When she emerged onto the scrubbed glistening deck, she was greeted by golden sunshine, and there was something in the air . . .

"It's summer! It's the tropics! It's glorious!" Betsy cried, running to the railing.

The ocean was sparkling and dancing as though it had never in all its existence caused a ship to lurch and roll. It was like her own prairie on a summer morning, Betsy thought. She could almost smell flowers.

"Oh, I'm so happy!" she confided to Taylor who was passing. "Honestly, I could tango down the deck!"

"Yes, Miss, I'm sure you could," Taylor answered politely. She was thin and rather stiff. Rosa was short, chunky, and cozy. Both of them were nice, but not so glamorous as Celeste.

Mr. O'Farrell immediately noticed the cap.

"You look like one of the little people of Ireland," he said. "All you need is a harp in your hair."

This was something else for Tacy! But Tacy not being available, Betsy sought out Maida.

"Can you imagine your Mr. Chandler saying a thing like that?"

"He might."

"Well, he wouldn't have a thrilling Irish voice to say it in!"

Quite as a matter of course today Betsy and Maida joined forces. They roamed over the ship with Betsy's square box camera. They tried their skill at shuffleboard. Together they called on Miss Wilson who lay in her deck chair, pale and apprehensive, but smiling.

"She teaches higher algebra," Betsy told Maida. "But you'd never guess it. She's a perfect peach."

Maida introduced Betsy to her mother who was playing bridge in the lounge. She was a slender, stately lady, very stiff at first, but Betsy was beginning to understand Canadians. Their characteristics had gone into her notebook along with Mrs. Main-Whittaker, Taylor, and Rosa.

Betsy told Maida about Celeste and Hortense. Maida cried that *she* wanted a maid, so they created Gabrielle. Betsy revealed that Maida had been Lady Vere de Vere. Exchanging these hilarious confidences, Betsy felt as though she were back in high school.

She was enchanted when Maida said "frocks" for "dresses," "boots" for "shoes." Maida, on the other hand, teased Betsy about "I guess," "cute," and "cunning."

"And you call everyone a peach. Why a peach? Why not a pear, or an apple, or a fig?"

"You're a perfect fig," Betsy said experimentally.

This chaffing was interrupted by visitors—Mr. Glenn, of course, and Mr. Burton. And Mr. Chandler was not the only officer to come to rest in their vicinity.

"My sister asked me," Dr. Wilson said at lunch, "whether you and Miss Bartlett held a fire drill down by

45

your chairs. It was a joke," he explained, "because there are always so many uniforms there."

Mr. O'Farrell looked at Betsy. "Ah, she didn't miss me at all! The flirt!"

"I did, as a matter of fact," Betsy replied.

But although the "fire drill" was held again after lunch, Mr. O'Farrell didn't put in an appearance. A purser, Betsy had discovered, was a very busy person.

"Why, oh, why," she wailed to Maida, "did I have to fall in love with a purser?"

They went to tea in Mr. Chandler's cabin; Maida's mother had given permission. He had a canary with which they made friends. He showed them photographs of his mother and sisters.

"I wish Mr. O'Farrell would ask us to tea," Betsy thought. "I'd like to know what *his* family is like."

Maida poured the tea and Betsy cut the Christmas cake—fruit cake and almond cake in layers, overspread with white icing and ornamented with candles, ribbons, and toy robins. They had a very good time, but Betsy remained loyal to Mr. O'Farrell.

That night he and Betsy lingered again at the table. They were talking about Betsy's writing. She told him about the small sales she had made, and how she kept her stories going out to the magazines and how they kept coming back.

"One story has brought in sixty-one rejection slips!"

"The deuce it has!" He was looking at her with attention. "I'd never be able to take it."

"Oh, I don't mind!" Betsy replied. "I think how fool-ish all those editors will feel when I'm famous."

Mr. O'Farrell burst into laughter. "We have an author . . . pardon me . . . another author on board. Did you know? A Mrs. Main-Whittaker. Would you like to meet her?"

"Well, I would normally, but in this case . . ." She didn't want to, because Mrs. Main-Whittaker knew Joe. It was idiotic. But Betsy's face turned scarlet.

Mr. O'Farrell changed the subject deftly. He was very tactful, Betsy realized—sensitive, too.

"That's why I like him," she thought later, on the up-per deck. "It's not just that he's so handsome and flings compliments around."

There were groups and couples on the upper deck looking at the stars. Betsy was with a group but Maida was with Mr. Chandler. "Fussing," Betsy accused her later down in Maida's cabin.

Maida's mother was playing bridge as usual and they had the small room to themselves. They had put on bath-robes and caps, rung for lemon squash and sandwiches. Again Betsy had the feeling that she had turned back the clock.

Maida was a little younger than herself, but it wasn't that. For Maida didn't usually seem younger. Mrs. Sims and Mrs. Cheney would never, Betsy realized, call Maida naïve. But she had gone to a private school and she had not, like Betsy, had boys around all her life—in the classroom, in the schoolyard, in and out of her home. She didn't understand boys as well as Betsy did.

"What's 'fussing'?"

"Flirting."

"I don't believe he's flirting, actually."

"That's it!" Betsy thought. "I'm only joking about having a crush on Mr. O'Farrell, but I'm afraid Maida is really falling for Mr. Chandler."

4
ENCHANTED ISLAND

"Seven o'clock and land in sight!"

These words of high romance were accompanied by a rattling of the stateroom door.

"Miss Wilson!" Betsy cried. "Do you hear that?"

"Yes, yes!" Miss Wilson was groping into a dressing gown. Betsy scrambled down the ladder and joined her at the porthole.

There romance was written along the horizon in a wavy line. It looked no more substantial than the airy cloud-built islands they had often seen at sunset. But this was a real island; it was one of the Azores.

"St. Michael's, probably," Miss Wilson said. She and her brother had stopped here before.

Excitement beat like wings over the breakfast table.

"Imagine," Betsy babbled, "finding islands out here in the middle of the ocean! Of course, I've always known they *were* here. But I never realized before how big the Atlantic was, and how brave it was of a little island to push right up in the middle of it."

"It didn't push," said Mr. O'Farrell. "It was flung up by a volcano. Eat your porridge, child."

"Porridge!" said Betsy scornfully. "I'm too uplifted to eat." But she poured the thick cream with a generous hand.

There were nine islands in the Azores Archipelago, Mr. O'Farrell said—all volcanic, mountainous, and rising steeply from the sea. They were farther from Europe and nearer to America than any other group of islands. Portugal had discovered them.

"Portugal!" The English lady didn't seem to believe it.

"Yes, Madame. It was in those adventur-r-rous days when Prince Henry, the Navigator, was pushing out the world's boundaries. And the islands had no human inhabitants when the Portuguese arrived."

"When were they discovered?"

"Corvo, the last one, around 1452. After that, men

kept on searching. They felt sure there was more land farther on, for some rocks on Corvo . . ." Mr. O'Farrell's voice warmed to the drama . . . "are shaped like a horseman pointing west."

Betsy felt shivers down her spine. "Did Columbus ever see that?"

"He may have."

"How simply, absolutely fascinating!"

Out on deck passengers gathered in the sunshine. Now the distant wavy line had resolved itself into mountains. They were the vivid green of grass after rain, divided off like a checkerboard by darker green hedges. And where the mountains swept down to the bay lay Ponta Delgada.

At first the little city was a splash of dazzling white. But nearer, it took on color. Many of the houses, all small and of similar shape, were tinted in pastel hues.

"It looks like a toy village! I want to sit right down on the floor and play with it!" cried Betsy.

"It's like a stage setting," said Maida.

Shortly they missed the throb of the engines. The *Columbic* had stopped and small boats were racing toward it. Betsy ran down to the stateroom for her jacket, cap, and camera.

"And some stout shoes!" Mrs. Sims warned her. "The cobblestones are fiendish."

"And your purse!" added Mrs. Cheney. "The embroideries are divine . . . and so cheap!"

Maida, too, sped below and returned with a flat sailor hat perched above her flowing hair.

The crew had let down a stairway from the lower deck, and the passengers descended to rowboats, manned by dark, barefooted boatmen. Their gibble-gabble was Portuguese, Dr. Wilson said. The boat tipped and joggled as though sharing the general excitement, and the little toy city came nearer all the time.

Landing at a rock platform, the visitors climbed stairs to the street and were at once surrounded by smiling, clamorous natives. Men and women alike were barefooted. The women wore bright shawls, and many carried black-eyed babies. Some attempted English. Little boys held out their hands with captivating grins, calling, "Mawney, mawney!" "I 'peak English. Give me mawney!"

Flowers were offered. Betsy bought a bouquet of violets and their wet fragrance intoxicated her. She looked around eagerly at the tiny streets—the little colored houses.

"Oh, this darling place! This dear, sweet, cunning, adorable place!"

Carriage drivers, with gestures, urged everyone to ride. But Betsy wanted to walk. She wanted to be on her own feet, able to stop and look about as often and as long as she chose. Fortunately, Dr. Wilson believed in exercise as much as he believed in raw vegetables. He and his sister would be walking, he said, and Betsy and Maida could go with them. Maida's mother took a carriage with

Mrs. Sims and Mrs. Cheney, and the girls agreed to meet them at Brown's Hotel for lunch.

The cobblestones were rough, as Mrs. Sims had warned, but Betsy was walking on air. And the steep streets were very narrow—many didn't even have sidewalks—but that only brought the travelers closer to the enchanting little houses.

These were built of dried lava, Dr. Wilson said; then plastered and tinted to suit the owner's fancy. They were pale green, blue, pink, lavender, and orange. They were striped, checkered, tiled like a bathroom floor. They looked like little frosted cakes or bricks of Neopolitan ice cream. They had second-story balconies with green wrought-iron railings that hung above the cobblestones.

"I love them! I adore them!" Betsy kept saying. "I'm going to come back and stay at least a month. Celeste and I are going to live in a pale green house with a balcony."

Maida laughed. "Just wait till you see Madeira!"

"But it can't, it *can't* be as nice as this!"

"Madeira is supposed to be the most beautiful spot on earth. It was probably the Garden of Eden."

Dark-eyed women smiled from the balconies where they sat working on the embroidery for which the Azores, as well as Madeira, were famous. Children, irresistibly pretty, peeped over the railings and crowded about the visitors in the street.

Betsy was taking snapshots madly. She snapped the

children. She snapped a Portuguese soldier, in gray and red, with a jaunty beret. She snapped an old man with a tassel cap, sitting on top of a load of brush that was sitting on top of a donkey.

There were donkeys everywhere, flanked with bulging panniers or patiently pulling two-wheeled carts. There were oxen, too, but very few horses.

Suddenly Maida stopped abruptly. "My word!"

Betsy turned her head. "Golly!" she breathed.

From among the brightly shawled women one had emerged wearing an unbelievable costume. It was like a nun's habit, blown out to a grotesque size. The cloak was as large as a tent, and the huge hood, shaped like a sunbonnet, was so contrived that the face could be completely concealed.

"That is the *capote e capelo*," Dr. Wilson said, "the traditional costume of the island. We are lucky to see one, for they are going out. The younger women object to them, I hear," he added regretfully.

"I should think they jolly well would!" Maida cried.

"But it's a perfect disguise! It might be convenient . . ." Betsy was already putting one into a dark romance.

"I think," Miss Wilson said, "the costume was devised on account of the showers." It was true that showers and little bursts of sunshine alternated every few minutes. "On our other visit I counted eleven showers and nine rainbows in the time we were ashore."

No one minded the rain. It was like a bright mist

through which struck quite plainly the little doll houses with their dainty balconies. After every shower there was a smell of heavenly sweetness.

"It must be freesias . . . or roses!" Betsy sniffed rapturously. "This place reminds me of California," she added.

The palm trees were indeed familiar, and she recognized the giant geraniums, red and pink, which had astonished her long ago in her grandmother's garden. In California, too, she had first seen bougainvillaea, which was pouring cascades of purple, red, and blue over these walls.

More and more houses had gardens now. The owners attempted to conceal them with high walls, but great masses of fragrant flowers surged up and over, to greet the passers-by.

"There seem to be so few people around these bigger houses," Maida observed.

"The upper-class women," Dr. Wilson replied, "lead lives of great seclusion. Men servants do their shopping for them. And when they go out . . . to church or to pay calls . . . they go in carriages."

"I don't blame them for staying in their gardens," Betsy said, pausing at a white wall where a white cat with yellow eyes sat in a torrent of yellow bloom.

Dr. Wilson wanted them to see some "sights," so they visited a public garden. Here were grotesque lava formations—caves and grottos and little hills—and more lavish vegetation. Orange trees with shiny green leaves, white blossoms, and golden fruit. Huge camellia trees, covered with red and white flowers. Magnolia trees, banana trees, figs, peaches, apricots. Mountains of cactus, forests of ferns, and oceans of flowers.

"It isn't hard to make things grow in these islands," Miss Wilson remarked. "The trouble is to keep them from growing too much. It looks untidy, doesn't it?"

But Betsy thought it was a garden out of a dream.

They went to the Old Jesuit Church. The portals were guarded by beggars; Betsy had never seen a beggar before. The church was almost three hundred years old, Dr. Wilson said, and she looked around with awe. The altar was astonishing. It was an enormous mass of cedar, carved with a multitude of little fat cherubs. Cherubs were as thick as leaves on a tree.

When they left the church, Betsy and Maida were too hungry, they told Dr. Wilson, to imbibe further education. He had brought his lunch in his pocket—a carrot and a slice of whole-grain bread—and his sister had a sandwich. They were going on to the Matriz Church.

"One of the doors is a very interesting example of the Manueline," he told them earnestly.

"But what *is* the Manueline, Dr. Wilson?"

"The Manueline style? It's like the Plateresque."

"Heavens! How much I have to learn!" Betsy said to Maida as they climbed to Brown's Hotel.

This modest white plaster building was situated on a

hill with terraces overlooking the city and bay. The showers had stopped and the air was very warm.

"Just think," Betsy said, "at home it's winter! The roofs and lawns are covered with snow, and Papa is out shoveling walks."

They were hot and tired. It was pleasant, when they went inside, to find the hotel deliciously cool. The Browns were English people, but their hostelry seemed very foreign, with high ceilings, bare, whitewashed walls, and cement floors.

The room to which the girls were escorted to rest was high, bare, and cool like the others, with long white curtains at the window, an iron bed, a wardrobe, a dresser, a washstand with a china bowl and pitcher.

"Not much like a room at the Radisson," Betsy said. "But then, the Radisson doesn't look out on a garden."

"What is the Radisson?" Maida asked, dropping down on the bed.

"It's a hotel in Minneapolis. That's near the Minnehaha Falls, in case you don't remember."

Betsy was as tired as Maida, but she couldn't leave the window. It was thrilling to stand in a strange room and look out into a flaming garden.

"I'm in a foreign land," she thought. "No wonder people love traveling!"

"Betsy," Maida said suddenly. "I want to talk something over with you. Why don't you get off at Madeira with us? You could go on to the continent later."

Betsy was too astonished to reply.

"You like the Azores so well," Maida continued. "And Madeira is even more beautiful."

"But would your mother want me?"

"Oh, yes! I asked her last night. She'd love to have you visit us."

"Why, why . . . that's the nicest thing I ever heard of! It's wonderful of you and your mother. But I don't know what to say."

"It would be ever so jolly to have you," Maida urged.

Betsy stretched out on the bed beside her, trying to imagine what it would be like to stay in Madeira—if Madeira were as beautiful as this. It would be like living in another world. But would it be sensible? What would her parents think? She'd have to write Miss Surprise.

Maida began to whisper confidences. "Mr. Chandler is really in love with me, Betsy. It isn't just a shipboard flirtation."

"Really?" Betsy was sympathetic. She couldn't help feeling secretly doubtful, though.

"He feels terrible that I have to get off at Madeira. Betsy, do you suppose Mamma would mind if I married a ship's officer?"

Presently they took turns at the washbowl and went out to the dining room where Mrs. Bartlett and others from the *Columbic* were waiting. Mrs. Main-Whittaker wasn't there. She had gone to the Portuguese hotel, someone said.

"Looking for atmosphere," thought Betsy.

All the guests ate at one table and they were served by two Portuguese women—one old, with a white turban on her head, the other, young and pretty with a pink skirt and a blue and white striped waist.

Conversation was in French and Portuguese as well as in English. Betsy rejoiced when she occasionally understood a *merci* or a *s'il vous plait*. She was almost rested after the fatiguing morning, and the cool, dim, lofty room refreshed her.

Moreover, the luncheon was delicious. They had first a thick soup, then a slice of beef with salad, then an omelet, with apricots and fresh pineapple for dessert. The Azores shipped pineapples everywhere, Mrs. Bartlett said.

No wonder! Betsy thought. She had never eaten one so sweet and full of juice.

After lunch she and the Bartletts went out to the terrace and Mrs. Bartlett repeated Maida's invitation.

"We have a villa rented . . . and servants arranged for. We'd love to have you."

"You're so sweet to ask me!" Betsy cried. "And it would be wonderful. But I don't know whether I ought to."

"The Wilsons are your chaperones, aren't they? They could speak for your parents?"

"Yes," answered Betsy. "I could do anything the Wilsons approved."

"The purser could arrange it very easily. This line permits stopovers. Another ship could pick you up and carry you on to Genoa in a month or two . . . say, in early spring."

"Then I wouldn't go to Munich at all." Betsy's head was whirling, but the plan tempted her greatly. Back at the quay she told the Wilsons about the invitation.

Dr. Wilson was dazed and dubious. He and his sister were charmed with the Bartletts, he said.

"But Munich is a great metropolis, a famous center for music and art. I really can't advise you to give it up merely for a picturesque island."

His sister agreed, and Betsy had an uncomfortable feeling that her parents would, too. And Julia wouldn't like her missing all that music.

"But it would be something," she insisted, "to spend six weeks in a perfect earthly paradise."

"Yes, of course! And if you want to do it, I can assure your parents that it would be quite proper." His reluctance was obvious, however.

They were all exhausted when they got back to the *Columbic*, laden with big bunches of flowers, pineapples, postcards, and embroideries. It was like coming home, Betsy thought, to return to the little stateroom. The stewardess scurried about making them comfortable.

While Betsy was taking a hot salt bath, she felt the engine begin to throb again.

She thought of the little island—such a tiny scrap of

land—melting from sight as the steamer moved away.

"Maybe it goes back into the ocean and rises up again when another steamer comes along. It's lovely enough to be enchanted."

If Madeira was really nicer than St. Michael's, she ought to accept Maida's invitation.

"I almost believe I will." She sprang out of the tub and rubbed herself until she tingled. "I'll ask Mr. O'Farrell to arrange it."

At dinner the orchestra was playing Strauss waltzes, and everyone was bursting with the day's adventures. The English lady, like the Wilsons, was talking of Manueline doors. Mr. Glenn had visited a pineapple farm. Betsy was delirious and knew it.

"It's the most entrancing little place I ever saw. Celeste and I are going to go back someday and live in a pale green house with a balcony."

"Celeste is your sister?" the English lady asked politely.

"Oh, she's my maid! I mean . . . she's my imaginary maid. I mean . . . aren't those balconies adorable?"

Mr. O'Farrell rescued her adroitly. "They're very important. The boy courts the girl there . . . from the street. He doesn't come into the house until they are engaged, and he doesn't see her alone until they are married."

"What kind of marriage would that be!" Betsy would have been glad to expand the subject of marriage. She had often wondered why anyone so charming as Mr.

O'Farrell had stayed so long a bachelor. But he kept the talk on island customs.

"Just wait," he said to Betsy, as everyone had, "until you see Madeira!"

Dinner was breaking up. They were standing by their chairs.

"I'm not only going to see Madeira," Betsy replied saucily. "I'm going to get off and stay there."

"I beg your pardon?" He was genuinely startled.

"With the Bartletts. They have invited me."

"Isn't this rather unexpected?" he asked slowly.

"I like to do things unexpectedly. Like Paragot going to Budapest, you know."

But although he admired Paragot so much, Mr. O'Farrell didn't seem pleased.

"Sit down," he said abruptly, pulling out her chair again, "and tell me all about it."

While she explained he sat looking at her, frowning. His eyes left her face and she felt them on her hands, clasped on the table under their lace frills.

"Have you made up your mind?" he asked without looking up.

"Not entirely. But it seems like a wonderful plan."

"I could arrange it, of course." Then his blue eyes lifted. They looked hurt, almost tragic. (And he was so very handsome with his shining black hair, touched with gray.)

Surprisingly he said, "Faith, and it's sad for me it will be if you leave at Madeira!"

He didn't seem to be joking . . . but he must be! Betsy felt her face flush.

Sometimes after dinner Mr. O'Farrell took her out to her chair although he never stayed there. But tonight she went out alone. She looked around for Maida, but Maida was with Mr. Chandler, leaning over the rail. Betsy, too, went to the rail. The moon was coming out, spreading a tremulous silver light over the water.

Madeira would be beautiful, of course, thought Betsy. But beauty wasn't everything. She pursed her lips judicially.

"I believe," she decided, "that it would be a mistake to miss a great metropolis like Munich for the sake of a picturesque island."

5
THE DELUGE

Madeira was beautiful, as reported. It was bewitching. It was idyllic. Yet Betsy didn't regret her decision to go on with the *Columbic*.

She regretted parting from Maida. Shipboard life had wrought its usual miracle, and the friendship of hardly more than a week seemed like the friendship of a lifetime. But Maida and her mother had affectionately extended their invitation to some time in Toronto.

"Why, of course! Toronto and Minneapolis aren't far apart. We'll see lots of each other," Betsy planned enthusiastically. She had seen very little of Maida, however, during the run to Madeira.

Maida had spent every available moment with Mr. Chandler. She and Betsy had not even had a stateroom spread on the last night, although Betsy waited up to a very late hour. The farewells must have been harrowing, Betsy thought. Mr. Chandler seemed to be in earnest after all.

Her own parting from Maida had been unsatisfactory. The *Columbic* was anchored off Funchal, and the passengers stood waiting for a tender to take them ashore, enjoying an exquisite view. The mountains were higher here than at St. Michael's. Against the verdant lower slopes the city shone radiantly white.

Betsy kept looking about for Maida but when she arrived on deck it was with her mother, and a boy carrying bags. Embracing Betsy, she whispered, "The parting was terrible! He's so in love! And I think I am, too. Don't answer! I haven't dared breathe a word to Mamma."

What a difference in mothers! Betsy thought. *Her* mother would have wanted to hear every word.

Mrs. Bartlett kissed Betsy. "Remember, you're coming to visit us sometime!"

"I'll remember. I'd love to, and thank you again. I'll

be writing," Betsy added to Maida. "And Celeste asked me to say good-bye to Gabrielle."

Maida's laugh rippled. "Gabrielle is desolated!" she replied, and she was gone, her long light hair floating behind her.

Watching her depart, Betsy mused on how the course of her own life might have been changed by staying on in Madeira. "I might have married an Englishman."

Madeira, she had been told, had a large colony of British and other foreigners, some attracted by the climate, others owning vineyards or sugar cane plantations. This was by far the largest and most populous of the Madeira Islands.

The Madeira Islands! Suddenly, without wishing to, Betsy remembered a visit she had made to Beidwinkles' farm back in Minnesota. She and Joe Willard had looked through a stereopticon set at "Views of Europe with Side Trips to Egypt, Algiers, and the Madeira Islands."

The memory brought a vision of Joe visiting a foreign place like this. She could see him walking about with his quick step. He would be asking all sorts of questions. Joe didn't just enjoy things in a dreamy way as she did, he always wanted to find out everything about them.

It took an angry effort to exorcise this vision. But she did it. She reminded herself—it was a dulcet thought— that Mr. O'Farrell had not wanted her to stop at Madeira.

She had told him casually, "I decided it would be foolish to give up a metropolis like Munich for a little island like Madeira."

"You were very wise, Miss Ray." There wasn't a hint in his suave reply of the feeling he had shown before.

She and the Wilsons had a wonderful day in Funchal. First, they rode in an ox-drawn sledge. Even Dr. Wilson was willing to forego the benefits of walking to test this curious vehicle. Wicker seats, set on runners, faced each other under a square red canopy from which white curtains fluttered down.

The Wilsons and Betsy wanted the curtains open so they could enjoy the quaint streets. The Portuguese driver, for a reason he could not communicate, wanted them shut. He would carefully tie those on the right, but as soon as he crossed to tie those on the left, Dr. Wilson would untie the ones on the right.

The driver jabbered and gesticulated. He was a small dark man with a worried face, wearing a short jacket over a yellow shirt. Dr. Wilson jabbered and gesticulated back until his white beard quivered. The tying and untying continued until Betsy, putting her head on Miss Wilson's shoulder, collapsed in laughter. Miss Wilson began to laugh, too, and the driver joined in, showing his white teeth. He rolled his eyes at the little professor, shrugged, and slapped the nearest ox.

"You have to be firm with these guides," Dr. Wilson said in a satisfied tone.

Certainly it was desirable to have the curtains open. In Madeira, too, the houses were tinted in rainbow hues. There was a sprinkling of English people on the street, and other Europeans in conventional dress, but as in the Azores there were comely natives, distressing beggars, and crowds of ragged adorable children.

Betsy took picture after picture of the children while she waited for a tram to carry them up the mountain. Each child had a rose or a camellia or a handful of violets, and wanted a penny in trade. One little olive-skinned fellow with a smile like Madeiran sunshine kept climbing up a post to throw roses at Betsy. He would cry with an ingratiating inflection, "Only one penny!" When her pennies were gone and she showed her empty hands, he kept on throwing.

The tram started its climb. Tinted houses draped with flowering vines stood one above the other. Wedged in, here and there, were native shacks. Fields of sugar cane began, and vineyards, and orchards. Mounting steadily, the tram reached the home of pines, and tangles of wild luxuriant growth broken only by streams and waterfalls.

"Oh, what a beautiful ride!" Betsy exclaimed for the dozenth time as they lunched in the lofty Monte Palace Hotel. The dining room commanded a view of mountain-side, city, and sea.

"But wait for the ride down!" Miss Wilson's face shone with pleasure at Betsy's delight.

"I know. Maida told me. We go on a toboggan."

It wasn't, she discovered, a toboggan in the Minnesota sense. It was like a broad settee on runners, cushioned, and extremely comfortable. Barefooted natives stood on either side, holding the contraption by ropes, and at a signal they began to run.

They ran like the wind down the steep precipitous slope. There was no track; they used the narrow cobble-paved street, and Betsy couldn't see how they missed the dogs, and children, and women with jars of water on their heads.

Plastered, flower-covered walls sloped down on either side. Above them the rainbow-hued houses flashed past, and arbors, and gardens. Leaning over the walls and out the windows were lovely laughing girls who pelted the tourists with flowers as they rocketed downward.

Back in Deep Valley, Betsy thought breathlessly, boys and girls were coasting down the Big Hill. They were rushing down an icy road between towering drifts of snow. And here she was sliding down a blooming mountainside under an avalanche of flowers!

"I never did anything so strange, so unusual, so fantastic in my life!" she chattered, climbing out at the foot of the mountain.

"I knew you'd like it," Miss Wilson answered, beaming.

"Very novel, very novel!" Dr. Wilson agreed.

They went shopping, of course. Shopping, Betsy had

already discovered, was one of the amusements of traveling. You were supposed to bargain with the merchants, and their prices slid down like the toboggans. With treasures of embroidery and wickerwork for gifts and a string of pink beads for herself, she went triumphantly back to the *Columbic*.

Mr. O'Farrell was nowhere to be seen. He was always busy in port, she had discovered.

"Celeste and I are coming back here, too," Betsy promised herself, and went below to leave her packages.

When she returned to the deck the weather had changed. It was beginning to rain, and the sea was misty and rough. Mr. Chandler joined her. He must be feeling terrible, Betsy thought sympathetically, but he showed no sign of anguish.

He took her arm gaily. "How about a spot of tea, Miss Ray?" And entering the cheerful lounge, where the orchestra was playing and stewards were moving about with appetizing little trays, he murmured, "If only that fellow Glenn will leave us alone!"

Betsy glanced at him sharply. "Of course he won't leave us alone. Why should he?" she asked. She was disgusted with Mr. Chandler. Here Maida was barely out of sight and he was already mooning around her! As soon as she finished tea, Betsy went below to be rid of him.

She couldn't forget Maida as Mr. Chandler apparently had. But even without her, she felt completely happy. Luxuriating again in a hot salt bath, her hair in curlers in preparation for dinner, Betsy reflected on it in perplexity.

She was always happy these days. She seemed to have shed all her bewilderments and perplexities. She wasn't homesick anymore, although she poured out her heart to her family each night in voluminous letters. Bob Barhydt had faded and even the stalwart figure of Joe was growing dim.

She liked shipboard life. She liked everything about it. But best of all—she couldn't deny it—she liked the dinner table!

She was increasingly aware that she looked forward eagerly to dinner. Not because it was the social climax of the day. Not because of the music or because everyone looked festive. It was because of the talk—and Mr. O'Farrell.

Sometimes, she admitted, she felt beyond her depth. The other people were so much older than she, so much more cultured, so much better educated.

Led lightly by Mr. O'Farrell, they talked of music, perhaps. Fortunately Betsy knew a good bit about opera because of Julia. And Julia had made her listen to modern music—Debussy and Ravel and Stravinsky.

But modern art! Betsy hadn't known anyone took that seriously. Talk of an International Art Exhibition in New York had reached Minneapolis, certainly. But Betsy remembered only one echo. "The Nude Descending the Staircase," at which everyone laughed.

And although she seldom missed a change at the local stock company and always saw stars, like Maude Adams and Otis Skinner, when they came to Minneapolis, she couldn't keep up with these people who went to the theater in New York and London and Paris.

She got on better with history. That had always been a favorite subject in school, and she had read Dumas, Hugo, and Scott. It was fun to sit and argue about Napoleon, or the Crusades, or Mary, Queen of Scots. She did well enough, too, when they discussed Irish home rule, international peace, President Wilson's policy in Mexico. Her father talked a lot about such things.

Betsy would get excited and flushed and turn her bracelets around and around as she defended her opinions. When Mr. O'Farrell talked, it was like a flame leaping.

"I never knew anyone who could talk like Mr. O'Farrell," Betsy thought. His wit was so nimble; his choice of words, so exact and colorful.

Their conversations weren't always profound. Sometimes, after the table emptied, Betsy told him about the Rays—her father's sandwiches, her red-haired mother's love of fun, Julia's singing, and Margaret's surprising turn of interest from cats and dogs to boys and girls. Mr. O'Farrell liked to hear about them.

He never talked about his own home.

"I wish I knew his story," Betsy thought. "He must have had some sad love affair. Maybe the girl died."

She took more and more pains dressing for dinner.

"How could I ever have thought I was in love with Joe?" she wondered, arranging her hair in three little heart-breaker curls on her neck. "I really prefer a man of the world."

That night the dinner conversation turned to women's suffrage. In the United States the campaign for votes for women had progressed without much violence. In Great Britain, too, at first, the women had merely paraded and made speeches. But then they had started picketing the House of Commons and breaking windows. They actually tried to be sent to jail in order to call attention to their cause by hunger strikes.

"Women," Mr. O'Farrell remarked, "are certainly ingenious at making themselves annoying. One window smasher up for trial kept her back to the judge and sang the 'Marseillaise' all the time he was talking to her."

"Good!" Betsy cried.

The English lady was startled, but not so much so as Mr. O'Farrell.

"You're not a suffragette!" he exclaimed.

"I certainly am."

"I don't believe it."

"Why, of course I am!" She was astonished that anyone could doubt it. "We're having a suffrage parade in Minneapolis this spring. I'd be marching if I were there."

"But you're not a militant?"

Betsy wasn't sure she was a militant, but she wouldn't back down. "I would be if I had to be."

Mr. O'Farrell's gaze turned mocking. "You, a militant!" he said. "You'd get your brick all poised to throw and then ask the nearest man, 'Oh, *should* I, or *shouldn't* I?'"

Betsy flushed crimson. "I would not!"

"You don't need to be ashamed of being feminine."

"I don't think I'm especially feminine. I can barely thread a needle."

"You're feminine! You're pure Victorian! You don't belong to the twentieth century at all, at all."

"Well, I can do the modern dances!" Betsy said indignantly, which made everyone laugh.

"Will you put me down for a Hesitation at the Captain's Ball?" Mr. Glenn asked. Mr. Chandler, who had stopped by her chair, spoke for a tango.

"Alas, all I can do is waltz!" said Mr. O'Farrell. He didn't ask her to save a waltz and Betsy didn't offer one. But she recalled with gratification that she was supposed to waltz exceptionally well.

She was exhilarated by the discussion and went out on deck smiling. A rain-filled wind was blowing now, but she had brought a cape. Wrapping it about her, she stood by the rail and went over in her mind everything Mr. O'Farrell had said to her and she had said to him.

"I wonder why he thinks I'm Victorian. But he said it as though he liked me."

She was annoyed when Mr. Chandler came out, taking her arm in that possessive way he had.

"We're in for a bit of a blow."

74

"So it seems."

"You're a ripping good sailor, though." He showed his big white teeth in an admiring smile.

"Not like Maida," Betsy answered pointedly.

He brushed that aside.

"How about a walk?"

"No, thank you. I have some post cards I must address."

Disengaging herself, she went into the lounge. But Mr. Glenn and Mr. Burton came up; she didn't write post cards after all. They played three-handed bridge with diverting lack of skill, and Mr. Burton ordered ginger ale, and the two stayed beside her all evening. It served Mr. Chandler right, she thought.

Her spirits were still high when she went below at eleven.

"I'll write my family a wonderful description of that suffrage fracas," she planned.

Miss Wilson, in a dressing gown, was standing at the porthole against which water was swishing heavily.

"This doesn't seem to be fastened properly," she said. "I'm fixing it, though."

"It's a cold night," responded Betsy, hanging up her dress. It would be cozy writing in her little upper bunk. "I'm going to go back to my warm nightie," she added, and pulled the ballooning blue and white flannel over her head.

She washed, brushed her teeth, wound her hair on curlers, and climbed to her lofty perch. Ready to begin her letter, she realized that she had forgotten her cap. Miss Wilson was still at the porthole; she would hand it up, Betsy thought, and leaned out to make the request.

The ship was really pitching now. A suitcase had toppled over; the towels on the washstand were swaying; and the boudoir cap, which usually hung on a hook with her bathrobe, had fallen to the floor.

"Miss Wilson," Betsy began, but stopped with a gasp. The porthole had swung open, and a roaring gray torrent rushed in, drenching Miss Wilson and flooding the stateroom with water to a depth of a foot or more.

Miss Wilson ran shouting out into the alleyway, and Betsy stared down in astonishment. Suitcases and bags were afloat. Her boudoir cap was sailing along, trailing its pale pink ribbons, as though on a gay adventure.

"Oh! Oh! And my best brown shoes!" Betsy began to wring her hands.

She heard excited male voices in the corridor. The door burst open, and in came a trail of agitated stewards.

Oh, dear! Betsy thought in panic. No boudoir cap, and the awful flannel nightgown! But, of course, stewards were used to seeing ladies in queer outfits . . .

An angry, all-too-familiar Irish voice froze her in horror! Mr. O'Farrell strode in, so handsome in his dress uniform with its swagger short jacket that Betsy could hardly bear it. She looked at him aghast.

Mr. O'Farrell's face twitched. "Miss Wilson has gone down to Number 87 to sleep. You must go, too," he said.

"I'll stay right here," said Betsy.

"You can't do that."

She tried for a crushing dignity. "My bunk is perfectly dry."

"It is impossible for you to stay. The men will be working here till morning."

"But I don't know where to find my bathrobe or slippers!" Tears rose and almost spilled over. She pointed an outraged finger. "*There's* my cap!"

"Get a wrap and go!" said Mr. O'Farrell, and he motioned the stewards to leave and went out himself, very quickly, shutting the door.

Betsy climbed down, sniffing back tears. She caught the boudoir cap, but it was too wet to wear. Her slippers swam beyond her reach. The bathrobe, still on its hook, was soaked around the bottom, but she put it on anyway and clutched both bathrobe and nightgown up to her knees.

The water was icy around her bare feet, but she couldn't resist stopping to look in the mirror.

"Oh, oh!" she moaned, recoiling. Wading to the door, she fled down the crowded corridor to Number 87 and Miss Wilson's arms.

"Why, why did I have to be wearing this hideous flannel nightgown?" she wept.

"It was very sensible, dear, on such a cold night!"

"But why couldn't I have been wearing a pink silk nightgown? Why couldn't I have had my cap on? Oh, these ghastly curlers!" Betsy was laughing now through her tears. "I'm *not* going to see Mr. O'Farrell again! Not ever! Not even if I have to jump off the boat!"

"Don't talk such nonsense!" said Miss Wilson, and hugged her warmly, and kissed her. "The stewardess has gone for hot tea, for both of us, and all our clothes will be sent to the tailor for pressing. Everything will be ship-shape by morning, she says . . ."

"Morning!" Betsy shuddered, and they both shook with laughter. "I won't go to breakfast! I absolutely won't!"

But she did, and Mr. O'Farrell strode in, smiling broadly.

"Do you know," he said, as he unfolded his napkin, "last night proved to me the truth of a French proverb. 'Even in the misfortunes of our friends we find a certain pleasure.'"

"What do you mean by that?" asked Betsy.

He poured his tea zestfully. "That stateroom was the drollest sight of my whole life! You were staring over the bunk, looking as though you'd seen a banshee, and down below, shoes and stockings and bags were floating around, and a little cap sailing like a lacy frigate . . ." Mr. O'Farrell choked with laughter.

"I don't see what's so funny," Betsy said, trying not to laugh herself, "about poor Miss Wilson being soaked, and both of us being hustled down cold halls . . ."

"Come on with the militancy!" Mr. O'Farrell cried.

The table was uproariously merry. Such wild tales were abroad that Betsy almost came to believe she had floated through the porthole onto an angry sea and been rescued from direst peril by the Captain, no less.

Mr. O'Farrell said that the Minneapolis papers would probably run extras with her picture.

" 'Minnesota belle in flood! Minded loss of cap more than salt water.' "

Catching Miss Wilson's eye, Betsy laughed and blushed.

6
THE CAPTAIN'S BALL

Mr. O'Farrell had seen her with her hair in curlers and he still liked her, Betsy thought joyfully, coming out from breakfast. The sea was smiling today. Rosettes of foam, scattered all over its surface, twinkled in the sunshine.

It was Sunday, and she attended Divine Service

again. She enjoyed it, although the clergyman always prayed for King George and Queen Mary, King Victor Emmanuel and Queen Elena, before he got around to the President of the United States!

Mr. Chandler continued to dog her footsteps. No snubbing deterred him, and Betsy was furious. Why, Maida had really liked him! She had wondered if her mother would mind if they got married! And now he was showing his big white teeth and tossing his wavy head, trying to charm her, Betsy.

He was always slamming Mr. O'Farrell.

"A deuced charming chap! Of course, he isn't an officer of the line."

"What do you mean by that?"

"Why, a purser just keeps the accounts, attends to freight and tickets! Sort of like a clerk."

"He wasn't much like a clerk in South Africa!" Betsy thought indignantly, but she didn't say it aloud. She wasn't going to discuss Mr. O'Farrell with Mr. Chandler!

She was delighted when his duties called him away, and she had a leisurely, lovely afternoon. She opened some of her steamer letters—she was three behind on Bob's daily epistles—and read cozily while Mrs. Sims chuckled over *Daddy-Long-Legs* and Mrs. Cheney perused *The Inside of the Cup.*

Part of the time she lay back in her chair and watched the water. Twenty-one from thirty-seven made sixteen! Was sixteen years' difference in age too much?

she wondered dreamily. She didn't think so. Husbands were proud of young wives.

"Faith, you're hardly more than a child!" she heard Mr. O'Farrell saying tenderly.

His word would be her law. She would listen while he talked with her eyes raised to his in adoration— almost.

"What a sweet ending!" Mrs. Sims remarked, closing *Daddy-Long-Legs* with a long, romantic sigh. Now *that* heroine, Betsy remembered, had married an older man!

After tea she went to the upper deck to watch the sunset. The western clouds were golden as the sun sank, but afterward they changed to copper-color and then to raspberry pink. She rested her arms on the railing and gazed.

Mr. O'Farrell came up behind her. "And do you see Proteus rising from the sea?" he asked.

Betsy turned a glowing face; she loved the Wordsworth sonnet. "The world *is* too much with us. I don't see half enough sunsets and sunrises, and I adore them both."

"I'm starting a little list of things Miss Ray adores: islands, balconies, sunrises. What else now?"

"Waltzing," said Betsy artfully, for it had been announced that the Captain's Ball would be held tomorrow night after they left Gibraltar. Mr. O'Farrell had once told her that he waltzed. But Mr. Chandler bounded up inopportunely, and Mr. O'Farrell strolled away.

That evening a crowd was singing on the upper

deck—Mr. Chandler next to Betsy of course. The stars were brighter than she had ever seen them, although they were familiar stars. She saw the Pleiades, in a dainty sisterly group.

Betsy loved to sing, and relaxed happily as they went from "Annie Laurie" and "Tavern in the Town," through "Down by the Old Mill Stream" and "Shine on Harvest Moon," to the newer song hits, "Peg o' My Heart," "Trail of the Lonesome Pine," and "Giannina Mia."

Surprisingly, Mr. O'Farrell joined them.

"And why not some Irish melodies, if I may be so bold?" he asked, resting lightly against a tier of lifeboats. Moonlight outlined his nautical cap, his slim uniformed figure.

They gave him "Kathleen Mavourneen," in parts.

"Would you be knowing 'The Harp That Once Through Tara's Halls'?" He rolled the *r* in "harp" and "Tara."

No one knew it except Betsy, who had sung it with Tacy long ago. But Betsy didn't mind singing it alone, although she wasn't a real singer, like Julia.

> *"The harp that once through Tara's halls*
> *The soul of music shed,*
> *Now hangs as mute on Tara's walls*
> *As if that soul were fled . . ."*

When the last note died away, Mr. O'Farrell touched her lightly on the shoulder. "It's a pretty good Irishman you are," he said, departing.

Gibraltar was overshadowed by the Captain's Ball. Britain's Rock was high, it was mighty, but it couldn't compare—for Betsy and the other young people who had slipped into Maida's place—with the only real ball of the voyage, scheduled for that evening.

There had been casual waltzing, fox trotting, and Castle Walking, but this was to be a real ball, with programs and everyone in formal dress. And next day part of the company would leave the ship at Algiers.

Of course, it was exciting to see Gibraltar. The *Columbic* was in the Strait when Betsy came rushing up, camera in hand. Mr. Chandler, lying in wait as usual, took her forward. The huge familiar Rock loomed against the horizon. Back of it curved the coast of Spain, and opposite ran the misty shoreline of Tangier. Europe and Africa, making a pathway to the Mediterranean Sea!

"Oh! Oh!" Betsy stared. The Rock looked just like the pictures, but something was missing.

Mr. Chandler chuckled. "I suppose you expect to see that dashed advertisement there."

That was it, Betsy admitted to herself. But she gave him a crushing look. "I was thinking," she answered with dignity, "about the Pillars of Hercules."

They had discussed them last night. Mr. O'Farrell had remarked that the great Rock and its companion on the opposite side of the Strait were said to have been tossed up by Hercules.

"He was looking for the oxen of Geryon!" Betsy had

84

cried. (There was some advantage, after all, in knowing the classics.) "It was during one of the Twelve Labors!"

The table had tried then to remember the Twelve. With much merriment, they had managed to name eight.

Mr. Chandler brought her back to Gibraltar. It was a British fortress and Crown colony, he explained; captured from the Spanish in 1704. They could see the city now, glittering white against the Rock.

Presently the *Columbic* passengers were on their way, in a big launch that was half fancy-work shop. Shawls, embroideries, drawn work, and hand-made lace were laid out for sale by importunate vendors.

"But don't buy a thing until you get ashore!" Mrs. Sims warned. "Shopping in Gibraltar is an occupation for the Gods!"

Ships from every corner of the world brought treasures to this crossroads port.

Barely off the launch, they were caught in a babel of beseeching tongues. Arabs held up wicker bags of tangerines and strawberries. Dusky children lifted flat baskets of roses, pansies, daffodils. And swarthy merchants, in open-fronted shops, flung out dazzling wares—shawls and silks, precious stones and Oriental scents, carved ivory and cedar.

The ladies from the *Columbic* were bargaining furiously. Taylor and Rosa, who had been permitted by their mistresses to come ashore, snatched at Malta lace collars.

Betsy bought gifts with reckless abandon, and for herself a pair of jade and silver bracelets.

"They're probably not real jade; they only cost sixty cents. But aren't they ducky, Miss Wilson?"

She would wear them tonight, she planned, with her maid-of-honor dress, at the Captain's Ball.

Because of the ball she did not regret that they had only two hours ashore. She and the Wilsons had time to drive, in a shabby little carriage with a fringed top, through the city and up to the fortifications.

Betsy looked eagerly around the crowded streets. There were Englishmen, Spaniards, Portuguese, Japanese, Chinese.

"Othello!" she whispered, squeezing Miss Wilson's arm, at her first sight of a Moor in a robe and turban.

In spite of the polyglot population and the semitropical vegetation, the place seemed very English. Statues of Wellington and Queen Victoria. Burly policemen. Rosy nursemaids. Tall, well-built soldiers pacing before the sentry boxes or lounging around the barracks that grew more frequent as they climbed the hill. An Anglo-Saxon air of propriety hung about the houses. These were of the Spanish type, but they looked English just the same.

Betsy remarked on the absence of beggars.

"They are allowed only on Friday and Saturday," Dr. Wilson explained.

"That shows the British influence, probably," Miss Wilson observed. "But this horse certainly doesn't."

Their horse was so pitifully thin and the road so nearly vertical that the Wilsons and Betsy got out and walked.

At the fortifications, Betsy surrendered her camera and they acquired a guide.

The Rock was tunneled out and the openings bristled with cannon. The British could certainly command the Strait in case of war, Betsy thought. But there was never going to be another war, so why all this fuss? She went back to the carriage where it was pleasant sitting in the sunshine, thinking about the ball.

The ball, when they were afloat again, triumphed over the Mediterranean, although this was blue, as reported. It was cornflower blue, and so was the sky, with boats spreading snowy wings against the brilliance. But Betsy was longing for the evening.

"I want to get those curlers out of Mr. O'Farrell's mind," Betsy confided to Miss Wilson when, at last, she was dressing for dinner. Miss Wilson was assisting. It was almost like having Julia to help her, Betsy said. She looked around.

"Where are Margaret, and the cat?"

And Miss Wilson laughed, for she knew the Ray family now. She knew how Margaret, pussy in arms, used to watch her older sisters get ready for a dance.

Betsy's hair was dressed, hiding her forehead and ears under soft shining loops. She shook pink powder on a chamois skin and rubbed it over her face while Miss

Wilson watched with interest. Miss Wilson never used powder, pink or white.

Under a frothy petticoat, Betsy's legs shone elegantly. (A pair of silk stockings had been in Julia's package today.) She slipped into green satin slippers, and Miss Wilson lifted the maid-of-honor dress carefully over her head.

It was a beautiful dress—filmy green chiffon over pink, with roses sewn into the bodice. The sleeves were short, ideal for her new bracelets. She wore them both on one arm, and they matched her jade and silver ring and the jade and silver pendant Julia had given her for a maid-of-honor gift.

After spraying perfume on her hair as usual, Betsy looked into the mirror and was glad—since only actresses used rouge—that her cheeks always flushed for a party. Assuming a blasé expression, she sank into the debutante slouch and revolved languidly.

"Don't I have an indefinable Paris air?"

Miss Wilson chuckled. "You look very nice."

Everyone looked nice! The English lady had bared her scrawny shoulders in a jet-trimmed gown. Miss Wilson was winning in prim black silk with a cameo in a nest of soft lace at her throat. Dr. Wilson and Mr. Glenn were wearing evening clothes, and Mr. O'Farrell was resplendent. Above the swagger dress uniform, his hair shone like satin.

Talk was all of the ball. Mr. Glenn reminded Betsy of their Hesitation. Mr. Chandler came up to hang over her chair and ask how many dances he could have. As many as possible, he pleaded, and one of them must be a waltz. Mr. O'Farrell said nothing. Leaning his head on one hand, a cigarette in the other, he smiled musingly.

Leaving the table, Betsy managed a gay hint. "My waltzes are going fast."

It didn't work.

"I'll not be spoiling your evening with my old-fashioned dancing," he replied. She smiled back (like a Cheshire cat, she told herself) to cover her disappointment.

The deck was hung with the flags of all nations. Red and green electric lights glimmered. The floor was waxed. There were cozy corners for fussers, and chairs at one end for lookers-on. The Mesdames Sims and Cheney, and Miss Wilson, sat there, self-appointed chaperones for Betsy.

The musicians started tuning up. They plunged with hearty jollity into "Over the Waves." Betsy danced with Dr. Wilson, who was as light as a puppet on strings—a puppet of a little professor with mustaches and a trembling spike of beard.

Dr. Wilson yielded her to Mr. Glenn, to Mr. Chandler, to Mr. Burton, and others. The sea was like glass, and moonlight poured over the world. In spite of Mr. O'Farrell Betsy couldn't be unhappy. She floated effortlessly, the skirt of the maid-of-honor dress caught lightly in her hand.

She loved the new dances: the graceful Boston Dip, the demure Hesitation, the rollicking Turkey Trot, and the absurd stiff-legged Castle Walk. Mr. Glenn, pale and slender though he was, proved to be marvelously adept. Mr. Chandler, too, was excellent, although he held her too tightly.

" 'Peg of my heart, I love you . . .' " he sang meaningfully.

She was taught the new Marjory Step by a New Yorker who said he knew the Castles. He studied Betsy through half-closed lids as they danced, and told her that she was a fascinating type.

"A tropical beauty!"

A tropical beauty from Minneapolis! Betsy thought, wishing Mr. O'Farrell could hear.

Mr. O'Farrell, she noticed, was being charming to the chaperones. She glanced at him now and then during the intermission, when sandwiches, lemonade, and chocolate ice cream were served. He was talking with Mrs. Main-Whittaker, who had doubled her feathers in honor of the ball. She wore a low-cut gown of raspberry pink.

Dancing began again, and now Betsy saw him watching her. Perhaps, she thought later, he noticed that she was a good dancer. Perhaps he noticed that she hadn't smiled or waved at him as usual. At any rate when the orchestra began the rolling opening phrases of "The Beautiful Blue Danube," he made his way to where she stood with Mr. Chandler to whom she was engaged for the dance.

Mr. O'Farrell offered his arm.

"Isn't this my waltz, Miss Ray?"

Betsy's face broke into joy. "Why, yes! I believe it is!"

Mr. Chandler was very angry. "Dash it all!" he cried. "What do you mean . . ." But his furious voice died away.

Betsy, in Mr. O'Farrell's arms, was dancing to the Blue Danube.

They didn't talk. Betsy didn't want to talk. His dancing *was* a little old-fashioned, but that didn't matter. He was dancing with *her*!

Over his shoulder, as the music wove its rhythmical enchantment, she looked at the golden moon. She looked down the quivering golden avenue it made across the water, and it almost seemed as though they were dancing on that avenue, circling and swaying to the cadence of the waltz.

But the music ended. As it died away, Mr. O'Farrell said, "Thank you, Miss Ray! Faith, for a few minutes there, I thought I was young again!"

He kissed her hand. Betsy had never had her hand kissed before, and she was transfixed into silence.

Mr. O'Farrell bowed and left, and the wrathful bulk of Mr. Chandler immediately filled his place. Betsy dreamily gave him the next dance, although it had been promised to Mr. Glenn. It didn't matter. Nothing in the evening mattered now.

"I believe, I believe, I'm in love with Mr. O'Farrell," she thought.

"What the deuce did you do that for?" Mr. Chandler demanded, backing Betsy around in the long-legged Castle Walk.

"Do what?" asked Betsy, gazing at the moon.

"Give my dance to that fellow O'Farrell."

"Was that your dance?" Betsy was still circling and swaying on that trembling golden path along the sea.

"You know deuced well it was my dance! See here! Will you listen to me for a moment?"

She shook herself out of a vision in which she was pouring coffee from a silver pot at Mr. O'Farrell's glittering table. She was definitely Mrs. O'Farrell, and the table wasn't in the dining saloon of the *Columbic*. It was in London, or Paris . . . or Dublin, maybe.

"Certainly," she said, and led the way to the railing. She was glad to be able to stop dancing. It was a . . . a desecration, almost . . . to dance any more tonight.

Mr. Chandler objected. "Why, we can dance! I don't have anything *that* important to tell you."

"Oh," said Betsy irritatingly. "I thought you did! I thought you had some great and important statement to make."

"Like what? A proposal, I suppose."

"Why not? Don't you propose to every girl you rush?"

Her teasing was light. She was too happy to be cruel,

even for Maida's sake. But it seemed to impress Mr. Chandler profoundly.

He turned and looked at her. He riveted his eyes on her with grimness and power.

"I see," he said. "I see it all!"

"But what is all?" asked Betsy, laughing.

"Why you've been treating me so. You think I've been fickle."

His expression softening, he drew her tenderly from the railing toward one of the dark corners arranged for fussers. "A man wouldn't be fickle to a girl like you. I know what you're thinking, though, and that explains a lot. I wondered how you could cut a dance with me for an old married man with five children."

"Why, I didn't . . ." Betsy started to say, but she stopped.

Mr. Chandler was curious. "You knew, didn't you, that O'Farrell is married?"

Betsy's world was whirling, but instinctively she hung on to her pride. She heard a voice, still teasing, coming out of the cozy corner in which they were now seated.

"Of course! We girls always assume that you men are married. How many children do *you* have?"

"I'm single. And I want you to get it out of your head that there was anything serious about that little flirtation with your friend."

"You did call her a Christmas angel though!" Betsy

heard a tone of sweet reproach. She heard herself say next, "Listen to that tango! Let's try it! If your tango is as good as your Boston . . ."

"Did you really like my Boston?" He stood up exultantly. She was dancing again, but only on the *S.S. Columbic,* not on an avenue of moonlight any more.

"You leave your family behind when you start out to travel," Mr. O'Farrell had told her.

7

THE *DINER D'ADIEU*

Algiers was the first place they visited to which Betsy
did not wish to return. It was beautiful enough at first
sight, spread out on a half moon of hills in the blazing
sunshine . . . white, flat-roofed houses, the dome of a
mosque hinting of the mysterious Orient, palm trees in
green rows. And the modern section was a perfect little

Paris, Mrs. Cheney told her as they went ashore. But Algiers frightened Betsy; it made her long for Minnesota.

In fairness it should be stated that she was in very low spirits. She was chagrined, furious with herself. Getting a crush on the first attractive man she met! Married at that! Five children!

Girls were always getting crushes, of course. People were amused by such affairs, but they weren't funny, really. They hurt.

"I feel as though I were coming down with the grippe," Betsy thought. But she wasn't, she knew, coming down with anything. She was getting over something.

In their stateroom after the dance she had told Miss Wilson merrily about Mr. O'Farrell's marital state. And up in her bunk she had confided the same news to her family. She worked rather hard over that letter.

"I guess my letters so far have had a decidedly O'Farrellish flavor. Don't worry! I haven't lost my young heart, but my wits have certainly been sharpened.

"He's thirty-seven years old and terribly attractive. (That fatal Irish charm, tell Tacy!) He's witty and full of blarney, with a dimple in his chin. He's traveled everywhere, was decorated in South Africa, speaks French, wears evening clothes just right, and knows how to manage waiters. Absolutely cosmopolitan!

"And the first little lesson I've learned on my travels, I've learned from him. Hold your breaths now. He's never told me he's married!!! He doesn't know I know it, but Mr. Chandler mentioned it tonight.

"The lesson? Not all married men are middle-aged and fatherly."

That had a fine light touch, she thought.

And sailing to Algiers next day over a sea that seemed spread with cloth of gold, she had covered her misery with gaiety. She had roamed the ship in carefree company, trying out new dance steps on the promenade deck, flirting with Mr. Chandler. Especially at luncheon, she had been all vivacity and sprightliness.

Mr. O'Farrell told of meeting ex-President Theodore Roosevelt, and that started the table talking of famous people. The English lady had seen Lily Langtry. Mr. Glenn had glimpsed the aged Longfellow. Miss Wilson, as a little girl, had presented a bouquet to Patti, and her brother had viewed President Lincoln in his casket.

"Well, I've seen Carrie Nation," Betsy said. And the famous termagant who invaded saloons with a hatchet made more of a sensation even than the Jersey Lily.

"Where?"

"Oh, she was out in Minnesota smashing up a few saloons!"

"What did she look like?"

"She wore a funny little bonnet and a shawl and spectacles. My friends, Tacy and Tib, and I were walking along the street when we heard mirrors cracking and bottles and glasses crashing, and out she came!"

"Did she have her hatchet?" Mr. Glenn asked eagerly.

"She shook it at us."

"Now, now!" Mr. O'Farrell admonished.

"I admit," said Betsy, "she was shaking it at everyone, but she looked so fierce I was sure she had us in mind."

"What happened next?"

"Our fathers found us," Betsy answered sadly. "We were only seven." And Mr. O'Farrell shook his head at her, laughing.

"Oh, Miss Ray! I derive such exhilar-r-ration from your company!"

Betsy gave him an enigmatic smile.

For Algiers she wore her suit. The red and green outfit admired by Mr. O'Farrell wasn't citified enough for a French colonial capital, she decided. Besides, it made her look too artless, too much like a girl who didn't know a married man when she saw one.

The blue suit with its cutaway coat and draped skirt rustling over taffeta seemed much more sophisticated, especially when she added a blue hat with a tall green "stick-up" on it, and her best kid gloves.

At first the city seemed very French. It showed a formal square, wide tree-lined avenues full of carriages and automobiles, and on the sidewalks, under awnings, little tables where people sat drinking wine or coffee. She saw Frenchwomen, chic on high heels; Frenchmen with tiny mustaches; French officers in ravishing uniforms of soft horizon blue.

"Why, it *is* a little Paris!" Betsy exclaimed, looking around.

But she soon became aware that it was the Orient, too.

She saw robed men in turbans. There had been a scattering of them in Gibraltar, but here they were everywhere. She saw her first veiled women!

Waiting for a tram (as streetcars seemed to be called) that would take them up to the old Moorish fortress, Betsy saw Moors, Arabs, Spaniards, Biblical-looking Jews in robes—but the veiled women were most fascinating of all.

They wore long, loose white bloomers, short jackets, and veils covering all their faces but their eyes. Even girl children were shrouded like that.

"The poor little things!" Betsy cried.

Some of the women were tattooed between their eyebrows. Betsy thought it was a pathetic attempt at adornment, but Miss Wilson said it was a mark of caste. Some of them stained their fingernails bright red.

"That's rather pretty," Betsy remarked.

At the Fort, they joined a group from the *Columbic* and secured an English-speaking guide for the trip through the Arab quarter. This was quite unsafe for tourists alone, they were told. Mrs. Main-Whittaker was in the party and Betsy met her for the first time.

The author was wearing a red suit. She loved bright colors, and was undeterred by the fact that she was short and stout. Her red plumes were even higher than Betsy's "stick-up." She was loaded with jewelry and moved in a cloud of perfume.

She talked all the time. Had Joe liked her? Betsy wondered, trying to see her with his eyes as the party descended into the native quarter. Soon the squalor, the misery, the eeriness of the Kasbah reduced even Mrs. Main-Whittaker to silence.

The tourists were on foot, for the passage was too narrow for a carriage. There were a few starved-looking donkeys around, and a good many starved-looking people. Sometimes the narrow street was only a flight of steps, lined by ancient houses which all but met overhead. It had a twilight dimness although the time was early afternoon.

The people lived in what seemed to be little dens scooped out of the walls. Some were quite open, so that you could look in. Others had doors bearing tiny iron hands on them—for luck, the guide said.

"Luck!" ejaculated Betsy, for it was almost incomprehensible that human beings should live in these unlighted, evil-smelling, filthy caverns and still hope for luck.

"Yes," said the guide. "And if they can't afford the iron hands, they paint some on the door."

Most of the people were so ragged, dirty, and emaciated that it was painful to look at them. The children, especially, almost broke Betsy's heart. They were pitiful, little, dirty, tangled creatures, some bearing still smaller children on their backs.

Men wearing flat round hats with tassels were smoking Turkish water pipes, or sat in circles drinking small cups of black coffee. A public letter writer was ensconced in a doorway surrounded with maps and papers. For a franc he would write a letter for you, the guide said. There were bakeshops where circular loaves were piled in the dust, fly-haunted meat and fruit shops.

"I don't think I can ever eat again!" Mrs. Sims whispered.

What made the awful place still worse was that everybody seemed to hate them. These people gave the visitors no sunny smiles or pleasant greetings such as had been general in the Azores and Madeira. The veiled women flashed hatred from their dark eyes, and the unveiled women motioned the visitors furiously not to look their way. All except the beggars drew away with sullen looks and mutterings.

"Why do they hate us so?" asked Betsy, almost trembling.

"We're aliens and infidels," Mrs. Main-Whittaker replied.

And perhaps, thought Betsy, holding the skirt of her suit above the refuse as she picked her way downstairs, they didn't like well-fed, well-dressed, comfortable-looking travelers coming to stare. But if such people didn't come—how would anyone find out that the misery existed?

The beggars were crowding about them now. Betsy had seen them first on the wharves among the clamorous guides and vendors. They had been bad enough there, but they were frightful now as they pressed close, screeching, whining, and holding out their hands.

Betsy held fast to Miss Wilson's valiant arm. She tried to think about Minnesota, about Deep Valley where she had grown up, the river, and the peaceful sunny hills. And at last they came out of the Kasbah!

No, Betsy didn't want to return to Algiers. She told Mr. O'Farrell so at dinner, where she was quieter than usual, thinking of the beggars and those unsmiling children carrying smaller children on their backs.

A few of the *Columbic*'s passengers had left and some new people had come aboard. One was a friend of the English lady, a Mr. Brown, but he sat at the Captain's table and Betsy did not meet him. He was a tweedy, undistinguished-looking young man, very thin and partly bald. Later she saw him circling the deck and she liked his swinging easy gait. He carried a cane which he swung in rhythm. He wasn't unattractive, but Betsy wasn't sorry they had not been introduced.

"Men!" she thought.

The first lesson she had learned on her travels had left her feeling cynical.

Dressing for the *Diner d'Adieu* was no such pleasure as dressing for the Captain's Ball had been. She didn't even begin until the bugle sounded. Then she jerked out a yellow satin formal. It was old, but it had made a hit at plenty of college parties.

As dinner began she had only that false sprightliness

that had been with her since Gibraltar. But the atmosphere of the dining saloon was irresistibly convivial. The musicians played with spirit: Waldteufel waltzes, the *Pink Lady* music, the "Pizzicato Polka" . . . And the nine-course dinner was elegantly described, with a sprinkling of French, on a souvenir menu. What fun to send it home!

She would underline her own choices: *hors d'oeuvres variés; consommé aux pain grillé; turbotin au chambertin;* calves' head *en tortue;* forequarter of lamb, mint sauce; roast guinea chicken *anglaise;* dressed salad; and the dessert—it was her favorite, *pouding à la St. Cloud!* Then would come coffee and cheese, of course. Betsy's spirits began to rise in spite of her.

People went skylarking from table to table. The Captain proposed toasts, and so did Mr. O'Farrell. And each table had its own nonsensical toasts:

"To Miss Wilson, heroine of The Flood!"

"To our Militant Suffragette!"

"To Carrie Nation!"

They drank them in *punch à la Romaine.*

Mr. O'Farrell looked at Betsy now and then with a slightly puzzled expression. He probably noticed that she seemed different, she thought. Or perhaps he was surprised that she was having so much fun?

"Probably he's used to girls who find out he's married, and are heartbroken about it. Well, he can see that I don't care!" And Betsy grew gayer and more audacious all the time.

He was chaffing her about saying something unkind to him after the flood.

"It isn't true. I never said anything unkind to you or about you either . . . oh, yes, I did once!"

"You did?" He was almost startled into seriousness.

"It was in a letter home," said Betsy.

"By all the saints I'll know what it was!"

"By all the saints you won't!"

She could see that he was really curious, and it was a satisfaction to be provoking.

"Miss Ray," he pleaded. "I asked the chef for this *pouding à la St. Cloud* just for you. I've noticed that it was your favorite sweet. Shouldn't such devotion be rewarded?"

"Oh, well!" said Betsy. "In that case . . . may I borrow your pencil?"

She turned over her menu card and wrote:

"And the first little lesson I've learned on my travels, I've learned from him. Not all married men are middle-aged and fatherly."

While he read it she looked at the ceiling and her color rose until even her ears were red. She didn't look down until his laugh burst out. It was a tremendous shout, and all of a sudden, Betsy felt elated and triumphant. He kept on laughing while the table smiled in bewildered sympathy, but at last he wiped his eyes.

"Ladies," he said, "and gentlemen, too, of course! Won't you do me the honor of coming to me cabin? I'd like to brew you some of me own coffee, which is superb, if you will par-r-don me saying so. And I wish to show Miss Ray a picture of the future King of Ireland."

"The future King of Ireland?" Miss Wilson asked, startled.

"Dennis Leo O'Farrell, aged four, and said to be the image of his father."

He was, too, Betsy discovered when the group was gathered merrily in Mr. O'Farrell's cabin watching his ritual of coffee-making. He was an enchanting little boy. Chubby, of course, but he had that laughing light in his eyes.

"Faith, and he's a spalpeen!" Mr. O'Farrell frowned at the radiant Betsy. "And so are you!" he added.

Mr. O'Farrell, Betsy decided, was a dear. After the party was over, she paused on deck to think about him. The *S.S. Columbic* was churning softly through the mild dark.

He had taught her a lesson, all right. She would watch out for married men.

"But he did more than teach me . . . that skim milk masquerades as cream."

He had awakened her interest in so many things—faraway places and strange languages, folklore and legends, pictures and books she might never have heard of, beauties of every sort. She would never forget him, although she wasn't in love with him any more—at all, at all.

It was strange, Betsy thought, how your estimates of people changed. Bob Barhydt seemed like a callow adolescent since she had known Mr. O'Farrell. Joe Willard stood up, though. No one could make Joe seem callow although he was young and had never traveled beyond Boston.

She wished she hadn't lost Joe.

"That was the most foolish thing I ever did," Betsy said in a small whisper to the rain and flying spray. "I wonder . . . if I wrote him . . ."

But she knew she wouldn't. She was too stubborn.

8

TRAVEL IS BROADENING

In the Bay of Naples a hateful sensation which Betsy had almost forgotten began to creep back into her body. It was that feeling of forlornness, of not belonging, of "What am I doing here anyhow?" that she had felt when the *Columbic* set sail.

At first she laid it to the weather, for a dreary drizzle

had begun. It was hard, too, to part with so many friends. What made it harder was their overflowing kindness. They all gave her calling cards, and Betsy offered her own in return. She seldom used them at home, but she had found out that they were important when traveling.

Mrs. Sims and Mrs. Cheney wrote down their Boston addresses and asked her to come and visit them sometime. Taylor and Rosa shook her hand, and Rosa had a little gift for her—a silk handkerchief with the Rock of Gibraltar on it.

Betsy promised them postcards of Minnehaha Falls. And Mr. Glenn asked for one, and so did the English lady. She invited Betsy to have tea with her in London. Betsy felt ashamed, for she had barely been aware of the lady's name. It was Mrs. Trevelyan.

Hardest of all was parting with the Wilsons, who were touring Italy and Greece before starting northward. She had grown fond of the humorless, kind, little professor. And as for Miss Wilson . . .

"Why, I love her!" Betsy realized in surprise.

They suggested again that she join them for some travel, and Betsy felt very different about the proposal than she had felt in Boston. She was even tempted to telegraph Miss Surprise that she was staying in Italy now. But she refused to yield to this unvalorous impulse.

"I'll write you from Munich, though. I'll write to you at the *Casa delle Rose d'Oro*." That was the Wilsons' first mailing address, the House of the Yellow Roses in Venice.

She promised them, and half a dozen others, to report her arrival in Munich. She was given instructions about changing money and getting through customs. Dr. Wilson was wiring a Thomas Cook agent to meet her in Genoa.

"And Mr. Brown can help her," Mrs. Trevelyan said, referring to the thin young man who had come aboard at Algiers. "He's going on to Genoa. Where is Mr. Brown?"

Everyone looked around for him, but he had already gone ashore.

Most of those who were continuing to Genoa fared forth with mackintoshes and umbrellas to see Naples.

"See Naples and die!" they reminded Betsy brightly, but she felt as though, in her case, that would be all too true.

"We could go to the movies," Mr. Burton urged, but she shook her head.

The deserted ship was uninviting; it was taking on coal. Betsy undressed, piled into bed under warm blankets, and rang for a pot of hot tea. She remembered that she had some steamer letters left and started to read them, but they made her want to cry. She opened Julia's present for the day, and that did make her cry. It was a small silk American flag! Just as twilight fell, she saw a great steamer, blazing with lights and flying those same dear Stars and Stripes, move majestically out of the harbor, bound for home. Home!

"Life is just too short," wept Betsy, "to spend a year away from home!"

But she felt different the next day.

The rain had stopped, and sunshine was pouring golden warmth over the world. On the upper deck, she got wind-blown and freckled, gazing at the Bay of Naples.

It looked startlingly familiar. The sky and water were as brightly blue, the amphitheater of hills as richly green, the city as white and shining, as in all the pictures. And there was Vesuvius, its summit wreathed in smoke!

"Oh, I wish I had time to see Pompeii! But I'll be coming to Europe often." She saw herself this morning as a woman of the world who would travel and write for many years before she married—if she married at all.

Mrs. Trevelyan's Mr. Brown strolled past, swinging his cane. He was almost good-looking, in spite of being bald. His tweed suit, although rumpled, sat jauntily on his bony shoulders. He gave Betsy a friendly look, but she didn't respond with her usual ready smile.

"Married, no doubt!" she thought tartly.

Mr. Chandler and Mr. Burton encamped on either side of her. As the *Columbic* sailed out of the famous bay, they pointed out the shore where St. Paul had landed in Italy, the hillside where Virgil was buried, the island on which Cicero had visited Brutus after the murder of Caesar.

The great names brought back hushed churches, dusty classrooms, a red morocco set of *Stoddard's Travel Lectures* in the bookcase at home. But here, today, the water rippled and gleamed; gulls were swooping; sails were bellying in the wind. It was alive! . . . and it had been like this for Cicero and Virgil and St. Paul. They had been alive! Betsy felt as though she had made a great discovery.

The olive-green islands showed shining towns, or melancholy ruins. The loveliest one bore only a castlelike building set in thick-clustering trees. She told Mr. O'Farrell about that one at luncheon where they had the table to themselves.

"Celeste and I are going to come back and stay there some time," she informed him.

"I hardly think you'd enjoy it," he answered. "The residents are all life convicts . . . the murderers of Italy."

"Oh, dear!" said Betsy with a laugh.

Mr. O'Farrell didn't laugh. "Miss Ray," he said gloomily, "you don't know enough about the world to be traveling around all alone."

"Why, Mr. O'Farrell!" She was disappointed in him. "I'm twenty-one years old."

"You're very young for twenty-one. Besides, you're too trustful."

Betsy glanced at him quickly. Was this a joke? She decided that it wasn't, for he looked really troubled, brooding over a cigarette.

"I don't see what could happen to me," she answered patiently. "I won't speak to strangers, or do anything I shouldn't. I intend to behave in Munich just as I did in

Minneapolis. But if it will make you feel any better, I am going to a friend of my sister's. She's promised to look after me until I'm settled."

"Faith, and I'm glad to hear that!"

"The only bad thing about traveling alone," Betsy confided, "is getting homesick."

Mr. O'Farrell looked up. "Do you get homesick?"

"Terribly."

"What do you do about it?"

"Just put up with it until it goes away."

He shook his head. "She's a naive intrepid spirit," he remarked as though to someone else.

"I wish to goodness," Betsy said with irritation, "that people would stop calling me naive!"

Then Mr. O'Farrell's face crinkled into its charming smile. "Miss Betsy," he said, "you're a very winsome girl!"

The rest of the day had a hurried unsettled feeling. She said good-bye to everyone she met. She thanked the stewards and stewardesses, and gave her modest tips, and Mr. O'Farrell asked her to come to his office, to exchange some American money for Italian *lire* and *centesimi*. When this was done, he smiled delightedly.

"I have a gift for you," he said, and spread a map of Europe across his desk. In one corner was a picture of the newest steamship of the line, a monster of forty-six thousand tons. Across the top was printed in red letters, "Six days from Munich to New York."

Betsy marveled. "Could I really get home in six days?"

"You could that!" He folded up the map and handed

it to her. "Now keep this handy for when you get home-sick!"

"Oh, I will! Thank you!"

But she did not forget the great lesson. It was brought home to her at dinner, for he ate hastily and seemed abstracted. Asking her pardon, he rose before dessert, and to her astonishment began to speak farewells.

"Why, why . . . I!" Confused, Betsy got to her feet. "I'll see you in the morning, surely."

"Alas, I'm afraid not! It's a madhouse here at the end of a voyage. But the Thomas Cook man will look after you like a father." He took both her hands with hurried gallantry. "I bless the saints that led me to put you beside me at table." He smiled and was gone.

Betsy sat down slowly. She understood! His wife would be coming on board!

"But I wouldn't have minded. I'd have liked meeting her." An unpleasant thought dawned. Maybe *she'd* have minded?

Mrs. Trevelyan's Mr. Brown smiled at her from the Captain's table. Betsy looked straight through him in a snub. Mr. Chandler dropped by her chair. He hinted pensively that it was beautiful on deck, but Betsy said she had to pack. Taking a leaf from Mr. O'Farrell's book, she put out her hand. She'd be busy in the morning, she informed him, smiling. His despair was flattering but she knew he was already wondering how many pretty girls would make the return voyage.

"Travel is broadening," thought Betsy.

Next morning she had to say good-bye to the *Columbic*. She hated to do it, for she had loved it all, down to the merry bugle that called them to meals. But a cruise had to end. Like a dance! Like a dream! Soon the deserted ship would be scrubbed and polished in preparation for another voyage—another escape from life, thought Betsy, for still another group of people.

She stood waiting with her suitcases piled at her feet, holding her handbag, camera, umbrella, and *Complete Pocket Guide*. Her heavy coat hung over her arm for she was traveling back into the winter.

"Yes, I'm Miss Elizabeth Ray," she said to the man from Cook's.

Mr. Feeney saw her ably through the customs. He guided her to the railway station, bought her tickets, and supervised the weighing of her trunk. With his help she sent a telegram to Miss Surprise, announcing her arrival the following morning. It seemed good to think that someone awaited her in Munich! And she was surprisingly glad to see dull Mr. Burton, who appeared with some chocolates for her.

He and Mr. Feeney put her into a first-class compartment which she occupied in solitary glory. She had planned to travel second class; first class was only for royalty and rich Americans, she had been told. But she was feeling too timid to protest any arrangements.

The little room opened into a corridor, and on the opposite side a window let down like a streetcar window for the admission of luggage. Mr. Feeney pointed out the dining car—the restaurant car, he called it. He reminded her that she changed trains at Zurich; she could get a sleeping car there. Then a bell rang. He jumped off, and the train began to move.

> *Down to Gehenna or up to the Throne,*
> *He travels the fastest who travels alone . . .*

She was alone again, all right, thought Betsy.

She went to the restaurant car in some trepidation, wondering whether she ought to be trying to remember German or French. "They couldn't expect me to know Italian!" She was both relieved and disappointed when the waiter greeted her in English.

"I work in Chee-ca-go. A ver' fine ceetee," he said.

"How do you suppose he knew I was an American?" Betsy thought, and looked studiously out the window as Mr. Brown came in.

While she was eating they went through Milan, and she saw the snowy dome of the great cathedral. Milan, she thought, was another place she must come back to. But she was feeling less and less like that adventurous woman of the world. Returning to her compartment, she plastered her nose against the pane.

There were mountains on the horizon, hazy as cloud mountains at first, but the train climbed past hillside pastures and sloping vineyards. Soon pine-clad mountains were rising all around her. Now and then a stream or waterfall caused Betsy to squeal with delight.

But the lakes choked her with their beauty.

"A lake at the base of a mountain is the loveliest sight in the world. It must be!" she thought.

Sometimes the water was a tranquil mirror reflecting its giant companion. Sometimes both mountains and lakes were veiled in blue-gray shadows. She leafed through her guidebook eagerly. Were these lakes Como, Lugano, Maggiore? The towns adjoining them seemed to be made up of glittering hotels.

She knew when they entered Switzerland because Swiss customs officials came in to examine her bags. They could understand her French, it seemed, but she couldn't understand theirs. Her questions brought forth a babbling torrent of words which seemed to bear no resemblance to anything she had heard in her French class.

"And I was an A student!" she thought disgustedly.

After they left, her door opened again, and Mr. Brown looked in.

"I don't believe we've met," he said, "but I was on the *Columbic*. My name is Brown." He had brown eyes, Betsy noticed, very alert and bright.

"How do you do?" she replied.

"I'm a friend of Mrs. Trevelyan," he added hopefully.

"And how many children do you have?" Betsy asked mentally. Aloud she responded in an icy tone, "Yes?"

He looked embarrassed. "I just wanted to say that if you need help with French or German, I'll be glad to interpret."

"Thank you," answered Betsy. "I've studied French and German." This sounded so childish that she flushed.

"Well, I'm in the next compartment if you need me," said Mr. Brown, and left her.

Betsy tossed her head. She went back to the window and told herself that these were the *Alps*. They were so high that she could scarcely see their summits. When she did crane her neck to view the rounded blue-white peaks, she saw more peaks rising behind them, and more, and more.

The cataracts leaped now from dizzying heights. Toylike chalets perched in terrifying niches, and down in the valleys were red-roofed villages. It was so *Switzeresque*! she thought.

"Oh, I need Tacy, or Tib, or Julia!" She needed some one to share it all with, to exclaim to. She was almost tempted to summon Mr. Brown. But she resisted even when daylight faded, and the lights came on, and she could no longer divert herself with views.

Her excitement subsided, and she began to feel increasingly forlorn. The beautiful *Columbic*, she thought, had been only an oasis in the desert of this awful trip. Here she was, alone in Europe, while her family sat heartlessly around the fire at home. . . .

The lights in the compartment blurred.

"I'm hungry; that's what ails me," she decided and walked down the corridor looking for the restaurant car, but it wasn't there anymore. She opened Mr. Burton's chocolates.

After a while the conductor came in and said something in German. It must have been German for she caught the word *Fräulein,* but the rest was as baffling as the French had been. Of course, she hadn't studied it since high school.

"What could he have wanted?" she thought when he went out. "Well, I should worry!"

She sat still and awaited developments, but nothing happened—especially nothing in the dinner line. They rattled along through the dark, and she grew hungrier and more wretched.

Presently Mr. Brown came in again, a checked cap in his hand.

"Please excuse me for intruding all the time!" His tanned face was so thin that his teeth looked large when he smiled, but the smile was very pleasant. "I suppose you understood that we have a stopover for supper?"

"Supper!" Betsy cried with joy, and flushed because she had almost given herself away. "That is . . . I wasn't sure."

"We have only fifteen minutes. I'm familiar with this station, and the restaurant. Could I help you?"

"Oh, yes!"

"You'll need your coat," he said and helped her into it and off the train.

On either hand, snow-clad mountains climbed to the sky, and above them stars twinkled in a narrow lane.

"Oh, this air! It's like Minnesota," Betsy cried.

"Do you come from Minnesota?"

"Yes. I'm going to Munich. My name is Elizabeth Ray."

He hustled her into the station restaurant. It was as clean as that air had felt pouring down her throat. The cap and apron of the waitress were as white as mountain snow. There was a rich smell of coffee.

Mr. Brown ordered in German without consulting her, and the dinner was delicious. They didn't talk; they were too busy eating, and when they finished he paid the waitress, for which she was grateful. Foreign money was as bewildering as foreign languages, almost. But back at her compartment, she opened her purse.

"I'd like to repay you for my dinner."

"Why, all right!"

She took out a handful of mystifying coins. He selected one or two.

"And thank you very much," said Betsy, in a definite tone of dismissal. Mr. Brown smiled and retreated.

She didn't see him again until they were entering Zurich. Then, quite as a matter of course, it seemed, he came to her compartment door. He assumed the burden of her coat and suitcases, called a boy, and got her settled in the station waiting room.

"What train are you taking out?"

"It leaves about eleven-thirty. I have to get a berth on the sleeping car."

"Maybe I can get it for you now." But it developed that he couldn't.

"The office is locked," he said, returning. "They open in plenty of time, though, the porter says. And by the way, when you get a chance, better get rid of your Italian money. French gold is a good thing to carry. Well, goodbye, Miss Ray." He held out his hand.

Betsy's heart dropped like a descending elevator.

"Where . . . where are you going?" she faltered.

"To my hotel. I'm stopping in Zurich."

"You've been awfully kind." She tried to keep the despair out of her voice.

"It was nothing at all," he answered. "You're going to love Munich. It's a cozy little city." And he went jauntily out of the station, swinging his cane, and followed by a porter with some bags and . . . of all things . . . a pair of skis.

Betsy sat straight and still in the almost empty waiting room. Money to change! A berth to get! And she couldn't remember a word of German except *Spinat mit Ei*. Why did she remember that? What would she want with spinach and egg at this hour of the night? She burst into a trembling laugh, and the sound frightened her and caused some of her companions in the room to look at her curiously.

She drew her belongings closer—suitcases, umbrella. camera, and *Complete Pocket Guide*. She gripped her purse and waited.

It seemed like an eternity, although it was just half an hour later by the loudly ticking clock, when the door swung open and Mr. Brown came in, looking like a tweedy angel. He sat down beside her, folding his gloved hands on top of his cane.

"What are you doing here?" Betsy asked tremulously.

He grinned at her. "Looking after you. You need to get a berth, and you never could do it alone. After I got to my hotel I realized that if I didn't see you on that train, I'd have it to worry about all the rest of my life."

"Oh, Mr. Brown!" cried Betsy. "How kind you are!"

"Kind nothing! Pure selfishness! May I smoke?"

They did a lot of visiting in the hour and a half before the train arrived. Betsy told him about Miss Surprise, and her own plans for seeing the world. She told him about Minneapolis. He had never been there and he, too, was interested in Minnehaha Falls. She told him about the Rays.

"What you've done for me . . . that's just what my father would have done. He'll appreciate it awfully. He'll write a letter to thank you, if you'll give me your address."

"I have a card somewhere," he said, and fished in his pockets but he didn't bring one out. He didn't tell her much about himself. He didn't mention his home. Perhaps he, like Mr. O'Farrell, left his family behind when he went traveling.

"Are you married?" Betsy asked suddenly. It was apropos of skiing technique and not very subtle, but she didn't care. It was a question she planned to ask freely from now on.

Her frankness went unrewarded, for just at that moment the ticket window was flung up. Mr. Brown ran to get his place, and he spent a fevered fifteen minutes with the agent. He beckoned for her money and changed some to French gold. He got her a berth, and that wasn't easy. She could tell by his emphatic German and the way he was waving bills around.

"And I've found an English-speaking porter. He'll look after you." They ran for the train. It was moving when he jumped off. She had to shout her thanks.

"I don't know your address . . . and my father . . ."

"Never mind!" he said, and waved.

She was sleeping before they were out of Zurich.

The German customs officer came in, in the middle of the night. Betsy unlocked her suitcases and fell asleep again before he had finished with them. But in that short moment of wakefulness, she remembered Mr. Brown.

How heavenly kind he had been! This berth! She never could have managed it without him.

"You don't know how kind people are until you go traveling," she thought. "Travel is very broadening."

9
MISS SURPRISE'S SURPRISE

When Betsy came back to her room after her first supper in the Pension Geiger in Munich, she shut the door behind her firmly, turned up the gas, walked to a capacious old-fashioned desk at the left of the window, and took Mr. O'Farrell's map out of a pigeonhole.

Lips quivering, she went to her bureau for pins,

unfolded the map, and affixed it to the wall.

"Six days from Munich to New York," read the slogan across the top.

Only six days!

"I could be home next Sunday. I could be home for some of Papa's onion sandwiches. Maybe I will be, too! Nobody's making me stay here."

She took off the maroon silk dress which had been so completely wrong at the pension supper table and hung it in the huge dark wardrobe. She put on her bathrobe, and stood stiff and straight, looking defiantly around the empty room. Then with a wail she flung herself across the bed.

Surprise checked her tears, for she sank down alarmingly. But when she realized that it was only because of a feather bed, she kept on crying. Clutching a pillow, she cried in floods until her face was bathed in tears.

"I want to go home!" she cried, and kicked the feather bed, which wasn't much satisfaction because it was so soft and yielding. "I want to go home!"

She had been in happy spirits, although a little fluttery inside, when she reached Munich that morning. There was no sign of Miss Surprise, but Betsy hadn't really expected her at such an early hour. She had gone boldly into the station restaurant.

"*Guten Tag, Fräulein,*" the waitress had said, smiling, and Betsy was pleased that she understood, "Good day, Miss." She did not understand anything further, but she received coffee, strong and delicious, with hot milk and little hard rolls and curls of unsalted butter.

An interpreter helped her get her trunk through customs; she wrote the address of the Pension Geiger on a card and, seated in an auto cab with her trunk on top and her bags around her, she rattled through the cold bright morning.

The streets were wide and very clean. They were being swept, she observed, by cheerful-looking old women in aprons. She saw a flower seller unpacking her basket. A group of soldiers in blue and scarlet uniforms passed at a dogtrot.

"I'm going to love Munich!" Betsy decided.

Nevertheless, she admitted to a feeling of relief that she was joining Miss Surprise. Independence was all very well, but it would feel cozy to be under somebody's wing for a while.

"Just until I begin to remember this darn language!"

Her heart was pounding when the cab entered Schellingstrasse and drew up before the Pension Geiger.

This wasn't too attractive. It rose straight from the sidewalk with a dreary courtyard at the side. Directly opposite, though, stood a wonderful house. Its walls were frescoed in lovely faded colors with kings and shepherdesses and cherubs.

"It's like a page from a picture book. Oh, I hope my room is on the front so I can look at it!" thought Betsy.

A servant girl came hurrying out. She was dark and

stockily built with pinned-up skirts, rolled-up sleeves, a key ring at her waist, and gold hoops in her ears. Nodding, bowing, smiling anxiously, and saying things Betsy could not understand, she seized Betsy's bags and ran into the house.

She returned in a moment with a tall, hard-featured woman dressed in shiny black who greeted Betsy politely and helped her pay the cabman. But neither she nor the servant spoke English, and Betsy understood none of their guttural talk except for a Fräulein Ray now and then.

"I'll certainly be glad to see Miss Surprise," she thought, and began to repeat the name. "Fräulein Surprise, please . . . *bitte*, I mean. Fräulein Surprise."

The pension keeper said, "*Ja*, Fräulein," and continued with unintelligible jargon. But she led the way inside, and the servant girl, to Betsy's amazement, hoisted the heavy trunk to her back and followed.

Betsy didn't like the hall, which had high bare walls and uncarpeted stairs. It was cold and smelled of cooking. But she liked her room, up on the second floor. It looked cozy with its thick bright carpet and worn velvet curtains over lace ones. There was a green tile stove—such a foreign-looking stove!—and a magnificent desk. She went at once to the window, and to her joy looked out at the picture-book house. Now, if she could just find Miss Surprise.

"*Wo . . . ist . . .* Fräulein Surprise, *bitte?*" Betsy asked again, and her hostess picked up a letter lying on the desk. It was addressed in a large angular hand to Betsy, who opened it eagerly.

Miss Surprise, Betsy discovered, had lived up to her name. She wasn't in Munich at all! She had changed to a singing teacher in Italy. Maybe Betsy would join her there?

"But I just came from Italy!" Betsy almost shouted.

This room, Miss Surprise continued imperturbably, with board, of course, rented for one hundred and ten marks a month (twenty-six dollars and forty cents).

"And don't let Frau Geiger charge you any more! She's an old shrew, as you can see from her face. But the house is respectable. It's a student pension which is probably what you want since you are a writer looking for material, Julia tells me . . ." Betsy read that over, bracing herself with Julia's proud phrase. "The food isn't bad and the place is near everything . . . galleries, theaters, shops. I'll be writing you from Florence, Minerva Surprise."

Betsy put down the letter uncertainly. Frau Geiger looked expectant. The servant girl was watching anxiously like a dog awaiting the word of command.

"Oh, for Mr. Brown!" thought Betsy, groping vainly for German. She nodded her head in confirmation and Frau Geiger brought a formidable-looking book for her to sign. She summoned a Fräulein Minnie, a short young woman with bushy hair, who knew a little English and helped Betsy fill out the blanks. They gave her a massive key, and left.

The servant girl followed, but almost immediately she was back, and now she was smiling a different sort of smile . . . as though sure of her welcome. Her hands were overflowing with letters which she tumbled onto the green felt ledge of the desk.

"Oh, thank you! *Danke schön!*" cried Betsy, and without removing hat or coat, she began to tear them open.

But reading them was almost more than she could bear. Her father and mother were entertaining their bridge club. Margaret had been asked to a high school dance. The family was going to the Orpheum for a vaudeville show. Julia and Paige would be home for Easter.

There was a letter from Tacy. Betsy opened it with avid fingers, but she read only half a dozen lines. It was a funny letter—about how Harry had asked some men friends to a venison dinner, and Tacy had never cooked venison, but didn't like to tell him.

"It was awful! I certainly wished you were here to charm them with your indefinable Paris air . . ."

"See here, I can't stand this!" said Betsy, and pushed the whole snowy drift of letters back into the desk.

The servant girl, who was building a fire in the stove, looked up timidly. Betsy forced a smile. She buttoned her coat, picked up gloves and pocketbook, and hurried out, trying to act as though she were late for an appointment.

She walked blindly up one street and down another. She didn't even pretend to look about. But gradually she became aware of broad, handsome avenues, pleasant squares filled with statuary, stately public buildings, and churches. One of these, with two round-topped towers, could be seen from everywhere.

Betsy walked on dizzily, and the streets began to seem theatric, as though she were seeing them on a motion picture screen—those old women still sweeping the pavements; policemen with shiny helmets; young men in flat, bright-colored caps; bare-headed girls carrying steins of beer, not one or two but half a dozen, foaming and spilling; and soldiers, soldiers, everywhere, especially officers whose blue and scarlet had an especial elegance and who wore swords at their sides.

Betsy walked and walked, and at last she realized that the sun stood overhead and she was very hungry.

"I'd better find a restaurant," she thought, for she had no idea where she was or how to get back to the pension. "I remember enough German to read a bill of fare."

She found one and went in. But to her dismay the menu was in German script. She had forgotten that completely—what she ever knew of it—and was floored for a moment.

The Mullers were German. She thought back to all the savory dishes she had enjoyed at Tib's house. How did you say beef stew or roasted chicken or hot potato salad? She could think only of *Spinat mit Ei.* And she didn't even like spinach with egg!

But she said it, and she must have said it properly for spinach with egg was produced. Triumphantly Betsy added, *"Kaffee, bitte,"* and the waitress brought an empty cup over which she poised two steaming pitchers.

She asked pleasantly, *"Dunkel oder hell?"*

Now what could that mean? Betsy shrugged and laughed, and the waitress, smiling, poured twin streams of coffee and hot milk into the cup.

When the bill was presented, Betsy spread out a pile of coins and the waitress, still smiling, selected some and left the rest. One of these Betsy pushed toward her, and the girl said, *"Danke schön."* She accompanied Betsy to the door with a singsong of farewells in which the other waitresses joined. Betsy had noticed that all departing customers were sent on their way to this chorus. Nevertheless, it sounded friendly.

And she felt better after she had eaten—even spinach. She thought how funny her experience would read in a letter home. And Miss Surprise's surprise certainly left her in an adventurous situation. What would the family say?

But after a while she grew lonely again. Everyone else on Munich's spacious streets looked so happy and content; they made her feel like an outsider, homeless.

"But I've got a home. It's my own nice little room. I'll go back and settle it," Betsy decided.

How to find it, though?

She remembered what Miss Surprise had said about the pension being near the galleries. The Old Pinako-thek was the famous one, of course. Stopping a woman who looked reassuringly fat, middle-aged, and plain, Betsy said, "Pinakothek?"

The kindly answer meant nothing, but the pointing finger was fine. Betsy followed it. She stopped a succession of estimable-looking females. "Pinakothek?" "Pinakothek?" "Pinakothek?"

She passed bakeries and caught the smell of coffee and the warm fragrance of cakes. Probably Munich had the afternoon coffee habit. Betsy had acquired it, visiting Tib in Milwaukee. She adored it, but coffee would be no fun alone.

Besides, she realized with a twinge of apprehension, it was getting late. The sun had sunk into some western clouds. Betsy walked and walked, saying "Pinakothek?" "Pinakothek?" "Pinakothek?" and at last, just as dusk fell in earnest, she spied the decorated house.

She ran into the Pension Geiger gladly. A door on the second-floor corridor was open, and she saw an artist working at an easel. She admitted herself with the massive key, and her room did, indeed, seem a heavenly refuge. A fire was roaring in the tile stove, the velvet curtains had been drawn, and the gas was lighted.

She took off her wraps, and unpacked and settled. It was good to have her familiar things around her! Soon the little clock was ticking beside her Bible and Prayer Book on the commode beside the funny wooden bed. At the foot stood a marble-topped washstand; and next to that a dressing table bore her jewel case, manicure set, comb and brush and mirror, and pictures of her father and mother. Then came her trunk with the steamer rug across it; and then the green tile stove.

Opposite, beyond the door, were ranged the wardrobe and a table covered with a spread on which were pictures of Julia and Paige, Bob Barhydt, Tacy and Tib. Mr. Burton's chocolates (what was left of them) sat there and her books: *The Beloved Vagabond, Little Women,* Emerson's *Essays,* some Dickens, Thackeray, and Dumas, and *The Oxford Book of English Verse.* Joe Willard had sent her that from Cambridge. There was another book Joe had given her, a limp leather copy of *As You Like It.*

Beyond a fat couch came the desk, which stood next to the window opposite the bed.

"At last," wrote Betsy, starting her letter home, "I have a big enough desk. It looks as though I were at least a congressman."

It had drawers and pigeonholes and shelves. Her writing materials were arranged with businesslike neatness inside. On top were "My Trip Abroad," and Margaret, and the American flag.

She told the family casually about Miss Surprise.

"I'll do whatever you think best but I'm sure I'm perfectly safe here. Miss S. said the pension was respectable, and I'm snug as a bug in a rug."

A piano broke in with a cataract of scales, and Betsy put down her pen to listen.

As in the early morning one bird is awakened by

another into song, so was a violinist somewhere inspired by the pianist to start tuning up. A cornetist began to blow; a tenor began to vocalize; and a clear soprano note rose from the room below.

After a scale, the soprano broke into an aria, and then started to rehearse an operatic scene. Ignoring the discord of piano, violin, cornet, and tenor, she pleaded and sobbed and went off into gales of artificial laughter.

Betsy went off into gales of laughter, too.

"This is a student pension, all right," she said, and thought of the artist painting madly in the room across the hall. Tomorrow, she, Betsy, would be writing a story. She had read of Munich's student life. Now here she was in the midst of it!

With some excitement she began to dress for supper. It was served at eight, Fräulein Minnie had said. Betsy was very hungry and not only for food; she was even hungrier for the camaraderie into which she expected to be welcomed.

She wanted a bath after the day's wanderings, but when she rang for the maid and said, *"Bad, bitte,"* she wasn't taken to a bathroom. She received a small jug of hot water. She primped a bit, heating her curling iron over the gas flame, donning the maroon silk dress and spraying perfume with her usual liberality. When a hollow clangor announced supper, she went downstairs with a pounding heart.

But supper was a bitter disappointment.

The high-ceilinged dining room was cold. A tile stove stood in one corner but it didn't seem to hold any fire; it looked clammy. The plaster walls were cracked and the floor was bare, so that the chairs scraped dismally. Faded, discouraged-looking curtains hung at the single window.

This was flanked by two small empty tables. A long table in the center of the room was half filled with young people who scrutinized Betsy as she entered. The girls were wearing sweaters or woolen dresses, and Betsy was embarrassed by her silk.

Fräulein Minnie came rushing up to seat her.

"Does . . . does anyone here speak English?" Betsy whispered.

"*Nein*, Fräulein. At dinner, *ja*. We have many peoples den from outside. But dese peoples who live in de house do not speak English. Only me." She was Frau Geiger's niece, she explained.

Seating Betsy at the big table, she said something in German and there was an anonymous murmur. The men half rose for hurried bows. After a lull, conversation swelled up in a mixture of tongues: German and French, but spoken too rapidly for Betsy's ear . . . Italian, she thought . . . Russian, maybe. German predominated, of course.

"This is the best thing in the world for my German," Betsy consoled herself, and tried to pick out phrases. But the enterprise lagged.

One girl looked German, another Italian, another was certainly Japanese. Which, Betsy wondered, was the aspiring prima donna? The artist, who was old and wrinkled, wore his hair to his shoulders, and a black Windsor tie. The other men were young with dark Slavic faces. They might be Bulgarians or Russians.

The tablecloth was not too clean. The dishes were thick and the meal was light. That dinner to which outsiders came in was clearly the substantial meal of the day. Supper offered only cold meat, bread and butter, a bit of salad, stewed fruit, and tea.

Fortunately, Betsy had lost her appetite. She was choked by that feeling of being an outsider. She cut the meat but couldn't put it in her mouth. She buttered the bread but returned it to her plate. She dipped a spoon into the sauce but carried to her lips only the smallest portion, and even that went down untasted.

One of the girls—the Italian—finished her supper and lighted a cigarette.

"She smokes it as calmly as—as Papa smokes his cigars," Betsy thought, shocked.

She rose as soon as she dared. Walking with leisurely dignity she left the dining room, but she ran up the stairs to Mr. O'Farrell's map on the wall.

Her pillow was soaked with tears when she heard a light knock. She didn't say "Come in," hoping that whoever was there would go away. Instead the door opened, and the servant girl who had carried up her trunk entered with a coal scuttle. Betsy turned her wet face back to the pillow.

But presently, after the rattle of coal subsided, Betsy felt a touch on her shoulder, and turned again. The servant girl stood looking down at her with a tender, pitying face.

She ran to the bureau and came back with Mrs. Ray's photograph. *"Mutter!"* she said, and thrust it into Betsy's hands.

She ran to the bureau again. This time she returned with Mr. Ray. *"Vater!"* she said.

She rushed across for Tacy and Tib. *"Schwester! Schwester!"* she cried triumphantly, pushing them all into Betsy's hands.

Betsy sat up, dashing the tears from her eyes.

"Nein! Nein!" She pointed to Margaret and to Julia. *"There* are my sisters. *Da ... ist ... Schwesters."*

The servant ran to get them, laughing.

She brought Bob Barhydt's picture. *"Schatz!"* she cried. But Betsy remembered this meant sweetheart, and shook her head firmly. That word brought only the image of Joe.

"Nein! Nicht Schatz! Freund! Freund!" she answered.

Both of them were laughing now.

"Was heisst ..." Betsy began, trying to ask, "What is your name?"

"Johanna," replied the maid, and added as though it were a nickname, "Hanni."

"Guten Tag, Hanni," Betsy said.

"Guten Tag, gnädiges Fräulein!" That meant "gracious Fräulein," Betsy remembered. How nice!

Hanni said something else with a rising inflection, but Betsy didn't understand. Hanni opened her mouth and put her finger in it.

"Ja, ja!" cried Betsy, bouncing off the featherbed. *"Ja,* I am hungry, *très* hungry. *Ich habe Hunger."*

Hanni beamed.

She rushed out of the room and Betsy jumped up and washed her face. She took down her hair and braided it, and sat down smiling beside the tile stove which was crackling now with heat.

"I just love this stove," she thought. "It belongs in a fairy tale, like that house across the street. And *what* a nice girl!"

Presently Hanni came back with a tray full of cold meat, bread and butter, salad, stewed fruit, and tea . . . everything there had been at supper, and more! Pickles and jam!

Betsy ate ravenously while Hanni replaced the pictures, turned back Betsy's bed, turned over the wet pillow, and plumped it up invitingly.

She picked up her coal scuttle at last and stood in the doorway, smiling.

"Gute Nacht, Fräulein."

"Gute Nacht, Hanni," Betsy answered. But just "Good night" wasn't enough. She looked up from her bread and jam with grateful shining eyes.

"Ich liebe dich, Hanni!" she cried.

And Hanni chuckled. *"Amerikanische!"* she said.

Betsy could hear her chuckling as she hurried down the hall.

10
BETSY MAKES A FRIEND

The next morning, of course, Betsy made a list. Lists were always her comfort. For years she had made lists of books she must read, good habits she must acquire, things she must do to make herself prettier—like brushing her hair a hundred strokes at night, and manicuring her fingernails, and doing calisthenics before an open window in the morning. (That one hadn't lasted long.)

It was fun making this list, sitting in bed with her breakfast tray on her lap . . . hot chocolate, crisp hard rolls, and a pat of butter. Hanni had brought it to her after closing the windows and pushing back the velvet draperies. Betsy felt like a heroine in one of her own stories; their maids always awakened them that way.

1. Learn the darn money.
2. Study German. (You've forgotten all you knew.)
3. Buy a map and learn the city—from end to end, as you told Papa you would.
4. Read the history of Bavaria. You must have it for background.
5. Go to the opera. (You didn't stay in Madeira because Munich is such a center for music and art???)
6. Go to the art galleries. (Same reason.)
7 . Write!

Full of enthusiasm, she planned a schedule. First, each morning, she would have her bath, and then write until noon. After the midday dinner she would go out and learn the city. She would go to the galleries, museums, and churches. She would have coffee out—for atmosphere.

"Then I'll come home and study German and read Bavarian history. And after supper . . ." she tried not to remember the look of that dining room . . . "I'll write my diary-letter, except when I go to the opera or concerts."

It sounded delightfully stimulating. Having finished her breakfast and tacked the list beneath Mr. O'Farrell's map, she rang for Hanni and said, *"Bad, bitte."*

She had her towel over her arm and her soap in her hand. That ought to make it clear, Betsy thought, that she expected a tub bath. But Hanni said, *"Ja, ja, Fräulein,"* as before, and came rushing back with a jug of hot water again.

Betsy felt disgruntled. A sponge bath didn't take the place of a tub. It simply didn't! She must get out her German dictionary and make it clear that she wanted her bath in a tub. Tub! What the dickens was the word for "tub"?

"I'll ask Fräulein Minnie," Betsy decided. When she was dressed she sat down importantly at the marvelous desk.

It was pleasant to look over at the picture-book house and start a story. What should it be about? If it was to have an author in it, she had seen an author. If it concerned a New York debutante, she knew two ladies' maids. Not able to decide between an author and a debutante, Betsy made her heroine a woman of mystery. She wrote:

"Meet Miss So and So."

A cute title, she remarked judicially.

Hanni came in to clean, and Betsy tried to explain that she would like that work done early before she started writing. She picked up her pen and wrote in the air. She pointed to a book.

"Ich verstehe," said Hanni, nodding eagerly, and tip-toed about, glancing at Betsy now and then with admiring awe. Evidently, thought Betsy, tickled, she wasn't the first writer to live at the Pension Geiger.

Going into Frau Geiger's office later (looking unsuccessfully for Fräulein Minnie to take up the subject of baths), Betsy met two officers coming out, resplendent in their blue and scarlet, with clanking swords. One was black haired, ugly, and thick-set; the other was young with blond mustaches twisted into peaks. He gave her a languishing look.

"I didn't suppose we had any of *those* gorgeous creatures here," thought Betsy, and looked for them at that one-thirty dinner to which Fräulein Minnie had said so many outsiders came. But they weren't there, that day or any other. Yet she saw them occasionally in the halls.

There was another mystery that grew as the days went by. At dinner, the two small tables in the dining room were occupied. Betsy still sat at the large table, listening in vain for the English Fräulein Minnie had promised, but the people at the small tables puzzled her.

Each sat by herself and neither spoke to the people at the big table. They bowed coming in, and said *"Mahlzeit"* going out. Everyone did that and Betsy soon learned to do it, too. But except for these formalities the two held themselves aloof.

One was a pleasant-faced lady in black who eaves-dropped cheerfully and smiled when the people at the big table laughed. The other, at Betsy's first dinner, was a girl of about her own age with a most disdainful expression.

She was tall but delicately built, with black hair and eyes and a pale soft skin—like white rose petals, Betsy thought. She wore a gray suit, a white blouse, and a crisp black straw hat. White gloves lay beside her purse. Everything about her was fresh and immaculate.

"But what a superior manner!" thought Betsy, progressing through noodle soup, stewed meat with dumplings, Brussels sprouts, hot potato salad, pudding with chocolate sauce, and a small side-dish of stewed fruit such as she had had the night before. This was the first thing served and the last taken away.

After her meal the tall girl stood up, murmuring *"Mahlzeit."* She walked out, erect and arrogant, and when she was gone, everyone started talking at once in scornful voices.

The next day, to Betsy's disappointment, the girl's table was occupied by a dingy woman in a shapeless veil-swathed hat and a worn suit with a soiled lace blouse beneath. Her dyed hair needed re-doing. Her skin had blotches and her nails were ill-kept.

The following day the tall exquisite girl was back. After that, she and the dingy woman occupied the table on alternate days. It was certainly a mystery.

"Story material!" Betsy thought, as she too said *"Mahlzeit"* (whatever that meant!) and left on her afternoon rounds.

She followed her schedule rigidly—except for the tub bath which she had not yet achieved. Hanni continued to bring only a jug of hot water and Fräulein Minnie forgot all her English whenever Betsy mentioned tubs. After the morning's writing, and her dinner, Betsy set out briskly, armed with camera, notebook, pencils, and *Complete Pocket Guide*. But it was a false briskness. In spite of her list, in spite even of Hanni, she was miserably homesick again.

Whether the sun shone or went under a cloud, whether it rained or snowed, Munich was the same to Betsy. She read in her guidebook that this was one of the most charming capitals of Europe, that Ludwig the First had laid it out in magnificent avenues and decorated it with copies of famous buildings and statues in Greece and Italy. Betsy didn't care.

The city stood on the green Isar, she read—that "Isar, rolling rapidly" of Campbell's poem. The river was bordered by landscaped paths, spanned by snowy bridges. Betsy walked the paths and bridges, aching for the Mississippi.

She discovered a park called the English Gardens. Miles long, it was like a tract of country put down in the middle of the city. It had a stream, a lake, waterfalls. She sat on a bench and watched the people.

There were whole families together, enjoying the February sun. There were lovers with their arms about each other, and schoolgirls in giggling pairs, artists in soft hats, and those young men she had noticed before wearing colored caps. And of course there were soldiers, soldiers everywhere.

"What do they want all the soldiers for?" thought Betsy. "There isn't any war."

There were almost as many dogs as soldiers—aristocrats led by chains, and curs bounding joyously ahead of their owners. Bicycles, too, crowded the paths.

"This park would be nice if Tacy were here," Betsy thought wistfully.

She strolled past the Royal Palace and loitered in its arcaded garden. She fed the pigeons in front of the Hall of the Fieldmarshals, but she felt self-conscious, doing it alone. She hunted up the Frauenkirche, Church of Our Lady, whose twin towers she had seen on the first day. This was to Munich what the Eiffel Tower was to Paris, she read. It was nothing to Betsy. But she sent flocks of post cards telling her friends that it was simply fascinating.

Americans were everywhere—smartly dressed, immersed in guidebooks, chattering. Some of them wore small American flags. They were all in twos or threes or fours and made Betsy feel lonelier than ever.

"I wander lonely as a cloud," she paraphrased Wordsworth, but she couldn't manage a smile. She felt desolate, even in the coffee houses. Oh, for Tib!

The guidebook made much of these convivial places, and of the overflowing beer halls. *"Gemütlich,"* it said, was the word for München, as the Germans called their city.

"*Gemütlich!*" That meant something like . . . cozy, which Mr. Brown had used in connection with the city. If there was anything Munich wasn't, Betsy thought bitterly, it was *gemütlich*!

Walking its streets was only better than being alone in her silent little room—at twilight when that din of practicing began. The prima donna was learning Madame Butterfly, one of Julia's roles. The familiar arias twisted Betsy's heart.

She still did not know which girl was the prima donna. The Italian? The Japanese? The plain little German with crimped hair? She looked too small, but Julia was small, and this girl carried herself like a singer.

In the evenings Betsy studied German fiercely.

"*Ich bin, du bist, er ist . . .*"

And she studied the history of Bavaria. It was quite distinct from Germany, she found, but its troops were at the Emperor's command. That Ludwig the First who had made Munich so beautiful had become infatuated with a Spanish dancer, Lola Montez. He had built her a palace and made her a countess. Finally, the people rebelled. She was obliged to flee, and Ludwig had to give up his throne. Not very edifying, Betsy thought.

She wrote notes to her *Columbic* friends and glowing letters home. She answered flippantly Margaret's reports on the stories she was sending out.

"It's too bad *Colliers* didn't appreciate 'Emma.' But

let's be magnanimous and give them a chance at 'The Girl with Lavender Eyes.' You might try 'Emma' on *Ainslee's* next."

She stretched the evenings out and out, for bedtime was a time to weep.

Hanni always managed to drop in. She wasn't much older than Betsy but she was as tender as a mother.

"Fraulein Ray *hat Heimweh,*" she would say, bringing the family pictures one by one, and Joe Willard's picture—Betsy had found one pasted in a kodak book, and had steamed it off and put it in a frame.

On Sunday Betsy went to the American Church. But the hymns, the dear familiar ritual, reduced her to tears and she rushed out without even speaking to the rector.

A day or two later she returned, for she had noticed a book-lined library. Here, over tea and toast, you could read American magazines, and the Paris edition of the New York *Herald.* She went there the next day and the next.

"But I didn't come to Munich to read the *Saturday Evening Post!*" Betsy told herself furiously, and rushed outdoors again.

She went to the Hoftheater and bought tickets for *Lohengrin* and *Tannhäuser.* She plodded through the galleries, beginning with the Old Pinakothek.

"But I don't know what to look for in these paintings," she thought despairingly, roaming past Raphael, Titian, Van Dyck, Rubens— The guidebook starred Rubens. She stared at his gigantic rosy figures.

"They're certainly fat!" she thought.

The New Pinakothek meant even less and the building wasn't heated. The Glyptothek had mostly sculpture, white and cold. In the Shack Gallery she found one painting she really liked.

A barefoot boy had thrown himself down on a hilltop. The sky was intensely blue, the grass was starred with flowers, and the boy was happily relaxed, one arm thrown over his eyes.

He reminded Betsy of herself and Tacy and Tib on the Big Hill back in Deep Valley. She could remember the warmth of the sunshine, the smell of hot grass, the hum of insects.

She bought a print of the Shepherd Boy—by Lenbach, her guidebook said—and put it up in her room. She loved it almost as much as Mr. O'Farrell's map.

Every night Betsy looked at that map and resolved to start home on the morrow. Every morning she decided to stick it out another day. But as though the situation weren't bad enough already, something happened to make it worse.

The street crowds began to grow fantastic. People were powdered, painted, masked; some were in costume. She ran into clowns, American Indians, court ladies, and girls in baggy trousers such as Betsy had seen in Algiers. Children were brownies and fairies. Even the dogs (and there were thousands of dogs, mostly squatty little dachshunds) had paper ruffs. Old men and women were selling bags of confetti. The air twinkled with dancing colored flakes.

It was the Carnival, Fräulein Minnie explained. It would last until Ash Wednesday. She herself had a shepherdess costume, she added, smiling broadly.

A carnival! But for a carnival . . . you needed to feel gay. It was awful if you didn't. And Betsy felt increasingly awful as the city turned into one huge masquerade ball. The crowds were laughing, shouting. They were orderly crowds, just childishly merry. But how could you be merry all alone?

Betsy tried. After half a dozen masks had showered her with confetti, she bought a bag and threw a handful. She didn't throw another. It was no good . . .

Giving her bag to a diminutive cowboy, she turned abruptly and walked toward the pension. She went faster and faster. She must, she must get home before she cried.

But back in her room at last, she didn't cry. She sat down and dropped her face despairingly into her hands.

"What I need is some friends," she said aloud.

She had never really appreciated friends before. Of course, she had always had them. Wonderful friends back in Deep Valley—Tacy . . . Tib . . . Carney. And at the University, Effie and Bob and the rest. She had always been surrounded with friends. She had taken them for granted. Never again, she thought, would she take friends for granted.

As usual at this hour the pianist with whose tireless fingers Betsy was all too familiar . . . the cornetist . . . the tenor all began to practice. The soprano struck a preliminary chord.

"Oh, not Madame Butterfly!" Betsy groaned. "Please! Not tonight!"

It wasn't Butterfly. The soprano began to sing a song so startlingly familiar that Betsy sat upright.

From the land of the Sky-blue Water
They brought a captive maid . . .

"Why, that's astonishing!" Betsy cried. She listened longingly. She could not tell whether the words were in English or German, but the tune was unmistakable. It was home itself put into song.

When Betsy went down to supper that night, she took along her German-English Dictionary. She slipped into her seat with the usual *"Guten Abend,"* and waited for a lull in the mingled German, French, Russian, Bulgarian, and Italian. Then she spoke boldly.

"Who," she asked in laborious German, "who sings the song about the sky-blue water?" She repeated *Wasser* so many times that the waitress hurried to bring her a glassful, and everyone else looked bewildered.

Betsy began to sing it. *"From the land of the Sky-blue Water . . ."*

She caroled as though she were standing beside the piano at home.

The girl with the crimped hair began to smile. She

had a monkeyish, cute little face. She leaned excitedly across the table. "Me," she said. "I sing dat."

Betsy put a careful finger on her breast. "I," she proclaimed, "I come from there . . . from the land of the sky-blue water."

"Was? Was sagen Sie?"

She tried to say it in German but the Bulgarians, the Japanese, the Italian, the little German did not understand. Betsy had an inspiration.

"Minnchaha Falls," she said loudly. "I come from Minnehaha Falls."

She might have been back on the *Columbic.* "Minne-ha-ha," everyone repeated, with long "ah-h-hs" of interest, and Fräulein Minnie hurried up.

"Fräulein Ray. You have seen de Minnehaha Falls?"

Poetry, Betsy thought, was wonderful! Longfellow was henceforth her favorite poet.

"I live there," she proclaimed. If they thought she went over the falls in a barrel every day, who cared?

She turned back to the small prima donna.

"Where . . . ?" asked Betsy, speaking in English slowly, "where . . . did you learn that song?"

The girl threw up her hands in laughing mystification, and the table broke into a babble of helpfulness. In German, in French, in Italian, and in what Betsy thought was Bulgarian or Russian, everyone said something.

The soprano called Fräulein Minnie and Betsy

repeated her question. Fräulein Minnie turned it into German. The girl smiled and answered in German which Fräulein Minnie turned into English.

"After supper she vill explain. Vill you come to her room, please?"

The singer's room, too, looked out at the picturebook house. A grand piano stood in one corner and operatic scores and sheet music were scattered about. She was waiting with a calling card. "Fräulein Matilda Dienemann," it said. Betsy put her fingers to her breast again. "Betsy Ray."

Fräulein Dienemann went to the piano and took up a sheet of music. Before she put it in Betsy's hand, Betsy understood. Written across the title page in a black angular hand was the name—Minerva Surprise.

Fräulein Dienemann plunged into explanation, but Betsy got more from intuition than from the mixture of German and broken English. Miss Surprise had left this song behind, and Hanni had given it to Fräulein Dienemann.

"It was Miss Surprise who sent me here. She is a friend of my older sister. My sister is a singer, too." The two girls sat down beside each other on the couch, passing the German dictionary back and forth. A little French helped. In five minutes they were Tilda and Betsy to each other.

Tilda wasn't German, after all. She was Swiss. She showed Betsy a picture of a white stone house in St.

Gallen, and photographs of her father and mother.

Holding her new-found friend tightly by the hand, Betsy led her upstairs to her own family photographs. Tilda was enthralled with Julia in her costumes as Cherubino and Elvira.

Betsy waved to the big desk. "I write stories," she declared. She could not understand Tilda's answer, but she understood her warm delight.

Hanni came in to turn back Betsy's bed and a smile spread over her broad dark face when she saw the girls together.

Presently Tilda took Betsy by the hand and they went back to Tilda's room. She made tea on an alcohol lamp, and brought out rolls and sausage and kuchen.

Tilda studied singing at the Conservatory, she said. She took dramatic lessons, too. But there would be no school tomorrow; it was Shrove Tuesday. Could they spend the last day of Carnival together?

They could and did, and like the rest of Munich they were childishly merry. There was a parade with bands and flower-trimmed floats and carriages full of costumed people. Tilda and Betsy bought bags and bags of confetti and pelted passers-by.

They saw Fräulein Minnie, a happy, dumpy shepherdess, strolling home in the twilight. They saw even Hanni, who so seldom had a holiday. Everyone came out on the last day of Carnival, Tilda said.

Hanni wasn't in costume except for the confetti

clinging to her hat and coat, but her face was shining with excitement and pleasure. She was with a soldier.

"He's her sweetheart," Tilda told Betsy. "But they can't afford to get married."

11

BETSY TAKES A BATH

One morning Fräulein Minnie came into Betsy's room on some domestic errand, and Betsy closed the door and leaned against it.

"Fräulein Minnie," she said, "here . . . at the Pension Geiger . . . is there a bathroom?"

Fräulein Minnie, looking startled, nodded.

"A real, *echte* bathroom with a tub?"

"Sure, Fräulein! A beautiful toob."

"Then when, please," asked Betsy, "may I have a bath?"

Fräulein Minnie moved hurriedly toward the door. "Soon, *gnädiges* Fräulein."

"But I'd like one today," Betsy persisted, not yielding her strategic position.

"Ach, *Himmel!*" Fräulein Minnie looked around with a hunted expression. She was perspiring. "*Bitte*, Fräulein, not today! But it won't be long, I promise. Some day . . ."

"Some day! I can have a bath some day!" Betsy told Tilda that afternoon.

Their friendship had progressed by leaps and bounds. They spent their evenings in each other's room, usually in Tilda's because of the piano. She sang Betsy arias from the operas in which she had roles—*Madame Butterfly, La Bohème, Tales of Hoffman*—and Betsy taught her American popular songs.

"Peg off my hear-r-rt, I loff you . . ." Tilda sang.

They tried on each other's hats and looked into each other's books. Tilda had Goethe, Schiller, Shakespeare, George Bernard Shaw—but all in German.

She told Betsy about an artist who was in love with her. Wishing to be rid of him painlessly, she had invented a rich American fiancé. Betsy must tell her about rich Americans so she could convince August.

"Wonderful!" cried Betsy. "Say he comes from Pittsburgh."

"Pitts-burgh? *Warum?* Why?"

"Oh, the best millionaires do! Now, shall he be young and dashing or old and fatherly?"

Old and fatherly, Tilda decided when she understood. August was so jealous. "All gentlemens is jealous," she informed Betsy sagely.

And now, in turn, armed with the German-English dictionary and a French-English dictionary, Betsy brought the problem of her bath to Tilda.

At first Tilda was as horrified as Fräulein Minnie. "*Aber es ist unmöglich.* Impossible," she said.

Betsy leafed grimly through the dictionary. She stood up straight and slapped her chest.

"Nothing is impossible!" she declared grandiloquently, and Tilda burst into laughter.

"*Amerikanische!*" she cried.

She explained, while the books flew back and forth, that there really was a bathroom in the pension. There really was a tub. But it was downstairs in the officers' quarters. At least it was near their quarters.

"Is it their tub?" Betsy asked.

No, Tilda conceded, it was everybody's tub. But the officers didn't like anyone else to use it.

"Why shouldn't we all use it if it belongs to us all?"

"Oh, Betsy! *Offiziere!*" Tilda rolled expressive eyes. Springing up, she gave an imitation of an officer. She twisted mustaches, threw back a cape, put her hand on an imaginary sword.

"Germany is theirs," she said. "If Frau Geiger let you use their tub and they found out . . . !" Tilda drew the sword and ran it across her neck.

She spoke in German, but Betsy understood. She had noticed how important officers were in Germany. Germans stepped off the sidewalk to let an officer pass. Betsy didn't; and she heartily snubbed the young lieutenant who always ogled her when they passed in the halls.

"If it isn't their tub," she said stubbornly, "I'm going to have a bath."

"Very vell," said Tilda. "I vill speak to Frau Geiger. I vill tell her du bist Amerikanische und crazy. For you a yug off vater ist not enough."

"*Nein!*" cried Betsy. "Must be a toob for the crazy Amerikanisches Fräulein."

Wiping away tears of laughter, they ran down to the office.

Frau Geiger's smile vanished when Tilda explained. There was excited rebuttal and surrebuttal. Betsy didn't understand a word, but Tilda told her at last that Frau Geiger had promised to arrange things. When the officers went out, and she could be sure they would be gone for several hours, she would call Betsy.

"Then you must take your bath, *schnell, schnell!*"

"Like lightning!" Betsy agreed.

For several days she awaited a summons, but the officers seemed to be of most domestic habits. The days, however. passed quickly; Betsy's life was transformed because of Tilda.

To be sure, she was doing just what she had done before. She wrote in the morning and, after the noon dinner, went out to learn Munich. But what a difference, now that she had a friend!

Almost every day, she and Tilda met for coffee. Betsy learned what the waitress meant when she offered her steaming pitchers.

Dunkel meant "dark," and produced a brunette fluid. *Hell* meant "light," and resulted in an insipid pallor. Betsy learned to say, *"Mitte, bitte."* Then equal amounts of coffee and hot milk poured into her cup.

Choosing a cake from the rack of kuchen was a mouthwatering task, especially in the confectioners' shops, which were frequented chiefly by plump women.

Betsy and Tilda drank their coffee in all sorts of places. Austere resorts where orchestras played classical music. Smoke-filled rooms where chess games competed with racks full of German periodicals . . . sometimes, the Paris edition of the *Herald.* Humbler hostelries; one was very cheerful with geraniums and a parrot that cried, *"Hoch!"* Here they saw coachmen, off duty, playing cards, and fat old women knitting.

One coffee house was popular with students. These proved to be the youths with colored caps. The colors denoted their clubs, Tilda explained, and their faces were scarred from dueling. That seemed to hold the place in

German universities that football did at home!

The Café Stephanie was a haven of Bohemians.

"Why," Betsy asked Tilda, "do women have to cut their hair in order to paint and men have to let theirs grow?" For several women had their hair cut short, and others wore English bobs, like children, while the men affected flowing locks.

There were authors surrounded with inkpots and papers, writing busily. One man would pause, now and then, and rumple his bushy hair and stare wildly about and strike his brow. Betsy knew he was fishing for a word. She longed to lean over, fraternally, and suggest one.

"Oh, Tilda!" she cried. "Let's come here again! And I'll bring 'Meet Miss So and So,' and write."

Tilda agreed. But only in the daytime, she warned, and here Betsy must never come alone!

Betsy laughed. "Don't worry about me! I could never be a Bohemian."

She was too clean, and too systematic, and too orthodox, she wrote in the home diary-letter. "I can see a woman smoking now without batting an eyelash, but I wouldn't smoke myself. I like to get the atmosphere, though . . . for my writing."

She and Tilda always wandered a bit before starting home. There was no time for real sight-seeing; they planned to do that on Saturdays and Sundays which were Tilda's free days. But they patronized the flower sellers who stood on almost every corner. (Their baskets made little gardens in the February sun.) And they loitered near the Royal Palace hoping for a glimpse of the King and Queen, or even a princess. There were three princesses, all very plain, Tilda said. Plain or not, Betsy wanted to see one.

Sometimes there were errands. Tilda took Betsy to a shop where she could have her films developed. It was strange to see those breeze-blown snapshots from the *Columbic*.

"Which one is Mr. O'Farrell?" Tilda wanted to know.

She needed shoes, and the shoe shop fascinated Betsy. The owner's wife fitted Tilda. A grown daughter was fitting a man in the adjoining chair. A yellow-haired child, intent of face, buttoned and unbuttoned the shoes. The only one at leisure was the husband and father who strolled about impressively.

"Not much like *my* father and *his* shoe store!" Betsy thought.

Tilda always knew a good way home. Perhaps it would be through the Old City, those narrow streets around the Frauenkirche with tall, thin, high-peaked houses. On the nearby Marienplatz was the fourteenth-century Town Hall.

They looked in at the Hofbrau Haus, the Royal Brewing House. In this famous hostelry there was always a cheerful clatter. Maids were moving briskly about with racks of pretzels while men, women, and even children sat comfortably drinking beer.

München, Tilda told Betsy, strolling home along the Isar which reflected the first lights of evening, München was called the City of Art and Beer.

"It is *gemütlich*, München," she said, and Betsy was astonished to find that she agreed. Yes, knowing Tilda made a difference, and nowhere was this more apparent than at the pension table.

There was still that mixture of strange tongues, only now Betsy was trying to contribute to the conversation, and her efforts caused endless merriment. Again and again the company summoned Fräulein Minnie.

"Fräulein Minnie, was *heisst* . . . ?"

Slowly Betsy was straightening out the people. The Bulgarians were University students. There were several Austrians: a poet, the tenor, the indefatigable pianist. The Japanese girl studied composition at Tilda's Conservatory. The long-haired artist was the only German. The Italian girl was an artist, too.

She put a question to Betsy, via the poet who understood Italian and put it to Tilda in German who put it to Betsy in their peculiar patois.

There was an American boy at her studio, and he said continually, "Oh, how peach!" They had a pretty model, and he said, "She is peach." And someone sketched an old woman and when he looked at the picture he said, "It is peach." What, the Italian artist demanded, was "peach"?

"Here," said Betsy. "This is peach." And she took a

spoonful of the ever-present compote. She chuckled to herself, remembering Maida who had asked a similar question.

So uproarious was the conversation these days that even the arrogant girl at the small table listened. Betsy kept intending to ask Tilda who she was. But she had not yet remembered to put the question, when one day at dinner the girl spoke.

Betsy had been to the Old Pinakothek, looking at Greek vases. She was trying to say that one beauty, covered with fanciful figures, had made her think of the "Ode on a Grecian Urn."

"You know. By Keats. It must have been translated into German. 'Beauty is truth, truth, beauty . . .'"

No one understood. And in the bewildered silence, the girl spoke.

"I don't know whether that has been translated or not," she said in flawless and beautifully articulated English. She gave the title in German, and there was instant recognition of the poem from Tilda, who nodded curt thanks. Betsy, too, expressed her thanks, and after the meal she paused by the tall girl's table.

"I didn't realize that you spoke English."

The girl smiled, and her smile made her look younger and sweeter. "I am only half German," she said. "My mother is English. Won't you sit down?"

Betsy complied gladly. "I've been wishing I knew you. Are you studying in Munich?"

"Yes. The piano, but I am only an amateur. I live with my parents. I've just come to stay with them after . . . a long time away. You know my mother, perhaps. She eats here the days I don't come."

Betsy was too taken aback to reply. That dingy woman and this exquisite girl!

"We never come together because we cannot leave my father. He is ill." For no reason that Betsy could see, the girl flushed. "My name is Helena von Wandersee."

"I'm Betsy Ray. Would you like to go for a walk?"

"That would be very pleasant."

But in spite of her perfect English, Helena wasn't easy to get acquainted with. She was excessively formal. She was trying to be friendly, though. When Betsy began to call her Helena, she reciprocated with a timid Betsy.

Like Betsy, she was just getting to know Munich. That long time away from her parents had covered not months but years. She had been living with cousins in some distant place.

"I can't get used to so much freedom," she confided. "My cousins and I never went out alone. If my aunt could not go, a maid took us . . . or a governess. It is very strange to go about like this."

They looked at the shop windows which were showing the spring styles.

"Do you like clothes?" Betsy asked, admiring a floppy flower-trimmed hat. She loved that picturesque kind.

"I have never picked out my own clothes. My aunt

always bought what was suitable for us. It might be very interesting to make a study of one's own . . . type."

"You're the aristocratic type," Betsy volunteered. "I've never picked out my clothes either. My mother loved having three daughters to shop for. You must come up to my room and see my family."

"I'd like to, very much. Would you . . ." Helena's pale face flushed again. "I'm going to hear Gabrilowitsch, the pianist, Sunday night. Would you care to go?"

"I'd love it. Where do I go to get a ticket?" Betsy looked at her watch. "See here!" she said. "I'm meeting Tilda, Fräulein Dienemann, for coffee. I want you to get to know her. Won't you join us?"

"Thank you, but I really couldn't." In an instant the girl was stiff and cool again.

"I'm meeting her at the Hall of the Fieldmarshals. We always meet there because we can feed the pigeons if either of us has to wait."

"I'm sorry. I must go."

"I'm sorry, too," said Betsy, perplexed. "You can get a tram right here."

"I never take trams."

"You never take *trams*?" Betsy was astonished. How could anyone not take trams? And the streetcars in Munich were particularly nice. They were painted Bavarian blue, and the conductor lifted his cap and wished you good morning when you got on, and lifted it again and bade you farewell when you got off.

There was an awkward pause. Then Helena smiled, and that made her look sweet and friendly again. "I have so enjoyed being with you. And I'll pick up your ticket for Gabrilowitsch. Good-bye . . . Betsy."

After coffee Betsy told Tilda about her. "I've been wondering why she came to dinner only every other day. Her father is ill; she and her mother can't leave him alone."

"So she can't leave her father!" Betsy was surprised to see Tilda's piquant face harden. "Ask Fräulein Minnie!" she added satirically.

"Why? What do you mean?"

"Frau von Wandersee gives Minnie English lessons to pay for one dinner a day, and she and her daughter take turns eating it . . . because they like to eat."

Tilda was speaking German and Betsy was sure she had not understood. But when the dictionaries were produced, the remark remained the same.

"She doesn't seem poor," Betsy replied thoughtfully. "And those cousins she's lived with all her life were certainly rich. But poor or not, she's awfully nice. Let's include her in some of our bats." Tilda had learned the word "bat," a favorite with Betsy.

"She wouldn't go," Tilda replied coldly.

"Why not?"

"Because she's a snob."

They paused on a street corner over their dictionary, to put "snob" into English.

She was much more of a snob than the princess, Tilda went on angrily.

"The princess? What princess?"

The woman in black at the other small table was a princess, Tilda said. But she was very pleasant. The girl was unbearable, and she was only a baroness.

Again Betsy was sure she had misunderstood. "Who's a baroness? Not Fräulein von Wandersee?"

"She's the Baroness von Wandersee."

Betsy was flabbergasted.

"Heavens and earth!" she said, and began to laugh. "Well, I told her she looked aristocratic!" But Tilda didn't smile, and Betsy sobered. Speaking slowly, in their mixture of tongues, she assured Tilda that Helena was not snobbish at all. She was lonely; she would be delighted to go about with them.

Tilda snorted.

They had reached the pension, and when they entered the courtyard they saw Frau Geiger standing in the doorway. Fräulein Minnie was behind her. The two called out in agitated voices.

"What is it? What has happened?" Betsy asked, thinking wildly of a cable.

It was her bath!

The officers had gone out, Fräulein Minnie explained while Frau Geiger and Tilda jabbered in German. They were going to a dinner, to a most important banquet. This was her chance.

Elated, Betsy pelted up the stairs, Tilda behind her. They rushed into Betsy's room and Betsy undressed swiftly. She screwed her hair into a knot. She put on her cherry-red bathrobe.

Hanni knocked with a pile of towels, although Betsy had plenty of towels already. Tilda ran down to her room for a bottle of cologne. Laden with towels, washcloth, soap, bath salts, and cologne, Betsy stepped into the hall.

A sizable crowd had gathered. The Japanese girl said something in German to Tilda who exclaimed, *"Ach, lieber Gott!"*

"What did she say?" Betsy demanded.

The poet, Tilda replied, had taken a bath one time. He had told Susuki about it. When he came out, an enraged officer was lying in wait.

"You can't scare me!" Betsy cried and raced down the corridor, chanting,

> *"Half a league, half a league,*
> *Half a league onward,*
> *All in the valley of Death*
> *Rode the six hundred . . ."*

There weren't quite six hundred, but her bodyguard included all the servants, Frau Geiger, Fräulein Minnie, Tilda, the Italian artist, the little Japanese.

On they went, downstairs and through a door, to the strange sacred wing of the officers. They escorted Betsy to the bathroom itself. There, everyone but Hanni left her.

A round heater had been lighted, but the tub was filled with boots and swords.

"Those officers don't appreciate their blessings," Betsy thought as Hanni pulled out the grim impedimenta and attacked the dusty tin catchall. There were even cobwebs in it!

Hanni scrubbed, and the heater roared and gurgled. Betsy glanced at it apprehensively, afraid it would explode. At last the water was drawn, and Hanni backed out. She would wait in the hall, she said.

"I will be here, Fräulein. I will not leave you."

"Und I am here," called Tilda.

Betsy peeped out. Fräulein Minnie, her eyes popping, stood guard at the door of the wing. "And Frau Geiger," Minnie called, "is waiting at the outer door . . . in case . . ."

But that "in case" was too awful to contemplate. Betsy closed the door.

The heater had done its work too well. And Hanni in her excitement had let only hot water run. The cold water came in a feeble trickle. Betsy tested it with a finger, with a toe. She dumped in rose geranium bath salts. At last she was able to step in herself.

Betsy loved baths. She soaped luxuriously, and then lay back in the hot scented water. Her nervousness receded and she was flooded with peace. She lay dreaming. Should she go to Rome next? To Paris?

"Fräulein! Fräulein!" Hanni called.

Betsy started upright.

"The officers!" This was Fräulein Minnie's voice. "They are coming back!"

"But why? What for?" They must have forgotten a sword or something, Betsy thought. Perhaps one of the very swords she was stepping over now as she climbed out. She rubbed herself frantically.

"Hurry! Make haste!" Frau Geiger was delaying them, Fräulein Minnie explained, her voice shaking with fright.

Betsy hurried into the cherry-red bath robe. Gathering up towels, washcloth, soap, bath salts, and cologne, she opened the door. A gust of warm perfumed air came with her.

With Hanni scurrying ahead she got safely to the door leading from the wing to the main corridor. But there she met the officers. She met them face to face—the thick-set ugly one and his handsome blond companion!

Behind them stood Frau Geiger, her face stricken. Fräulein Minnie was a picture of terror and Hanni had that look Betsy had seen before, of a dog who has been ill-treated. Tilda had disappeared.

As for Betsy, there was no denying her guilt. The narrow passageway smelled of rose geranium, her hair was screwed into a knob, and her face, she knew, was moistly pink. In spite of herself, Betsy broke into a smile.

The young lieutenant who had ogled her so vainly smiled back in astonished delight. The dark, ill-natured-looking captain smiled, too. Both officers clicked their heels together. They bowed from the waist.

Betsy acknowledged this salute as graciously as she could, with soap, bath salts, and cologne in her hands and towels dripping from her arm. She trailed her cherry-red robe triumphantly up the stairs.

Tilda was trembling in a corner of the room.

"Look at me!" Betsy cried, revolving proudly. "Look at me! I have had a bath!"

12
THREE'S NOT A CROWD

At the concert, Betsy planned, she would see what she could do about bringing Tilda and Helena together. Tilda's attitude was most discouraging. She not only disliked the young baroness; she seemed stubbornly sure that Helena would never accept her as a friend. But how could that possibly be?

Tilda was engaging, well bred, well educated—her interests extended far beyond music. If money mattered—her father was a prosperous manufacturer. She didn't have a title, of course, but neither did Betsy. Betsy liked Helena. She didn't like her arrogance, but it was easier to forgive now that she knew Helena's story.

"Eating dinner only every other day! When she's a baroness, too!"

Betsy had always thought she would be overwhelmed with romantic excitement by a title, but she wasn't. The baroness was just a nice girl whom she liked and wished she could help.

She must make Helena and Tilda and herself into a threesome, she decided. Three made a crowd, in more ways than the old adage indicated. It made a Crowd.

"Look at Tacy and Tib and me!" Betsy argued.

She thought about it all through the concert while the Polish Gabrilowitsch with dazzling skill played Beethoven, Chopin, Mendelssohn, and his pretty wife, once Clara Clemens, sang German songs. It was thrilling to be seeing Mark Twain's daughter.

Betsy planned to begin her campaign on the walk home, but Helena's mother was waiting, wearing the same rusty veil-swathed hat, the same worn suit, the same soiled blouse. "Doesn't she ever wash it?" Betsy wondered.

She didn't like Frau von Wandersee. Her manner and her soft, purring voice were both insincere. On the walk home she asked questions about the concert . . . but not the music. She was curious to know what celebrities and society figures had attended. Had Betsy known any of them?

"Won't you sit at my table tomorrow?" she asked Betsy when they parted. "I should like to get to know you. My daughter is happy to have found a new friend."

"So am I," Betsy answered. "I've found two wonderful friends at the Geiger. Helena, and Tilda Dienemann."

There was no answer from Helena or her mother.

The following day, to Tilda's good-humored scorn, Betsy did eat dinner with Frau von Wandersee and, more than ever, Betsy did not like her. She had a sly way of maneuvering the conversation to bring out that her husband had once been wealthy, that the cousins with whom Helena had been raised were countesses and lived in a castle.

All through dinner Betsy had the feeling that Helena's mother was trying to find out how much money she had. Every question she asked about Betsy, or anyone else, bore on financial standing. Yet she made it clear that Helena would never play the piano professionally, and that her husband did nothing at all.

"How can she love money so much and yet despise the good hard work which earns it?" Betsy wondered.

The next day Helena and Betsy made a plan to visit the National Museum. This time Betsy didn't suggest meeting Tilda.

"And afterward, let's go out for coffee," she said. For a coffee table with its atmosphere of leisure and relaxation would be ideal for a talk.

"I'm sorry. I never go into a coffee house."

This was even more amazing than the tram. "But, Helena! They're such fun! And we'll need nourishment after the museum."

"Mother will make us a little lunch," Helena replied. "If it isn't too cold we can eat it outdoors. There are some quite secluded places in the Gardens."

The National Museum was near the English Gardens. A rambling conglomeration of turrets, wings, arcades, and courtyards, it housed a renowned collection of Bavarian antiques.

"You'll love it, Betsy. Each room illustrates a period. They run from the Stone Age to the death of King Ludwig the Second. Let's go through them in order!"

"Oh, you Germans!" Betsy teased. "Such thoroughness! You know, don't you, that there are over a hundred rooms?" But she agreed and they passed through the Prehistoric Ages and the Roman invasion of Bavarian soil before they found themselves ready for Helena's lunch.

It was very dainty, with small linen napkins lying on top, each sandwich wrapped separately, and fresh cookies beneath. And they were able to eat in the Gardens for the sun was very warm. Buds were swelling; and robins, sounding just like those in Minnesota, were singing with abandon.

"Tilda would adore this," Betsy plunged. "You must get to know her, Helena. The three of us can have such good times."

The young baroness was silent for a moment. Then she said in a strained voice, "Betsy, I may as well tell you. We Europeans feel differently than you Americans do about some things. Fräulein Dienemann may be very nice but she isn't in my world and never could be."

"Why not?" Betsy asked. "She's studying music, just as you are."

Helena paused. "Betsy," she said, "I'll be frank. Her father is in trade."

Betsy burst out laughing. It was hard to take this remark seriously, but Helena looked as though she had just announced that Tilda's father was a murderer.

"Forgive me!" Betsy said. "It isn't funny, really. You may want to break off *our* friendship. *My* father is in trade. He runs a shoe store."

"I expected he did something like that," Helena answered calmly. "But you are an American."

"Do you really mean that you can associate with me and yet you can't associate with Tilda?"

"That is exactly what I mean," said Helena frigidly.

Betsy was angry. In their short friendship, she had come to love Tilda. If she had to choose, she would certainly choose Tilda. It might be best to choose now, and be done with it.

But when she looked up she saw something in Helena's face. It was an almost pleading expression. She was too proud to say, "Betsy, I'm lonely." But Betsy saw it shining in her eyes. And Betsy had learned since her trip started what it meant to be lonely. She reached over and gave Helena's hand a quick warm pressure.

"I wish you'd change your mind," she said. "But whether you do or not, you and I are friends. You must let me fix the sandwiches sometimes."

"Oh, no!" said Helena. "We have a kitchen." She turned her head and Betsy knew she was winking tears away.

"Helena," asked Betsy, "why do you object to a perfectly respectable coffee house?"

"For one in my station," Helena answered stiffly, "it is not suitable. If I could afford a private room at a fine hotel, yes. But I could not eat with common people."

"And the tram?" asked Betsy gently.

"If I can't have a private carriage, I prefer to walk." Now tears rushed into Helena's eyes too freely for her to conceal them. She touched them with a snowy handkerchief.

"Betsy," she said, "you don't know what it is like to be in my station and be poor. At the castle I had my own bedroom, my own sitting room and bath, my maid. There was a coachman to take us everywhere."

"Do you like being in Munich?"

Helena spoke in a low voice. "It is wonderful to be with someone who loves me. My aunt was kind but I never came first. With my mother, I come first."

She did not refer to her father.

Betsy took her hand again and squeezed it. A feeling of thankfulness welled up in her at her decision not to choose.

And so Betsy's days came to be divided between Helena and Tilda. Tilda didn't mind. She only joked a little about decayed aristocracy, and when Betsy said that Helena was nice, Tilda made a face.

Betsy and Tilda began on the galleries, and the Old Pinakothek was very different for Betsy with Tilda beside her. The German and Netherlandish pictures were the ones to study here, Tilda said—the Holbeins, the Dürers.

"The most important picture in the Pinakothek is Albrecht Dürer's portrait of himself."

She told Betsy stories about the Nuremberg goldsmith's apprentice who had made himself Germany's first great painter. Betsy looked at his self-portrait respectfully but she liked best Van Dyck's "Flight into Egypt." She bought a print of that and put it up beside Lenbach's "Shepherd Boy."

Tilda took her to an exhibition of ultra-modern paintings. She was interested in everything—like Julia and Joe, thought Betsy, watching her squint with lively curiosity at all the cubes and angles. Betsy remembered the *Columbic* dinner table, and how she had wished she knew something about the new art movements. She tried to understand these Cubist and Futurist pieces, but they seemed perfectly crazy.

They dropped into churches and sometimes Tilda explained the architecture. Often in the candle-lit dimness they just knelt to pray.

Once they looked through an iron fence into a small enclosure with a shrine and two rows of graves. It had been a cemetery for some monks, Tilda said. Late sunlight lay on the plain black crosses, and green shoots of crocuses were pushing up from the graves. It was strange, thought Betsy, the stillness in there, when the world was so giddy with spring.

She did not speak, but Tilda pressed her arm.

"The spring . . . even there," she whispered.

One day they visited the golden Angel of Peace, poised atop a column beside the Isar, and afterward, they scrambled down to the river where children were wading and sailing boats. Betsy knew just the squashy, gritty, muddy, tired loveliness they felt. She remembered wading in the streams of melted snow that ran down the Big Hill.

"I wish I could go wading."

"I, also."

"I hate growing up."

And they fell into silence.

They made a trip to the gigantic statue of Bavaria and ascended into her head to get the view. That night Tilda got to talking about Bavarian history.

They always ate and made tea on the alcohol lamp before going to bed. This was quite in the German tradition, Tilda said. Germans in their homes ate six meals a day: breakfast, second breakfast, dinner, afternoon coffee, supper, and in the evening tea or beer with sandwiches and kuchen. Betsy, in the cherry-red bathrobe, and Tilda in a blue one, feasted merrily.

The second King Ludwig (a dull Maximilian came in between) had been gloriously mad, Tilda said. He was dark and very handsome. On top of the Royal Residence in Munich he built a winter garden where, clad in silver armor, he used to float in a swan boat like Lohengrin's. This mad Ludwig was the patron of Wagner.

He built fabulous castles in lonely mountain spots. They often had French salons and gardens, for he was in love with Marie Antoinette.

"But, Tilda! She was beheaded before he was born."

"He loffed her," Tilda declared.

He used to ride through the mountains in a carriage drawn by four white horses. In the winter his golden sleigh was shaped like a swan. He would drive all night through snow and storm. The villagers in their beds would hear him rushing by. Or they caught glimpses of him, his face pale, his eyes blazing under a diamond-studded cap.

"Tilda! You're scaring me!" But Tilda kept right on.

The peasants loved him, she said, in spite of his extravagances, and when he died . . .

"What did he die of?" Betsy interrupted.

He drowned himself, Tilda answered, because he was forced to abdicate. The peasants made a hero of him then. To this day young mountaineers wore his picture in their hats.

"There's a song about him," she added, and began to hum it. *"König Ludwig der Zweite . . ."*

"It's like a fairy tale," said Betsy. "A dark sort of fairy tale . . ." She paused uncertainly but Tilda understood.

"Ja," she agreed. "It is of the dark Bavarian mountains!"

History was less thrilling, more accurate, and much more arduously imbibed going through the National Museum with Helena. They proceeded slowly through relics of the Early Church, Guilds, the Reformation. Betsy liked the Knight Errantry room. It was lined with suits of armor, and there were life-sized models of armored men on horseback. She thought how much Joe would enjoy it.

Helena explained everything exhaustively. She was very well educated. In addition to German and English, she spoke French, Italian, and Spanish.

"You and Tilda make me feel so ignorant," Betsy said. She never lost a chance to bring Tilda's name into the conversation, but Helena always coolly changed the subject.

On rainy days they took their afternoon sandwiches in damp and drafty halls. But there were rewards. Betsy got Helena to talking about the castle in which she had lived . . . the powdered servants in livery, bowing on the terrace; the great entrance hall which was a bower of growing plants with statues gleaming through; Englander, her riding horse. Listening was like reading the beginning of a novel.

Frau von Wandersee took them to hear the orchestras. The concert halls were usually crowded with tables. During the music, the people were reverently silent, but when it stopped, everyone started smoking and eating and drinking beer.

Betsy was delighted one day when Tilda offered her concert tickets which she was unable to use. She rushed off eagerly to the von Wandersee apartment.

She had never been there before, and at first she wondered whether she had made a mistake. It was such a shabby place with dirty stairs and hall. But she found the card of the Baron von Wandersee tacked over the door.

His wife answered the bell. She was wearing a soiled bathrobe, and she didn't ask Betsy in. In fact, she pulled the door half shut behind her. Speaking in her usual purring voice, she said that Helena was out, but a strong odor of alcohol made Betsy suspect that the baron was in.

"Is that why Helena never mentions her father?" Betsy wondered. She felt sick inside.

Frau von Wandersee refused the tickets, and Betsy got away quickly. A few days later Helena, head high, told her that they would be moving soon.

"We have had such trouble finding a pleasant apartment. We've moved three times," she said.

Museums, galleries, concerts were all very well, but Betsy liked the opera best. She had awaited her first one with some trepidation. Julia loved opera so much, and had chosen it for her career. How awful, Betsy thought, if she didn't like it! But she liked it beyond words.

She went to the Hoftheater straight from afternoon coffee, for the operas began early, sometimes as early as six. There was always a line of people waiting for "standing places"—shabby, humble-looking people, and soldiers, and students. Yet inside, the great auditorium glittered and shimmered with fashion. Everybody went to the opera in Munich.

The conductor was greeted with thunderous applause but there was a solemn silence when the lights dimmed. Betsy began to cry as soon as the overture started, and she never knew quite when she stopped. The music carried her off on a golden tide.

She was a Wagnerite from the moment when Lohengrin, godlike in silver armor, floated on stage in his swanboat.

"I don't blame the Mad King for trying it," she thought, munching sausages in a crowded lunchroom during the intermission. "I'd like to myself."

This opera and *Tannhäuser*—with its mountain castle and shrine and the steep dark path down which the pilgrims marched, made her think of Tilda's stories.

Tilda always waited up for her, and they talked the opera over while Betsy ate her supper. Hanni brought it to her whenever she came in; that was the custom.

"You must hear something besides Wagner," Tilda said, and Betsy bought tickets for *Carmen, Madame Butterfly, The Barber of Seville*. She slipped in *Die Meistersinger*, too. She bought these tickets early Sunday morning when the cheap seats went on sale.

"You won't be a Münchener until you have stood in line with the crowd on Sunday morning," Tilda said. So Betsy got there at eight, but there were two or three hundred ahead of her. Some people stood from Saturday midnight on. Others hired street porters who would stand for them for a mark.

Betsy considered herself quite a Münchener now. She had seen the plain princesses going to church, and the King and Queen in a gala street procession, with martial music and gentlemen and ladies-in-waiting in carriages of vivid light blue. The royal carriage was drawn by eight black horses.

The King and Queen were old and dull. They hardly acknowledged the cheers of the crowd, just smiled in an absent-minded way. Nevertheless, when the Queen threw her bouquet, Betsy scrambled for some violets.

"I want to send them to Margaret," she told Tilda sheepishly.

On Sunday Betsy went to the American Church; now she knew the rector and his wife. Afterward she crossed to the Hall of the Fieldmarshals for the band concert, when all Munich promenaded. She met Tilda, who was a Lutheran, or Helena, who was a Catholic (but never both of them together), and they promenaded like true Müncheners.

And sometimes, also in München fashion, Betsy took her writing to a coffee house. It was "The Disappearing Dancer," now, for "Meet Miss So and So" had gone on its way to Margaret. Scribbling with a coffee cup beside her, she flattered herself that impressionable American tourists would write home that they had seen an authoress composing a masterpiece in public.

Betsy was devoted to the coffee houses. But she was disturbed by the little-boy waiters, wearing diminutive dress suits and running about with heavy trays. There was too much child labor in Munich. She could not forget that yellow-haired little girl buttoning and unbuttoning shoes, nor a pale little boy she had seen in a watch shop. Wearing an apron, bent over some delicate work, he had looked like a little old man.

She didn't like it that Hanni worked so hard and that she couldn't marry her soldier. Hanni was so good to her! She polished Betsy's shoes, mended her clothes, and often brought little bouquets for her desk.

"Celeste is quite jealous," Betsy told Tilda, who knew all about Celeste.

Tilda was well acquainted with all Betsy's friends. She knew about Tacy's gay struggles with housekeeping, and Tib's affairs of the heart. Bob and Effie wrote from the University . . . about quizzes and spring track and who was leading the J.B.

"*Was ist* 'J.B.'?" asked Tilda, and received a glowing account of the Junior Ball.

Tilda admired Joe's picture, for even a snapshot showed how blond and muscular he was. She noticed also that although it stood at Betsy's bedside, there were never any letters from him.

"He used to be my beau, but he isn't any more. I don't have a beau."

It was true, and a strange situation for Betsy. But it was restful, she told Tilda, not to have to curl her hair. She hadn't curled it since the first night in Munich. And she was getting fat.

"Haven't I the most beautiful arms?" she asked, turning in front of the mirror. "And my shoulders aren't bony any more. I can hardly wait to wear a formal."

Munich agreed with her. But she must leave it soon to live in and learn another place. Her father and mother, aghast at first at Miss Surprise's surprise, had accepted the fact that Betsy seemed safe, living alone in Munich. But they didn't want her to try it in a second city. They had advised her to join a Thomas Cook party, make the Grand Tour, and come home. Betsy thought this would be horrible.

Fortunately the Wilsons had written, suggesting that she come to Venice. They were leaving for Greece, but the *Casa delle Rose d'Oro* was charming—run by three tiny old ladies, unmarried sisters, always dressed in black.

"You would put them into a story, Betsy," Miss Wilson wrote. "And they would be ideal as chaperones." Betsy could stay with them through May, and in June join the Wilsons for Switzerland and Paris.

Her parents approved this plan and Betsy loved it.

"Imagine me," she said, "floating along in a gondola and feeding the pigeons in St. Mark's Square!"

"For Venice," Tilda pointed out, "you will want a sweetheart."

"Pshaw!" said Betsy. "I'm going to study the stones like Ruskin did."

13
DARK FAIRY TALE

Tilda was in bed with a cold and Betsy was having supper with her. Hanni had set a low table between them. In the center was a bouquet of hyacinths from the corner flower seller, and that wasn't the only assurance of spring. The windows were pulled open to admit balmy air. And out in Schellingstrasse children were playing games with a joyful racket that took Betsy back to Hill Street.

"I remember," she told Tilda, "how I used to run in the house every two minutes and beg Mamma to let me take off my winter underwear."

"I have been thinking of summer clothes all day," Tilda replied.

"This weather is bad for work." Betsy sighed, for "The Disappearing Dancer" wouldn't disappear; she wouldn't dance; she wouldn't even budge. "No mail either," Betsy added as though this too could be blamed on April.

Tilda sat guiltily upright. "Betsy, I am a wretch! You were out, and Hanni brought a letter for you here." She fished it from the pile of books on her bed.

It was addressed in Mrs. Ray's dashing hand.

"Not very plump," Betsy observed. "Do you suppose my family doesn't love me any more?"

"*Ja*, I am sure! You should come and live in Switzerland. We will keep cows."

" 'Cows, cows, beautiful cows!' " As Betsy ripped open the letter, an even thinner slip of paper fell out. She took it up. She stared at it. She threw her napkin into the air and shrieked.

"Tilda! Tilda! *Ainslee's* have succumbed!" Betsy spoke in English for she couldn't remember any German.

"*Was ist Ainslee's?*" Tilda cried.

"It's a magazine, Tilda. They've bought one of my

stories, 'Emma Middleton Cuts Cross Country,' for one hundred dollars!"

Betsy flew over to the bed and they hugged each other until they were breathless. Hanni, coming in with fresh tea, stared in bewilderment.

"Hundred dollars!" Tilda cried. "Betsy, that's four hundred marks!"

"Is it? Oh goodie! Goodie!"

Tilda told the amazing news to Hanni.

Betsy looked up from her letter. "Papa wants me to spend this money for anything I like. Something I couldn't afford out of what he sends me. And, Tilda, I know what it will be! I'm going to travel around a little. I've been wishing I could, before I go to Venice."

"Wunderschön!" Tilda exclaimed. "Und to von place, I vill go mit."

"You will?" Betsy asked rapturously, and danced about the room.

" 'Added hours had but heightened the wonder of the day,' tra la!"

" 'His gray gaze was inscrutable,' yo ho!"

"Betsy, *bist du* crazy?"

"They're excerpts from the immortal manuscript," said Betsy. "One hundred dollars, Tilda! I never got more than ten before." She ran for Mr. O'Farrell's map.

When she returned Hanni had pulled the draperies and lighted the gas and put a kettle over the alcohol lamp. This important discussion required more tea, of course. It was fascinating to take meditative sips over the rival charms of medieval Nuremberg and Wagner's Bayreuth.

"Pshaw! I'll go to both!" Betsy cried—after all, a hundred dollars! And she would go to a little town called Sonneberg which the rector had told her about. It was the doll center of the world.

Tilda was going home for the long Easter holiday, but afterward, they agreed, they would meet in Oberammergau. It wasn't a Passion Play year but they both wished to see the famous village.

"Will your parents mind your traveling alone?" Tilda asked.

"Not this tiny jaunt! Germany is as safe as my own back yard. And you know, Tilda, I speak the language now."

"*Ja,* magnificently! Of course, you call everyone *du,* even the policemen, and that is supposed to be only for family and friends."

"The way to talk German," answered Betsy, "is to talk German. If I bothered with forms, and genders and cases and tenses, I'd be tongue-tied. I just string along the words I want to say, and put *Nicht wahr?* at the end. Of course, I must have a new hat."

"With a hundred dollars? *Natürlich!*"

Next day Betsy cashed her big check at the bank where she cashed the checks her father sent each month. Then she bought presents: A pipe rack for her father, a pewter platter for her mother, carved bookends for Julia and Paige, a watch for Margaret, a pink enameled pin for Anna, the hired girl. She bought Tilda a print of Willem Key's "Pieta" which both of them loved, and Hanni, a lace collar and jabot.

Helena went with her, and she was a great help in shopping. There was something about her that made everyone jump. The milliner rushed for her finest creations, and Betsy bought a large black straw. One end touched her shoulder, the other shot off toward the sky, and under the skyward edge, next to her hair, was a luscious pink rose.

"It's a little extreme," she admitted, "but why shouldn't it be? I'm a famous lady author. You wouldn't like some coffee, would you?" But even to celebrate "Emma" Helena would not go into a coffee house. Betsy bought her a box of marzipan.

She and Helena finished up the National Museum. Betsy grew maudlin toward the end. Bavarian history, she said, was coming out her ears.

"But I do thank you, Helena! I wouldn't have missed it."

Easter was coming near. The streets were full of little girls in white dresses carrying candles. The shop windows showed rabbits, eggs, and chickens. Tilda would be leaving soon. Betsy put aside "The Disappearing Dancer"; Tilda skipped all the classes she dared to; and they set forth exuberantly every day.

All Munich was out to celebrate spring. The squares were crowded with people, talking and drinking beer. The paths along the Isar were filled with loitering families.

"Nobody works in Bavaria," Tilda remarked.

"Except Hanni."

"Oh, *ja*! The servants!"

At Nymphenburg where the Mad King was born, they drank coffee out of doors. After that they did it every day. In the rustic English Gardens. In the Hofgarten, where the spring hats rivaled the tulips. In humbler parks where there were fewer tourists, artists, students, but more fat Müncheners, bicycles, and dogs.

Strolling home through the sweet spring twilights, Betsy and Tilda talked of their careers. They made plans for touring Europe in 1917. Sometimes Tilda talked about August. She liked him better than she admitted, Betsy perceived. Betsy at these pensive moments always thought about Joe.

In no time Tilda was packing for home. She and Betsy parted crying, *"Auf Wiedersehen!* Until Oberammergau!"

On Easter Betsy and Helena made the rounds of the churches. In the Frauenkirche, lofty and grim in spite of candlelight and lilies, the people sang while the organ rolled out paeans of gladness. Thinking of Easter at home, Betsy wept a little.

She was grateful for Helena, who ate dinner at the

pension that day. Afterward they walked to the English Gardens and took snapshots under the trees. Helena had brought sandwiches as usual, but when four o'clock came, Betsy paused by the white-covered tables. Waitresses were rushing about with their moneybags jingling.

"Let's have coffee here! Please!" she pleaded.

Helena raised her pretty eyebrows. "They're very common people."

"So am I common. I'm terribly common. And, Helena, do you know what Abraham Lincoln said? 'God must love the common people because he made so many of them.'"

Helena laughed. "Come," she said, taking Betsy's arm. "I will drink coffee here. Not for the sake of your Abraham Lincoln, but because you are leaving so soon."

With their coffee they had sweet spirals of *Schnecken*, and above them birds were singing on frothy green boughs.

"I don't see why they call these *English* Gardens," Betsy grumbled. "The count who laid them out was born in Massachusetts. Of course, I know he was a Tory and George the Third knighted him. Still, this is very like America."

"Everything good you claim for America."

"Come and see it, and you'll understand. Why don't you come, Helena? I'll matchmake you to a nice American boy. Of course, he'll be in trade," Betsy teased.

Helena smiled. But suddenly over the empty cups and

plates and the white cloth on which blown maple wings were lying, Betsy saw that her eyes were full of tears.

"I am in love with my cousin Karl," she said.

"Why, Helena!" Betsy reached across and touched her hand. "Is he in love with you, too?"

"Yes."

"And will you be married?"

"Oh, no!"

"Why not?"

"My aunt wants a good match for him. It is quite right that she should. He is a lieutenant in the army."

"But you'd be a good match. You're pretty and clever and talented."

"I am poor."

"Well, he has plenty of money."

Helena shook her head.

"And Europeans were always saying that Americans liked money!" Betsy thought.

"Why don't you just get married?" she asked. "You could live on his salary."

But Helena, drying her eyes, did not bother to answer so preposterous a question.

"Helena," asked Betsy, "is this why you came to Munich?"

"Yes. There is talk at the castle of whom Karl will marry. My aunt thinks I behaved very well. I could go back. But, Betsy, I won't leave my mother."

"You could see her often."

"No, I couldn't." Helena's pale cheeks colored faintly. "I never saw my mother until I came to Munich. Not to remember her. You see . . . my father's family didn't like the marriage. My mother was English . . ."

And far beneath him, Betsy felt sure, the story unrolling like a scroll.

"They . . . cast him off. And it wasn't good for him."

Betsy knew. She had known since the day she went to their apartment.

"I didn't understand until I came to Munich, but now . . . I couldn't leave my mother. Things are hard for her, very hard. And she's so good to me . . . you can't imagine!" Helena's face glowed.

Betsy tried to remember that glow, for Helena's story left her with a heartache. Helena and her mother were so different. Tall and proud, Helena looked like a true aristocrat. She always made you think of something white— snow on a mountain, or moonlight, or lilies.

The next day Frau von Wandersee suggested that Betsy eat dinner at her table, and she was as dingy, frowsy, sly as ever.

"She must have something fine about her, and I ought to be able to dig it out," thought Betsy, but she couldn't seem to.

Frau von Wandersee talked on as usual about how much money people had . . . or didn't have . . . or used to have. But during the meal there came one moment of revelation.

She was saying that her daughter would miss Betsy. "She considers you a real friend. And she hasn't friends enough." The purring voice seemed to change, to strengthen. "Sometimes I'm afraid she ought to go back to her aunt."

"She doesn't want to, Frau von Wandersee."

"How do you know?"

"She told me. She said she would hate to leave you. She loves you very much."

Frau von Wandersee looked up. She looked straight at Betsy, which she didn't often do, and her eyes were luminous, beseeching.

"If I make her go back . . . it won't be that I want her to go," Frau von Wandersee said. After a moment she added in her usual tone, "She will be over tonight to say good-bye."

There was one last party in Munich. Betsy took Hanni out for afternoon coffee. She had to battle Frau Geiger, but the bath episode had given this lady respect for Betsy's perseverance. When she saw that the crazy American Fräulein was really in earnest, she gave in.

Hanni's face was one big smile. She wore a monstrous summer hat, several seasons old, and the lace collar and jabot Betsy had given her. She wouldn't say where she would like to go, so Betsy selected the zoo. Betsy was obliged to decide whether they would have coffee or tea and what kind of cakes. Hanni would only say, "As you will, Fräulein."

They discussed a favorite subject, Hanni coming to America. In the early days, Betsy had tried to plan how Hanni could marry her soldier. He could earn a little extra money, or leave the army and get another job.

"It is impossible," Hanni always said sadly. "I will come to America to you."

She loved to talk about this, telling Betsy over and over how hard she would work, how Betsy would have her clothes mended and her hair brushed and her breakfast in bed. She would live in Paradise, Hanni declared.

"Fräulein, when you are married, send for me, and I will come."

"And if I don't marry," Betsy said now, "when I get to be a famous author, we'll go around the world together."

"I'll have to write Tacy," she thought with a chuckle, "that I'm firing Celeste."

She took Hanni's picture, and the servant girl was transfixed with delight. She stood as straight as her soldier, smiling fixedly beneath the monstrous hat.

"I'll send you some prints from Venice," Betsy promised. Secretly she resolved to have one enlarged for Hanni's sweetheart.

For the last time Betsy heard the din of music practice at the Geiger. She said good-bye to the cold bare dining room, to Susuki, and the Italian artist, the Austrians, the Bulgarians.

It was starting to rain and Betsy was afraid that Helena might not come, but she knocked at Betsy's door and came in smiling, wearing a raincoat glistening with drops. She carried a package.

"I can't stay. I know you are busy packing, but I wanted to say good-bye. Betsy, I wish we could keep in touch."

"But of course we will! I'd love to correspond, and I write enormous letters."

Helena offered the package. Her sensitive face quivered with pleasure while Betsy unwrapped it. There emerged a tall china cup, striped in pink and gold and blue.

"It is a cup the poet Goethe drank from."

"Why, Helena! How . . . how marvelous!"

"It's come down in our family. We haven't very many such things left; we've moved so much. But my mother and I thought you would like this because . . . you're a writer, too."

"I'm overwhelmed by it!" cried Betsy. "It will be one of my dearest treasures always." She threw her arms about Helena, wanting to cry.

For a second Helena's arms closed around Betsy. "You've helped me," she whispered, then drew back stiffly. She left soon after with "auf Wiedersehen" only, for Betsy assured her that she would be coming back.

While she packed, Betsy kept remembering that "You've helped me."

"I don't see how I helped her! Why couldn't I have liked her mother!" Betsy thought in self-reproach.

Packing was a complicated operation. Her trunk was being shipped to Innsbruck; only the bags were going on the fortnight of travel, and every article was shifted from bags to trunk and from trunk to bags, as Betsy decided now that she couldn't live without it and then that she would have to. Everything breakable had to be wrapped in something unbreakable, but there seemed to be more breakable than unbreakable objects. Goethe's cup had the steamer rug to itself. At the end the trunk would not shut although Betsy jumped on the lid. Hanni came in and sat on it.

The rain pounded, and in the wavering gaslight the dismantled room looked strange and unfamiliar. Ready at last to slip beneath her featherbed, Betsy opened the windows and looked out at the decorated house.

Helena had said she had helped her, but it seemed to Betsy that she hadn't helped anyone in Munich. Germans were hard to help. They were all so pessimistic, so sure that reduced circumstances could never be bettered nor difficulties solved.

Betsy remembered what she had told Tilda, that Bavaria made her think of a dark fairy tale. It did. In its wild mountains there were more sorcerers and ghosts and goblins than helpful fairies.

She thought of Helena locked in the prison of her title, and of that princess in the dining room who sat by herself, and of Hanni who worked so hard and couldn't marry her soldier. Although Munich was so *gemütlich*, it seemed to have a spell upon it.

But in the morning Hanni was smiling down at her above the breakfast tray. To the usual chocolate, hard rolls, and butter, she had added *ein bissel* marmalade. The rain had stopped and the air that the casement admitted was full of happy promise.

"A good journey, *gnädiges* Fräulein," Hanni said.

14
A VERY SPECIAL DOLL

Betsy was in a bus riding toward Krug's Hotel in Sonneberg deep in the Thuringian Mountains.

She had visited the festival city of Bayreuth. Opera was not sung at this season, but she had seen Richard Wagner's great Opera House, and his home, the Villa Wahnfried. In fact, she had trespassed in the garden there and had been ejected by no less a person than Wagner's son Siegfried.

At Nuremberg she had walked in enchantment around the old gray wall that encircled the medieval city. She had strolled the cobbled streets, looking up at the gable-roofed houses pierced by dormer windows . . . especially at the fifteenth-century house in which Albrecht Dürer had lived, and at the house of Hans Sachs, right out of *Die Meistersinger*. The cobbler poet had not always stayed at home, though. He had traveled the open road with a stick and a knapsack.

"Like I'm doing now," thought Betsy, ignoring the bulging suitcases piled around her feet. She was all alone in the bus and bounced like a piece of popcorn.

She had been surprised, at the Sonneberg station, to see a uniformed driver from Krug's Hotel. She had expected only a primitive inn in the little Doll Town and looked out curiously as the bus joggled along through a wide mountain valley. But the town was at some distance from the station.

Betsy caught her reflection in the bus mirror. She was beaming like Hanni at the coffee party.

"Pretty pleased with yourself, aren't you?" she asked. "Well, no wonder! I'm pleased with you myself."

She was pleased, for one thing, because her mail was being forwarded from Munich. There should be lots! Since leaving Munich she had had her twenty-second birthday. A strange birthday with no cake or presents, just the wine of traveling alone . . . seeing strange places, meeting new people, struggling with a foreign language! Her present, the family had written, was a check to be spent for new clothes in Paris. But there would certainly be some letters here.

"What a place," Betsy thought, "to be getting mail from Minnesota!" A town in the Thuringian Forest that had been making dolls since before Columbus!

But Sonneberg was a little like Deep Valley, she discovered as they entered. The mountains seemed no taller than the Big Hill and its companions had seemed to her and Tacy when they were little girls.

"Tacy would love this crazy expedition," Betsy thought.

Krug's Hotel was something of a shock. It was an imposing white stone building with gardens and shaded verandas. Betsy's room had electric lights, and steam heat flooded it with summery warmth, quite different from the limited circle of heat thrown off by porcelain stoves. Most surprising of all, there was a bathroom.

"Glory of glories!" Betsy cried. Her one and only bath in Munich was a long time behind her now. "What? No boots?" She smiled down at the gleaming white tub.

She was in wonderful spirits, in spite of the fact that there had been no mail awaiting her. It would come! And the clerk had spoken English!

"I might be in the Radisson Hotel in Minneapolis," Betsy thought.

The reason for this cosmopolitan atmosphere was, of course, that Sonneberg was the center of the doll trade. It drew buyers from London, Paris, New York. Betsy was made aware of this again, when, having freshened up, she went for a walk before supper.

On cobblestone streets, where oxen were more common than horses, she passed well-dressed, clean-shaven men wearing Derby hats, swinging canes.

"Heavens!" she thought. "I should have curled my hair!" But even with straight hair, she attracted attention enough. In her smartly cut suit and the big slanting hat with the rose—and, of course, the debutante slouch which she did not forget to assume—she seemed as surprising to the buyers as the buyers did to her. The Americans especially looked at her unbelievingly, and some even seemed on the point of speaking. But Betsy was cool and unresponsive.

The air, piney and fresh, was as stimulating as the unwonted admiration. The streets ran up the side of a mountain, but just a little timid way. Above them, where a stretch had been cleared of trees, old women with baskets on their backs were stooped over, gathering fuel. Higher still, the slope was darkly wooded and a bench had been placed to catch the view.

"Like the bench on Hill Street where Tacy and I used to take our suppers when we were little. Dear me, Tacy ought to be here!" Betsy mourned.

The newer streets had modern shops and villas, carriages, and even a few automobiles. But there were old streets, too. Streets so narrow that the gable-roofed houses almost touched overhead. Streets that were nothing but winding paths or steps up the side of the mountain.

Many people wore baskets, such as the old women had worn, fastened to their backs. Some of these were filled with wood; others, with groceries. But most of them were covered with white cloths and Betsy could not see what they contained.

Some of the women carried their babies tied on with shawls. Betsy smiled at them but they looked blank.

"People don't seem very friendly," she observed. Tilda had told her that the North Germans were different from the dark, vivacious, warm-hearted Müncheners, and it was certainly true.

Not the children, though! They gathered about her, smiling and nudging one another. Betsy tried out her German, and they bent their heads to conceal delighted chuckles. They were rosy and fat. All the little boys seemed to be outgrowing their jackets. The little girls wore aprons over their dresses, and thick black stockings, and stout shoes.

"But none of them are carrying dolls!" Betsy was puzzled. There certainly ought to be dolls on the streets of the doll metropolis! She couldn't look into the matter, for now the quick upland twilight fell. It was cozy to return to the warm luxurious hotel, but there still wasn't any mail.

The dining room was spacious with glittering chandeliers and potted palms, and the traveling men were already eating when Betsy came in. Her entrance caused a flattering commotion, and although she strove for a bored air, she was charmed with the proximity of the American men. Their voices, their slang, took her across the wide Atlantic—to her father, to Joe, to college dances and gaieties at the Ray house.

Eavesdropping as intently as she could while remembering to act blasé, she heard them discussing the States. They even mentioned Duluth, Minnesota. Betsy wanted to lean over and say, "Boo! I come from Minneapolis!" But she resisted.

After sauntering out like a woman of the world, she hurried to her room lest she be tempted into some indiscretion. She knew the rules for safety in traveling alone, and they didn't include picking up strange men acquaintances—even Americans!

She wrote home jubilantly, pouring out the day's adventures. And naturally she took a bath. She had had one before dinner, but she took another now and planned a third in the morning.

"Goodness knows when I'll see a bathroom again!"

She was glad, though, that Krug's Hotel was not too modern for a featherbed and slipped beneath it gratefully for the night air was sharp. In the morning the snug warmth of steam heat returned. She ate breakfast in her room, and presently in suit and hat with camera, notebook, and pencil, she was down in the cool invigorating morning.

Everyone was either at work or going to work. Sonnebergers, both men and women, hurried along with those large wicker baskets on their backs. All the baskets now seemed to be covered with white cloths. The buyers, freshly pressed and shaven, were heading for the doll factories—*Puppen Fabriken,* the desk clerk had called them.

There weren't many factories here; that was the reason the air was so pure, he had said. No smoking factory chimneys as in Nuremberg where they made their toys by machinery. In Sonneberg, manual work in the homes was most important.

Betsy, too, headed for a *Puppen Fabrik.* The large modern buildings were easy to identify on Sonneberg's picturesque streets.

A crowd of children had already gathered behind her. "I feel like the Pied Piper," Betsy thought, turning to smile at them. One little girl put her hand shyly into Betsy's. She was the only thin one in the lot, elfishly thin, with a shock of pale straight hair and vivid eyes. Her name was Gretel.

At the door of the *Fabrik* a youth of tender years stood moodily with folded arms. Betsy asked in her best German if she might go through the factory. Before replying he astonished her by going through all the motions of brushing up a mustache, although his pink and white face looked as smooth as a girl's. Studying him closely she did catch a bit of fuzz.

A trip through the *Fabrik*? Impossible, he said, and brushed up the mustache again.

Betsy explained in a torrent of bad German that she came from the United States, that she was a writer, that she loved dolls and expected to have a large family of children who would also love dolls. Surely he would like to have her able to tell her children that she had seen the famous dolls of Sonneberg—*nicht wahr?*

He blushed. "Oh, I was calling him *du!*" Betsy thought in consternation. Tilda had warned her over and over that *du* was only for family and intimates.

He said something, bowed, and went inside. He would be back, the children told her, jumping up and down and laughing. They all waited.

He returned accompanied by a larger and more substantial young man with a florid face. Betsy repeated her speech, watching out for *du*'s. At the end he bowed again and now both youths disappeared.

The pair returned with an older man. He had a paunch with a gold watch chain across it and piercing eyes behind thick spectacles.

"I must be careful not to call him *du*," Betsy warned herself, repeating her speech with care.

When she finished he too bowed. He turned upon the two young men with rapid words; she thought he was calling them donkeys. Then he said in careful English,

"Gracious young lady, it makes us very happy that you wish to see our dolls. Have the goodness to let these two young men accompany you!"

So the two young men took her through the factory. It made dolls' heads, she found. These were sent to the homes.

"In baskets!" Betsy cried.

"*Ja*, in baskets, covered with clean white cloths!" In the homes the eyes were put in, the hair was pasted on, bodies were attached; the dolls acquired dresses, hats, and shoes.

"Do the children help?"

"*Ja, natürlich!* Whole families."

"And do the children . . . still like dolls?" It would be too sad, she thought, if they didn't; if that was the reason she had not seen any little girls playing with dolls!

But the young men were baffled by this question and hurried her off to the showroom. Here she saw finished products, samples of dolls that would come out next Christmas. There was a dazzling array! Blonde dolls and brunette dolls, large dolls and small dolls, dolls of every kind, type, and costume.

"Oh, what a beauty!" Betsy cried, reaching for a large, yellow-haired charmer. It was dressed in pale blue and wore a straw hat with a high pink plume, pink gloves, and pink shoes and stockings!

"Tacy and I would certainly have bonied this one," Betsy thought.

When she and Tacy were children they had loved to look at the dolls in the Christmas shop windows, pressing their noses against the plate glass while snow fell and sleighbells tinkled all up and down Front Street.

"I bony this one!"

"I bony that one!"

"So do I."

Betsy stood with the big doll in her arms thinking about Tacy. At last she put it down. "I really must go now. Thank you for showing me the factory." The two young men glanced at each other, and the slender one began to twirl his invisible mustache into fascinating spirals.

"And this evening?" the florid one asked softly. "Would the Fräulein enjoy a ride?"

"Or a little walk?" suggested his companion.

"A glass of beer, perhaps?"

Betsy shrugged as though she did not understand. *"Ich verstehe nicht,"* she said brightly. "Good-bye. Thank you again."

The children had disappeared. Were they making dolls? she wondered, walking back to the hotel. She hoped Gretel had a doll. There was still no mail, and after dinner, during which she happily impressed the buyers with her aloof sophistication, Betsy went to the Historical City Museum.

She saw the dolls that over past years had won prizes for the Sonneberg makers. A life-sized Gulliver covered with tiny Lilliputians. A miniature Kirmess, complete with merry-go-round, fortuneteller, dancing girl, clowns, fruit vendor, crowds of people, even dogs.

There was a display of period dolls beginning with rude figures cut from wood. Each successive generation was dressed like the children who had played with them, and Betsy saw dolls in costumes of the Civil War era who looked like Meg, Jo, Beth, and Amy. She saw dolls in accordian-pleated skirts, in long-waisted dresses that looked like herself, or Tib, or Tacy.

She and Tacy had been funny about dolls, Betsy reflected. The most important thing to see on Christmas morning, poking out of a stocking, or sitting under a tree, was a big curly-haired fancily dressed doll. But after Christmas they used to put these dolls away. They preferred paper dolls cut from magazines. And Tacy, of course, preferred real babies.

Tacy had always been crazy about babies. She used to help Betsy take care of Margaret, and Tib take care of her little brother Hobbie. She even used to ask the neighborhood mothers to let her take their babies out riding in their carriages—just for fun!

"Why am I thinking about Tacy all the time, for goodness' sake!" cried Betsy, and went out into the sunshine. She wished to get a peek, if she could, of the doll-making in the homes, and in the old part of town the streets were so narrow that you couldn't avoid looking in the windows.

She made her way to those ancient houses with

dormer windows sticking through the roofs. The streets were clean and cheerful. Ducks waddled along the cobblestones. There were pink and white fruit trees at every turning and multitudes of children.

The children made a rush for her. Gretel put her hand into Betsy's as a matter of course, smiling elfishly through pale wisps of hair. Betsy took snapshots of them all and asked an older boy to write down their names and addresses so that she could send them pictures.

Loitering along with her bodyguard, she saw men and women sitting in the windows, and they *were* making dolls. One flaxen-haired woman was gluing on a flaxen wig. Another was seated at a table covered with doll hats. A man wearing an apron was wiring eyes into rows of china heads.

Betsy turned to the children. "Do you have dolls?" she asked. "*Puppen?*" She rocked one in her arms.

They stared at her for a moment. Then the little girls turned and ran. Gretel ran into the house where the woman was gluing on wigs. They all returned with shining faces, and each one was holding a banged and battered doll.

"Look, *gnädiges* Fräulein!" Gretel's vivid eyes were snapping as she exhibited a headless treasure. "*Meine Puppe.* She is called Victoria."

So! That was settled. It was all right. But returning to the hotel in the late afternoon Betsy admitted a craving that had been growing all day. She wanted a doll! She wanted one even though she *was* twenty-two years old. Moreover, she knew the very doll she wanted. The yellow-haired charmer with the pink plume on her hat.

It wasn't easy to buy it, although she found her two cavaliers without difficulty. They were delighted to see her, thinking at first that she had reconsidered about the drive, the walk, the glass of beer. But when she explained her real reason for returning, the florid one frowned and the slender one tugged sternly at his mustache.

"Please! *Bitte!*" Betsy waved her purse. "I can't leave Sonneberg without a doll. The gentleman who spoke to me this morning . . . maybe *he* would sell me a doll." She hoped they would remember that he had called them donkeys.

She won, and marched out triumphantly with the pink and blue beauty. "She looks just like Lillian Russell," Betsy thought. But before she reached the hotel she began to feel a little foolish. A doll did look strange on the arm of a girl in a picture hat with long rustling skirts.

"Crazy *Amerikanisches* Fräulein!" she could imagine people saying.

"Of course," she told herself, trying to find a sensible motive, "of course I bought her for someone. My little sister . . . ?" But Margaret, in high school now, was more interested in boys than dolls.

"Who could she be for?" Betsy wondered. She couldn't seem to remember a single child of doll-playing age.

What made it worse, the buyers were in the lobby

smoking and reading their newspapers. They all looked up and some of them grinned. It was hard to saunter by like a lady author with your arms full of pink and blue doll. Betsy blushed crimson and thought she would never reach the desk.

Once there she forgot her chagrin. She forgot the doll, everything! For there was an enormous stack of mail—from her parents . . . Julia . . . Margaret . . . Cab . . . Tib . . . Tacy . . .

"I'm going to open Tacy's first," Betsy planned. "I've been thinking about her all day."

Up in her summer-warm room, she put the big doll against the pillows of her bed and established herself blissfully in an armchair by the window. Smiling in anticipation, she opened Tacy's letter and started to read. But in a moment she put it down on the bed. She clasped her hands in her lap and tears came into her eyes.

Tacy was going to have a baby!

Tacy! Betsy could hardly take it in. Why, she could remember Tacy at her own fifth birthday party, bringing a gift of a little glass pitcher, so shy that she held her head down and her long red ringlets fell over her face! But it was wonderful. It was just right. Tacy had always loved babies. Betsy had been remembering that all day.

"Only, I wish I could be there! I wish I didn't have to be so far away!" said Betsy, and she leaned her head on the bed and her tears flowed over Tacy's letter, making it quite soggy. Betsy sat up when she realized that, for she hadn't finished reading it yet, and her gaze fell on the big doll with its pale blue dress and coat, and its hat with the pink plume, the pink gloves, and the pink shoes and stockings.

Betsy caught it into her arms.

"*That's* why I bought you!" she cried, and her tears came faster and faster, but they were happy now. "*That's* why I bought you! I knew you were a very special doll."

A very special doll, for a very special baby! Tacy's baby! Maybe she would have red curls like Tacy's?

Betsy had an awful thought.

"But what if it isn't a girl?"

"Well! It had better be!" cried Betsy.

15
A SHORT STAY IN HEAVEN

Tilda was waiting at the Oberammergau station. She and Betsy flew into each other's arms.

"Betsy!" Tilda whispered ecstatically. "Here is Heaven!"

Betsy breathed deep of the mountain air. She looked around at the houses—white-plastered, green-shuttered,

red-roofed—and up at the rolling hills that were buttressed by pine-covered slopes. On a rocky height overlooking the village stood the famous Cross of Oberammergau.

"So it's Heaven!" Betsy replied. "Well, I've certainly been climbing to reach it!"

She had come by way of Munich, and her train had started climbing soon after the towers of the Frauenkirche melted into the blue. It had wound around mountainsides, past shining lakes and waterfalls, higher and higher, until the skyline wore royal crowns of snow. Far below, the valleys were dotted with villages, each one a cluster of red roofs about a spire. Oberammergau was swung like the others in a green hammock of valley.

Betsy had heard of it all her life. She knew that almost three hundred years before, when the Black Death was ravaging the Bavarian highlands, these villagers had promised that if God would spare them they would perform every ten years the drama of Jesus' Death and Passion. No man, woman, or child had fallen to the plague after the vow was made, and it had been faithfully kept by succeeding generations. Given at first in the churchyard, the play now required a huge auditorium. Every tenth year, from May to September, throngs of people from all over the world poured into the village—and then went away, leaving it to the peaceful isolation which Tilda and Betsy now disturbed.

The girls had engaged rooms with Herr and Frau Baumgarten. They were already, Betsy found, Uncle and

Aunt to Tilda who had arrived the day before. *Tante* Else was a spindling old lady with a smile almost as broad as her white cotton umbrella. *Onkel* Max was tall, too, and knobbily thin.

"And that's Hedwig!" Tilda smiled at an apple-cheeked servant girl who was bundling Betsy's belongings into a handcart.

Accustomed to the geometric arrangement of an American middle-western town, Betsy was charmed by Oberammergau's streets. They ran without rhyme or reason under flowering fruit trees, pink and white. There were no sidewalks.

On many of the whitewashed houses Biblical scenes were frescoed in bright colors. Shrines looked down from almost every door. Crosses spread benignant arms above rooftops, in gardens, at street corners. The people looked Biblical, too. Many men wore their hair long, and beards were everywhere—black, brown, yellow, gray.

"*Natürlich!*" Tante Else said. "In the Passion Play, the actors would not wear wigs or false beards, any more than they would powder and paint."

"And Betsy!" Tilda said. "They call each other often by their names from the Passion Play . . . Judas, Pilate, even Christ."

"*Ach, ja!*" said Onkel Max. "Christus Lang. You must meet him this afternoon."

Even more suggestive of holiness than the Biblical scenes, and beards and names, were the smiles that welcomed Betsy and Tilda. *"Grüss Gott!"* everyone said.

"God bless you!" What a wonderful greeting!

Children ran out to take their hands and curtsy. There was a pervading air of friendliness, of love.

"Maybe there's one place in the world where people really live up to their religion," Betsy thought, looking around.

"Wait until you see our *Haüschen*," Tilda kept saying. At last she cried, "There it is!" And Betsy let out a joyful cry.

The lawn was smartly green. White stones edged the graveled paths, and peach trees in radiant bloom stood out against the lath and plaster walls. A balcony ran around the second story, and a smaller one stretched across the front, up under the eaves.

"Oh, that sweet balcony! The little one!"

"It's outside your room," said Tilda. "I remembered you liked balconies."

Onkel Max and Tante Else smiled proudly.

Up two flights of stairs they clattered, followed by Hedwig with the suitcases. They went through Tilda's room and into Betsy's, which had a puffy white bed and a *Herr Gott* worked in brightly colored yarns on the white-washed wall. They pushed out to the little balcony.

"Nice! *Nicht?*" asked Tilda.

"Darling!" Betsy looked down in delight.

Sunlight danced on the clear River Ammer winding through the village. Out in the fields oxen were dragging ploughs and old women with white scarves on their heads bent to their work. Beyond the fields, blossoming meadows climbed to dark masses of pines, and in the distance the skyline was topped with a white meringue. The balcony faced the towering cross.

"How it glitters!" Betsy exclaimed.

"It is covered with zinc," Tante Else explained. "It catches every ray of light. We can see it before dawn and after sunset, even. But now you must have second breakfast. Here on your balcony."

She and Onkel Max retreated. Hedwig of the apple cheeks brought hot water in a thin-necked pitcher. And while Betsy washed, and drank coffee and ate *Pfannkuchen,* and finally unpacked, she and Tilda talked, talked, talked.

"Whatever are you doing with that doll?" asked Tilda when Betsy lifted the radiant creature out of its box.

Betsy told the great news of Tacy's baby.

"And me unmarried at the ripe old age of twenty-two!"

"You had your birthday all alone!"

"I felt very philosophical. I planned out my future all the way to when I'm an old lady. I'm going to wear a cap and sit by the fire."

"We'll fatten you up for it," said Tilda. "Here we eat all day. And never did you taste such cooking!"

Running downstairs and outdoors, they crossed a rustic bridge to those slanting meadows strewn with daisies, forget-me-nots, violets, and buttercups. They sang "Peg o' My Heart." They raced through the grass like children.

"This air goes to my head," said Betsy, smoothing her hair as they walked back, more sedately, to dinner. It was such a meal as she remembered from the Mullers, rich, heavy, and delicious. Tante Else loved to work in her kitchen as her husband loved to pull weeds from his velvety lawn and whitewash the stones along his graveled paths.

After dinner they all went over to the Langs'.

Anton Lang lived in a rambling house, plastered in white like its neighbors and bearing above the door a shrine and the scrolled name of its master. He was a potter and his workshop was attached.

In the yard, which was full of fruit trees, children, and confusion, they met Frau Lang, a small plump woman with rolled-up sleeves who greeted them in English. She had bright black eyes, ready dimples, and a chuckly voice.

Cheeriness seemed to be the keynote for the family. There was Anna, Anton's sister, tall, energetic, and over-flowing with fun. She was one of the Three Weeping Women in the Passion Play.

"But I can't imagine her weeping," Betsy whispered.

There was Matilde's father, a one-time director of the Passion Play chorus, and little Martha, the baby and pet of the family. The white-haired old man and the tod-dler were as jolly as the others.

Anna said, "Come on in and see Tony!" And they all trooped into a workshop filled with the tile stoves, plates, jugs, and vases that Anton Lang made. There were several men in the shop, but Betsy recognized the Christus before he put down his tools and turned to greet them.

Back home, the pictures of this large bearded man had aroused in her a slight unreasonable resentment. It had seemed presumptuous in any human being to appear in the role of Jesus. This feeling melted before his warm unaffected smile.

He was slightly stooped, and wore work clothes, dusty from his craft. He had flowing light brown hair and beard, and a strong face with keen, humorous, light-blue eyes. His stoop was humble but his whole manner expressed a simple natural dignity. Like his wife, he spoke in English.

"What a happy family!" Betsy commented as she and Tilda and the Baumgartens walked home.

"Tony is a good man," Onkel Max said. "No man is chosen for the Christ unless his life is blameless."

"In Passion Play summers," Tante Else added, "he goes into another world. It is very hard, the part . . . so full of strain. Imagine the fatigue of hanging for twenty minutes to the cross! And the self-control he must exercise when he is taken down for dead, and the blood comes rushing painfully back into his arms."

"There are other times when he must show self-control," Onkel Max broke in. "The adoration of the crowds would spoil some men. People besiege him; often he hides out in one of the mountain grottos to escape them and Anna brings him his meals."

They spoke in German, but Tilda quickly translated the words Betsy did not know. For both of them, the Passion Play had come out of books into life.

Tante Else went on to say that Herr Lang had refused huge sums to play his role elsewhere. Once, an American manager came all the way to Oberammergau to ask him to star in a play, "The Servant in the House."

"Tony would not think of it, of course. And the manager was astonished. He thought every man had his price."

Through coffee in the garden and supper back at the dining-room table, they talked about the Passion Play. They kept on talking until they grew sleepy, and then Tante Else urged cookies and milk. Out on their balcony before going to bed, the girls drank in the country dark and silence.

Breakfast was served back in the garden, dazzling in morning freshness. Second breakfast, Tante Else announced, each one took where he pleased.

"You'll never again be able to lament that I haven't seen German home life," Betsy told Tilda. For they were treated like daughters. They scattered their belongings from end to end of the Haüschen, and if they went across the Ammer they were given picnic lunches and enough cautions to have brought them safe out of Daniel's fiery furnace.

Kindly proud guides, the Baumgartens took them to the church and the great Passion theater that stood on the edge of the village. The stage was in the open air with the natural background of mountains. They went into the dressing rooms. They saw the basin in which the repentant woman bathed the feet of Christ; the table and chairs used for the Last Supper; the cross. They inspected the costumes which were all of the finest materials.

"They are made by the villagers themselves, copied from famous paintings," Tante Else said.

They called on Ottile Zwink, the Virgin Mary of the last Passion Play. Married now, she would not play the part again. She met them at her door in a spotless apron. Betsy, who had expected a pink and white beauty, was surprised.

"You'd hardly even call her pretty," she and Tilda agreed later. But she had a sweet tender mouth—like Tacy's—blue eyes and wavy brown hair.

Her little parlor was full of Passion Play mementoes. Shyly, she showed them pictures of herself as Mary and autographed one for each.

As the days went on the girls met many of the actors. They even met the ass used in the entry to Jerusalem. In every home they were shown photograph albums.

"Family albums, Oberammergau style!" Betsy wrote in her diary-letter. "Instead of 'This is my aunt's cousin who was killed falling off a stepladder,' we hear, 'This is my brother-in-law. He played Herodotus in 1900.' "

Only natives of the village were allowed to take part in the play.

"How sad for a little girl whose family just moved in!" Betsy exclaimed. "All her playmates would probably be seraphims with three sets of wings apiece, and she couldn't be even a little old baby angel with one pair."

"Ach!" said Tilda. "You're always making up stories."

Every day, wherever else they went, Betsy and Tilda walked through the twisting streets, past curtsying children and their smiling elders, to Anton Lang's house which was the friendly center of the village. Here too, in Herr Lang's workshop or Frau Lang's shining kitchen, the Passion Play was discussed.

In Oberammergau time was marked not by years but by tens of years. As the villagers made their pottery, or their fine wood carvings, or tilled their fields and gardens, they talked of the Passion Play summer that was fading into the past and of the one that was looming ahead. They presented minor plays now and then.

"Fine training," Onkel Max explained, "and a good way to discover talent. It helps the judges decide who shall be picked for the great Passion Play."

For this purpose, every tenth year a committee of villagers met in the Town Hall in secret session. It was a solemn religious occasion. Betsy felt prickles along her spine as she listened to Tante Else tell how Anton Lang had been chosen.

"Nobody expected it. He was only twenty." His modest hope, Tante Else said, rose no higher than the part of St. John. And he only dreamed of that, talking in secret with his father of how wonderful it would be to play the Beloved Disciple.

He was at supper in his father's house. The committee had been in the Town Hall all day. Everyone was on edge. And suddenly shouting neighbors were tapping at every window, and others were crowding through the doorway.

"Tony is to play the Christus!" they cried. "The committee has picked Tony."

Tony's face went white, Tante Else said. Without a word he rushed into his bedroom.

One sparkling morning, Betsy and Tilda set off for the monastery of Ettal. It was from Ettal, Herr Lang had told them, that the Passion Play had sprung. The monks had written the earliest known version in 1662.

Their way led up piney mountain paths. Betsy and Tilda picked flowers and laid them on the roadside shrines. Once they stopped in a meadow for Betsy to teach Tilda the tango. And when the lesson was ended, Betsy ran to an apple tree and broke off blossoms for their hair.

"These make me think of Joe Willard."

"Vy?" Tilda wanted to know, for she was always interested in Joe. "Betsy," she said in English. "You loff him. For vy you fight?"

But instead of answering, Betsy swung Tilda into the tango again.

At Ettal their mood changed. The ancient monastery with its enormous church was startling in this lofty solitude. And the cool hushed cloisters were strange after the blazing spring sunshine.

The monks who had lived here long ago had done more than write the Passion Play. They had taught the villagers to act by putting on those miracle and morality plays so popular in the Middle Ages. They had taught them music. They had taught them to carve in wood and ivory. The library with its thousands of volumes had been a source of culture.

"Ettal explains a lot about Oberammergau," Tilda said thoughtfully, walking homeward, and Betsy agreed. It explained why the people of that village were so different from the run of mountaineers. It explained their gentle manners, their dignity, their cultivated voices. They were even unusually handsome.

"It doesn't explain everything though," Betsy added, and Tilda understood. How about that simple goodness that filled the village like soft air?

Betsy remembered something Onkel Max had told them. "Generations of boys have grown up here with just one ambition, to play the Christ."

They walked on silently for they seemed to be touching the hem of a mystery.

Tilda said at last, "I wonder how long Oberammergau can keep itself unspotted from the world."

"Always," Betsy answered confidently.

"Could it survive a war?"

Betsy faced her, laughing, hands on hips. "You Europeans! There's never going to be another war."

On the last day, of course, they went to say good-bye to the Langs. They were in the workshop talking, when a clatter sounded in the street. Excited voices lifted, and Betsy looked out to see a cloud of dust and a low-slung expensive-looking automobile.

For a moment she was delighted. The young man in the car was obviously American. She was reminded happily of dating and dancing. "Of my gay young days," she thought and wondered where he came from. But when children ran in shouting that the foreigner wished to speak with the Christus, Betsy's pleasure fled.

The young American sprawled behind the wheel, smoking a cigarette, waiting with condescension for Oberammergau's world-famous Anton Lang to come out into the street and greet him.

"*I'm* going out!" Betsy said furiously. "I'll tell him to go home and learn some manners!"

But Herr Lang smiled and said, "No, please!" He put down his work, dusted off his hands, and went out to stand bareheaded in the sun and chat with the young tourist who did not remove his hat, did not unsprawl, and acted, Betsy thought, as though he were inspecting animals in a zoo.

"I'm ashamed!" she raged to Tilda who, although she was indignant, too, was a little amused at Betsy.

"It is the first time you have ever admitted that anything American was less than perfect," Tilda said.

Betsy kept looking through the window, at Anton Lang in his rough clothes standing in the dust beside that automobile. He didn't even seem annoyed, although there was a quizzical look in his eyes.

Anton Lang gave Tilda and Betsy each an autographed picture, and a little pottery angel signed with his name. The Baumgartens loaded their charges with flowers, and presents, and packets of lunch, and half of Oberammergau took them to the station behind Hedwig's rattling cart.

The girls weren't leaving together. Tilda, who had to get back to her school, was going by train. Betsy was going by bus, for she wanted to see the Mad King's castle of Linderhof nearby, before she went over the Brenner Pass to Italy.

"*Liebe, liebe* Betsy!" Tilda kept saying as they waited for the train.

"Dear, dear Tilda!" said Betsy. "But I'll be coming back in 1917." That was the date of their planned reunion.

To keep from feeling weepy, Betsy started a chant such as they used at football games at home.

"*Neunzehn siebzehn! Neunzehn siebzehn!*" Nineteen seventeen! Tilda fell in with it, of course.

Her train arrived; they hugged and kissed, and in a flurry of good-byes she climbed to the platform. Short, erect like a singer, very graceful, her plain little face made lovely by a smile, she called her last farewell. And as the train pulled out, she and Betsy took up the chant again, waving, laughing, crying a little.

"Neunzehn siebzehn! Neunzehn siebzehn!"

Yes, Betsy resolved, she was coming back in 1917 and nothing could stop her.

16

BETSY CURLS HER HAIR

It was not quite evening when Betsy's train shot out between sky and water to the City of the Sea.

She was tired, having left Innsbruck early that morning. She was exhausted, too, by her enthusiasm over the Alpine scenery. And there had been an emotional wrench when she left Austria (which seemed just like

Bavaria) and descended to Italy's vineyards and olive orchards, and the air grew warm, sweet, and lazy.

She had changed trains at Verona. Grateful to find that she shared her compartment with nuns, she had relaxed completely, fully believing that she would not begin to savor Venice until after a good night's sleep. But sweeping across this bridge into a crystalline world jolted her awake.

In a moment they were in a bustling railway station and Betsy, clutching her handbag, camera, umbrella, and *Complete Pocket Guide*, looked about for one, two, or three Signorinas Regali.

"They shouldn't be hard to find," she thought. "Little old ladies in black." But while she still stood looking around, a young Italian approached, his straw hat in his hand.

He was very good-looking, with thick black hair, just slightly wavy, and expressive dark eyes that seemed darker and brighter because of heavy brows and lashes. He was olive skinned, clean shaven; white teeth shone when he smiled. To her surprise he spoke in English.

"Are you Miss Ray?"

"Yes, I am."

"I am Mark Regali. My aunt asked me to meet you, and some other guests for the *Casa delle Rose d'Oro.*"

They shook hands and he beckoned the boy with her bags.

Emerging from the station, Betsy gasped. Of course

she had known that Venice had streets of water. Yet it was a shock to see gondolas and motor boats crowding about the quay like hacks and auto taxis and to hear boatmen crying out for fares. She flashed a delighted look at Mr. Regali.

They joined two plump ladies—Miss Cook and Mrs. Warren from Philadelphia—and Mr. Regali helped them all into a gondola. This looked excitingly familiar, curving out of the water at both ends, with a small covered cabin in which they seated themselves. The gondolier stood at the stern, his oar in his hands.

They glided off into the Grand Canal. Dusk had fallen, but there was a moon. It turned the street of water into an even more incredible street of trembling silver. When the clamor of the station died away, there was no sound but the soft plash of an oar and some distant music. Betsy spoke of the silence and Mr. Regali said, smiling at her, "The Grand Canal is in the shape of an *S*. Italians say this stands for Silenzio."

At that moment a shrill whistle blew and a loaded steamboat hurried past, churning up a noisy wash of water. He and Betsy both laughed.

"That's a *vaporetto*. They are our streetcars. They're very convenient even though they do spoil my story." He was nice, Betsy thought. She wondered how he happened to speak English.

Moonlight shimmered over the snowy palaces that rose on either side. They rose straight from the water.

Betsy had expected a scrap of lawn or sidewalk in front, but there was none. Just steps, lapped by the waves, and some tall striped posts. These were hitching posts for gondolas, Mr. Regali said.

As they glided along he pointed out houses in which Wagner had lived, and Browning and Byron. The ladies from Philadelphia peered out and asked, "Where? Which one?" But Betsy was speechless with rapture. She sat with her hands squeezed together, looking at the glimmering city. Byron was right. It did seem to have come from the stroke of an enchanter's wand.

"Oh, I love it! I love it!" she thought. "How lucky I am to be here."

Mr. Regali looked at her now and then.

They traversed a network of shadowy small canals and arrived at the House of the Yellow Roses. It was one of a row of white houses and had iron window grilles through which lights were streaming. There were no yellow roses in sight, but there was a sidewalk!

In the tiny office, crowded with new arrivals, all was confusion. The three Signorinas Regali—small, dark, and dressed in black, as described—welcomed Betsy kindly. One spoke English, and asked her if she would have dinner. She had dined in Verona, Betsy answered. All her fatigue had come back. She was longing for her room—and her mail.

"Miss Ray has a great deal of mail," Mr. Regali reminded his aunt and brought it out from the desk at which Betsy was registering. There was a glorious thick pack, bound with a cord. Betsy smiled luminous thanks, and clutching her treasure, she followed the maid up to her room.

She didn't even take off her hat before diving into the letters . . . the first she had received since Sonneberg. Having finished them, she undressed and dropped into bed without even unpacking. It seemed no time at all until sunlight was flooding into her windows along with the hum of bees and a sweet, sweet scent.

Betsy jumped up. Her room overlooked the garden! And the white walls that enclosed it were covered with climbing roses. *There* were the yellow roses, and pink and red ones, too! Below her, little paths intersected flower beds, and in a patch of lawn, tables were ready for breakfast.

Her room had a desk. "Hooray! I'll lay a story in Venice. A love story, of course."

She could hardly wait for her trunk, to get out her books and writing materials. She would go to the Custom House this morning, she planned. Meanwhile she unpacked her suitcases and ran downstairs to breakfast.

The House of the Yellow Roses was different from the Geiger. Here were no impecunious European students but prosperous American tourists, with flags in their buttonholes and guidebooks open on the table— Miss Cook and Mrs. Warren, four college girls, a doctor with his family, a young man from Harvard and another from Princeton. There was one lone Englishman.

"Sort of broken down," Betsy decided. He was well into middle age with a red dissipated face which had once been handsome but wasn't any more.

They were all talking of what they would see today— cutting up Venice as though it were a sausage and their days were sandwiches, Betsy thought. No one planned to stay more than a week. Half that time was more common. She was offered numerous sight-seeing schedules, and people acted astonished and almost resentful when she said she planned to stay six weeks.

Mr. Regali, who ate with his aunts, strolled past and said good morning.

"Don't get a crush!" one of the college girls warned Betsy. "It won't do you any good."

"What made you think I was going to?"

"Everyone does. But he's not susceptible."

"And he's busy making drawings."

Harvard turned to Princeton. "Do you suppose they talk *us* over like that?"

Mr. Regali strolled past the table again.

When they rose, the Englishman said to Betsy, "May I offer my services, Miss Ray, in introducing you to Venice? I have a gondola ordered for ten."

"Oh, no thank you!" said Betsy hastily. She groped for an excuse. "I have to go to the Custom House to see about my trunk."

"I'll take you there. It will be a pleasure." He bowed quickly as though the matter were settled.

Flushing, Betsy glanced around. Mr. Regali was listening, his black brows drawn together. She would consult his aunts, Betsy thought, and went to the office, but it was empty. Mr. Regali followed her inside.

"See here!" he said. "Excuse me! But you can't go out with that fellow."

"Oh, dear! I know it. But what am I to do?"

"You are in my aunts' care. They would never permit it."

"Of course not. But what can I *say*?" Betsy wailed.

His answer was stern. "Go back and tell him that you've changed your mind. Tell him you don't *think*"—he stressed the word—"you'll be going out today. Then as soon as he's out of the way, I'll take you to the Custom House myself."

"All right," said Betsy meekly. It was wonderful to have broad shoulders to drop her problem on.

When the Englishman had departed, she and Mr. Regali took a *vaporetto* to the railway station. It was a sunshiny morning with a breeze, and Betsy's spirits rose like a balloon in the bright Venetian blue. Mr. Regali's kept pace. Leaning over the rail, they laughed together at the neatness with which they had extricated her from her predicament.

The Grand Canal was crowded with watercraft, and all around them was a babble of Italian.

"How do you happen to speak English?" Betsy asked.

"I lived in the States until I was fifteen."

"*You did*? Where?"

"Princeton, New Jersey. My father taught in the University. When my parents died, I came here to my aunts. So Venice has been my home for eight years."

Then he was twenty-three. Just a year older than she was!

"Of course, I've been off at college," he added. "Rome."

"Finished?"

"I'm an architect. And I was lucky enough to be put on a research project. I was sent right back here with some very interesting work laid out. I'm making drawings now of the choir stalls at San Giorgio Maggiore."

"Do you . . ." Betsy broke off, laughing. "Really," she said, "I was brought up not to ask personal questions. I know I shouldn't be hurling them at you. It's just so wonderful . . . to be out with someone my own age who speaks English. I'm so happy!"

"So am I," he answered.

After getting her trunk through customs, they ordered it sent to the pension and Mr. Regali said, "Why don't we look around Venice a little before we go home?"

Because it was near, they went first to the Rialto. The old marble bridge was lined with cheap little shops. The proprietors stood in front haggling over prices with women in black shawls.

"All the treasures of the Orient used to be spread out here," Mr. Regali remarked.

"And Shylock used to come!"

They took another *vaporetto* to St. Mark's Square . . . the Piazza, Mr. Regali called it. It looked just as it did in all the pictures, except that the colors of the marble buildings were richer and the Grand Canal sparkled as it never did on canvas.

Tourists were going in and out of the rosy Doge's Palace and St. Mark's Cathedral with its oriental-looking domes. They were looking up at the clock tower and the golden angel on top of the Campanile. They were lunching at the open-air cafés, and feeding the pigeons that kept circling down in glossy waves.

"Oh, I wish we'd brought my camera! I want my picture taken feeding the pigeons."

"If you really do," said Mr. Regali, "I'll take it the next time we come. I believe we've passed lunchtime. How about stopping here at Florian's?"

They lunched at that famous café, outdoors. Betsy kept looking around at the brilliant busy square.

"They have music in the evenings."

"Oh, that would be too celestial!"

"You must let me bring you soon."

They walked from the Piazza to the Piazzetta, and between two stately columns, topped by St. Theodore and the famous winged Lion of St. Mark, down to the quay. The Grand Canal was full of gondolas, barges, yachts, and ferries. The gondoliers began to call: *"Una gondola, Signor! Una barca!"*

Mr. Regali nodded across the water. "See that tower? It's on the church of San Giorgio Maggiore."

"That's where you're drawing the choir stalls."

"Yes. And the view from the tower is the finest in Venice. Let's go over; shall we?"

"Oh, yes!" Betsy said.

So they took a gondola to San Giorgio Maggiore. The gondolier wore white with a green sash. They swept gently over the water and landed at another domed church. Palladio had built it in the sixteenth century, Mr. Regali said, and going inside he showed her pictures by Tintoretto, and the choir stalls. "Magnificent baroque!"

They climbed what seemed like a hundred thousand dark steep steps, but when they came out into the sunshine, Venice was spread out below like a map, glistening white, the water dotted with the orange sails of fishing vessels.

"Oh, oh!" cried Betsy.

"Ripping, isn't it?" came a British voice. There was another visitor in the tower. The Englishman of the House of the Yellow Roses lifted a soft hat.

"Why . . . how do you do? I *did* go out after all," said Betsy.

"So I see."

"We attended to the trunk," said Mr. Regali.

Then, forsaking the view, he and Betsy turned and clattered down the stairs. Laughing, they ran as though pursued, down through the vertical darkness and out into the light and back to their gondola.

"Wasn't *that* a horrible moment?" Betsy asked.

"He's a horrible person. The idea of his thinking he could take you out all alone on your first day in Venice!"

Simultaneously they realized that it was just what he himself had done, and they broke into laughter.

It dawned on Betsy that they had been laughing all day.

"I laugh with him like I do with Tilda, and Tacy and Tib," she thought. She felt as though she had known him forever. It seemed completely natural to be wandering around with him, but it came to her now that perhaps it hadn't been quite proper.

"I was having so much fun I forgot about everything."

She had even forgotten how she looked. She hadn't so much as glanced in her pocket mirror. Taking it out now, she tucked her hair beneath the red and green cap, buttoned her red jacket, and smoothed the skirts of her pale green cotton dress.

"If I'd known we were going to stay all day, I'd have worn a hat, at least."

"I like you the way you are," said Mr. Regali. "Do you know," he added thoughtfully, "there's a full moon. *This* might be a good night to go over to St. Mark's Square."

"And it might not," said Betsy, and laughed, and he laughed, too. He knew she had realized belatedly that they had been together for a very long time.

Reaching the pension, Betsy went straight to her

room. She rested and bathed and changed into a white dress. At dinner she talked animatedly to her fellow Americans. (The Englishman ignored her.) And in the evening she took pains to join the college girls in the garden. Mr. Regali walked past them once or twice.

She went to her room early, for her trunk had arrived. She unpacked, and settled her desk, and got out her photographs and Goethe's cup and Tacy's doll, and put the American flag over her mirror. She wrote her home letter and told the story of the day, not forgetting the embarrassing situation on the tower at San Giorgio Maggiore.

"Mr. Regali is a perfect dear," she was writing when she heard a knock. She opened the door to find one of the maids with an enormous armful of pink roses.

"Oh, thank you! *Grazie!*" Betsy cried. But she knew from whom they came. She put them in her water pitcher, for none of the vases in the room would hold them. They filled the entire room with fragrance.

Standing before the mirror in her pink summer kimono, brushing her hair, Betsy's expression grew thoughtful. She opened a drawer in which she had arranged her toilet articles and began to hunt for something she had not used for a long time.

A short time later, chuckling, she went back to her letter and added a postscript.

"I just put my hair up on curlers," she wrote, "for the first time in Europe. You've heard about emotion coming in *waves*??? "

17

FORGETTING AGAIN

In exactly five days Mr. Regali told Betsy that he loved her. And after that he told her every day in Italian, French, and English.

"When I saw you standing in the railway station," he said, "with all those bags, I fell in love. I didn't admit it, though. I said to myself, 'Oh, I hope she will be stupid!'

But in the gondola I could see that you weren't. I knew I was a goner."

"It's perfectly ridiculous," Betsy replied with a joyful sensation spreading through her body. "You only imagine it!"

"I wish I did. I didn't want to fall in love. Why couldn't you have stayed in Oberammergau?"

Until this revelation he had continued to be only an extremely kind friend.

"He's my guardian angel," Betsy wrote home.

He explained the monetary system and helped her change her money. He pointed out the American Express Company, and Thomas Cook's, and the English Church. He bought her a map of Venice and checked the steamboat stations and the ferries.

"But getting around Venice on foot is complicated," he said. "I'd better show you in person."

There were no streets except canals. Walking, you went up and down bridges, and along tiny alleys, spanned by clotheslines full of washing, and across picturesque courts where people were always hanging out the windows in vigorous conversation. They shouted; they gesticulated.

"What's the matter with them anyway?" Betsy asked.

Mr. Regali laughed. "Oh, they're just saying it's a beautiful day!"

You dodged around old houses, time-stained to mellow hues. You went through lanes with vines climbing over the walls and hints of gardens behind. With Mr. Regali, Betsy explored every tantalizing nook.

And always in the end they came out on the Grand Canal. The palaces lifted their airy arches, balconies, and columns above water that changed color all the time. It was oftenest a vivid blue, but it could be sapphire blue and lilac blue. It could be grass green and emerald green and bottle green. It could be iridescent, enameled, pearly, silky.

"I don't see how you put up with me!" cried Betsy. "All my raving and ranting! I know I bore you, but I just can't help it."

"You don't bore me."

He took pictures of her feeding the pigeons. They bought a paper bag full of corn, and the pigeons perched on her shoulders, her arms, her fingers! The Harvard man passed by and yelled something scoffing.

"I know it's a touristy trick, but I don't care," Betsy said.

"He's only ignorant," Mr. Regali assured her. "He doesn't know how important these birds are. They're direct descendants of carrier pigeons that helped us win a victory over the Greeks five or six centuries ago."

They peeked in at St. Mark's Church, dim and glittering. St. Mark was buried here, Mr. Regali said. His body had reached Venice after many strange adventures which were told in mosaics over the entrance door. They went up to the galleries to see them, and on a balcony overlooking the Square stood four bronze horses.

"The only horses in Venice!" he announced. They were trophies from Constantinople. Napoleon had taken them off to Paris, but after his downfall they had been returned. Betsy had her picture snapped beside them.

They went next door to the rosy Doge's Palace. Its stones were red and white, but the effect was pink. Going inside, they climbed the Giants' Staircase and wandered through lofty halls which were carved and gilded, with gigantic paintings by Tintoretto, Titian, and Veronese covering the walls and even the ceilings.

They walked through the Palace to a bridge which led to an ancient prison next door.

"Recognize this?"

"The Bridge of Sighs! But, oh dear, I don't feel like sighing!"

"Neither do I. There isn't a sigh in me. I think Florian's would be more suitable for us."

So they went back to the Square and drank coffee and ate *casata di Siciliano,* a delicious concoction with chopped fruit and nuts and layers of chocolate in it. They talked about the Wilsons, who were having a fine studious time in Greece, and about Betsy's travel plans, and—of course—her family.

"All those letters that were waiting for you. Were they from your family?"

"Not all of them."

His expressive eyes grew thoughtful.

New sets of tourists were feeding the pigeons now, and going in and out of the Palace and the Cathedral, and shopping in the arcades of other marble buildings around the Square.

"I just adore this place," said Betsy.

"Then when are we coming in the evening?"

"Oh . . . sometime!" She wasn't sure it would be proper to go out with him alone at night. And she was trying to be very discreet.

Partly because her *Italian Self-Taught* proved to be inadequate, and partly because study took time which might otherwise be indiscreetly spent, Betsy had started Italian lessons. One of the aunts, the one who spoke English, was her teacher.

Mr. Regali spent her lesson hours in his rooms, a few houses away. He had been climbing around Venice gathering data, he said. Now he was working on his drafting board, transcribing notes.

"The sort of notes an architect takes . . . with pencil, scales, and caliper."

Betsy alternated walks with him and sight-seeing trips with her fellow Americans . . . to the Accademia to look at masterpieces or to Murano to see the glass works. If she went out with him in the morning, she was careful not to do so in the afternoon. But every evening they walked down to the nearby Giudecca Canal to see the sunset.

Sunsets in Venice were twice as beautiful as ordinary

sunsets because they were doubled. All the splendor of the sky—the flaming crimson, violet, and gold—was spread on the water too. And all the tender after-colors, the pastels, the fading silvers were repeated.

Battleships, merchant vessels, yachts, and gondolas were moored on the Giudecca. Artists were sketching on every bridge and barge.

"They'll be putting us into their pictures," Betsy said.

"Let's fool them Sunday night and go to the Piazza."

Betsy hesitated. "I'm not sure we should go out at night unchaperoned. In America, of course, I'd think nothing of it. But in Italy . . ."

"You're an American."

"Yes, but your aunts . . ."

"We'll ask them," he said, and when they returned to the pension they hunted up the Signorinas Regali.

Betsy had straightened them out now, although they looked much alike. All were small, and submerged in black garments, and had their nephew's thickly lashed dark eyes. They consulted each other on everything, like chattering birds.

Signorina Eleanora was a little shorter than her sisters but she was more forceful. Signorina Beatrice was a little taller but she had a quicker sense of humor. Signorina Angela, Betsy's Italian teacher, had the softest heart.

"We'll ask Aunt Angela," Mr. Regali said as they walked back to the House of the Yellow Roses. But they found all three in the little family parlor.

The aunts, whose home was full of Americans from one year's end to the next, understood American ways. They made no objection to Mr. Regali's plan.

"Americans think nothing of such things!" Aunt Beatrice tossed it off.

"You must bring her home early," Aunt Eleanora warned, looking at her nephew.

"Marco is a good boy," said Aunt Angela lovingly.

It was agreed that they might go. But as it happened Betsy did not, after all, have her first glimpse of St. Mark's Square by night with Mr. Regali. He received a telegram from a group of professors under whose direction he was doing his research. They were visiting at Padua and they wished him to come on Sunday for a conference.

Betsy was surprised at how much she missed him. She went to the English Church in the morning, and after dinner she went to the Frari and looked at Titian's tomb. At supper Miss Cook and Mrs. Warren asked her if she wouldn't like to go over to St. Mark's Square; they had heard it was delightful in the evening. Betsy accepted, and then she had a miserably guilty feeling.

"Why under the sun should I feel guilty?" she asked. "Mr. Regali didn't invent Venice."

But while she was putting on her hat in her room, she heard a whistle from the garden.

For, I adore,
I adore you, Giannina mia . . .

It was their signal, formally adopted several days before. He had heard her humming the song and had been charmed with the Italian phrases. She went to the window and there he stood, looking hot, rumpled, and triumphant.

"*Ecco!*" he cried. "I had to run out on a whole flock of bigwigs, but here I am! And there's going to be a band concert."

"Oh, Mr. Regali!" Betsy faltered. "I'm so sorry! Miss Cook and Mrs. Warren asked me to go with them, and I didn't know you were coming back . . ."

The joy went out of his face. He didn't speak.

"I'm so terribly sorry!" Betsy repeated. She was. She wanted to cry.

He said something in Italian; it sounded despairing. And he pushed his fingers through his hair. But then he looked up with his shining Italian smile.

"My fault!" he said. "But will you promise not to look at a thing?"

"Not a thing," answered Betsy tremulously.

"And not to listen to the music?"

"I won't listen."

"And tomorrow," he said, "you'll go out with me on a bat?" Like Tilda, he had picked up Betsy's favorite word. "And no talk about hurrying home to write letters or study Italian!"

"But I have a lesson in the morning," Betsy reminded him, laughing.

"*Bene!* You may take it. But I'll be waiting for you when it's over." And he picked a rose and threw it through the window, and Betsy went slowly out to meet Miss Cook and Mrs. Warren. They were nice; they were very full of fun. But Betsy wished they had never started traveling.

At St. Mark's Square she tried not to look or listen, although on a platform in the center a band played rousingly. Everything was brightly lighted, and there were crowds of people promenading across the marble pavements, strolling in the arcades, and eating and drinking at little tables. It seemed as though the rest of Venice must be entirely deserted, and no one anywhere sleeping.

The Grand Canal doubled all the lights and the beauty and the fascination. It was full of gondolas, some of them strung with lanterns, and their occupants were singing and strumming guitars.

"Oh, dear!" mourned Betsy while she ate ices with the jolly middle-aged ladies. "It would have been so nice to see it with him!"

The following morning she put on her prettiest dress, white, with a tiered skirt, green buttons down the front, and a flat green bow at the collar. She wore the green bracelets she had bought at Gibraltar, and her jade ring, and her slanting black hat with the green leaves and the rose.

Mr. Regali was waiting when her lesson was over, and they took a steamboat to the Lido.

The large island contained a city of hotels and

bathhouses. Smartly dressed crowds strolled its walks, while vendors of flowers and fruits called their wares. The beaches were scattered with bathers, and children were digging in the sand.

Betsy and Mr. Regali sat down on a bench and looked out at orange sails floating on the water. It was here he told her that he had fallen in love.

She was astonished, delighted, and half-unbelieving. How could even a romantic Italian fall in love in five days! But with the sun flooding down on the Lido, she wanted to believe him, even though she realized that she didn't know—now that he had ceased to be a friend—how she felt about him. He relieved her by not asking for an answer.

"Understand," he said, "I don't expect you to feel as I do! Not yet! But you're going to be here six weeks. That ought to be time enough . . . in Venice."

He asked her again about the letters. "The ones that didn't come from your family. Were quite a few from some one person?"

"No," answered Betsy, smiling.

"You aren't in love with anyone?"

"No."

"Have you ever been in love with anyone?"

"I thought I was one time." She told him about Joe. "He's a wonderful person. I liked him all through high school and college. But we quarreled."

"How could anyone quarrel with you?"

"It was my fault."

"I don't believe it."

"It really was, Mr. Regali . . ." But he didn't want to be called Mr. Regali any more.

"I am Marco for the Saint, and the Cathedral, and the Square, and Marco Polo. He was born in Venice; I'll show you the court."

"All right, Marco. My name's Betsy."

"It's Elisabetta, and I shall call you Betta." He had another inspired idea. "After this, I shan't whistle just two lines of our song.

"For, I adore,
I adore you, Giannina mia.

"I shall always whistle four lines.

"More, more and more,
I adore you, Giannina mia."

Betsy was enchanted.

But that night when the whistle sounded . . . unexpectedly, for she thought he was working . . . there were only two lines.

"For, I adore,
I adore you, Giannina mia."

"He forgot!" Betsy thought in disappointment. Glancing at the mirror, she went to the window. But when she put her head out, the four college girls were grinning up at her.

Fortunately, they moved on the next day to the Italian Lakes, and after that there were always four lines whistled, and it was always Marco, leaning against an arbor, gazing up.

"Only an Italian could do it," Betsy often thought, for he was never awkward or self-conscious but always graceful and at ease.

He was usually asking her to come down and go some place, and she usually went.

They saw a wedding—and a funeral. The funeral had a band, and the mourners carrying the casket to the black-draped gondola marched in time to the music, followed by boys with candles, and a priest. The silent gondolier, standing behind the casket, dipped his oar and Betsy thought of the Lily Maid of Astolat floating downstream. But this boat was one of a long procession. The cemetery was on a nearby island, Marco said.

"I believe we've seen every one of those hundred islands you told me Venice was built on," Betsy remarked, for on foot and by gondola, steamboat, and ferry, they had traversed the city from end to end. "I'm glad people thought of building this heavenly place. They were running away from the Huns; weren't they?"

"Yes. Back in the fifth century. And they built a cluster of reedy little islands into a great Republic. I wish we could have seen it in the days of the Doges, Betta."

"It couldn't," Betsy answered positively, "have been any nicer than it is right now."

She was happier than she had been since she left home. Up to now a nagging homesickness had been with her all the time . . . except when she was with Tilda or Helena. But here she was completely free of it.

And how grand, she thought, to have a man to bat with! Because she had known no men in Munich, she had seldom gone out at night and hadn't had a single party. It was glorious to dress up and curl her hair and go to St. Mark's Square in the evening with Marco.

They went whenever the band played, and they drank coffee, and ate *casata,* and watched the crowd. Marco knew many of the people who went by, artists and musicians and some architects like himself.

They always took a gondola home. From the Grand Canal the lighted Square stood out like a stage setting. People floating around them were singing . . . everything from *Il Trovatore* to "Funiculi, Funicula." Betsy and Marco sang with them.

When their gondola left the Grand Canal and went gliding down dark waterways to the House of the Yellow Roses, they kept on singing.

Although he had told her he loved her, and repeated it every day in Italian, French, and English, Marco never touched her, which pleased Betsy, for if he grew mushy she would have to stop seeing him. And oh, she didn't want to have to do that!

"Dear darling family," she wrote home. "To say that I'm happy as the day is long doesn't express it. I wake up happy. I go to bed happy. Oh, my beautiful, beautiful Venezia! (As Marco likes me to call it. That's the Italian name.)"

She liked her Italian lessons and studied two hours every day. She tried this new language on the maids and in the shops. (German seemed like an old friend now. One day at Florian's she heard some people speaking German and for a second she thought they were speaking English, because she could understand.)

She loved the garden at the House of the Yellow Roses, and often had it to herself. She sat in a low wicker chair, pretending to write, but really dreaming, enjoying the scent of the flowers, the buzzing of the bees, and the circling of white butterflies.

The other guests were out sightseeing, of course . . . rushing about in the heat, staring up at the ceilings of the Doge's Palace, marching through St. Mark's Cathedral with their Baedekers in their hands. How sensible she was, thought Betsy, just to live in Venice, to dawdle about this sunny garden, and take walks and stroll down with Marco to watch the sun set over the Giudecca!

They were doing that one evening when they saw a steamer starting for Fusina, the nearest point on the mainland, and on an impulse they boarded it. They didn't get off at the little town but came directly back. Venice was outlined by lights against black sea and sky.

Betsy and Marco stood out in the bow gazing.

"What is it like at Fusina in the daytime?" Betsy asked.

"I'll take you someday, and you'll see."

18

THE SECOND MOON IN VENICE

One morning when Betsy was studying Italian, she heard "Giannina mia" under her window and looked out to see Marco smiling up at her. The sun was shining on his wavy black hair, his eager face.

"How about a walk?"

"I'm working."

"So was I, but I stopped. Besides, I can teach you Italian down on the Giudecca."

"Will you hear me say verbs?" asked Betsy, and she caught up her red jacket and ran down to the garden where the aunts were shelling peas, looking as alike as peas themselves. Smiling at Marco, Betsy said *"buon giorno"* nicely as Aunt Angela had taught her.

"Bene!" cried Marco, and Aunt Angela gazed at them fondly. Aunt Beatrice twinkled at them, but Aunt Eleanora, Betsy thought, looked a little grave. Aunt Eleanora liked her, she felt sure. And she had done nothing the aunts had not approved. Could Aunt Eleanora be worried for fear she and Marco were getting serious? Didn't she know it was just that they were young, and in Venice in June?

On the Giudecca there was a lively breeze. The water was rippling, boats were rocking. The clouds, Betsy remarked, all seemed to be going some place.

"We ought to do the same," Marco replied. And just as before, they heard a steamer whistling its departure. "Here's your chance to see Fusina in the daytime."

"Marco Polo! I'm not even wearing a hat!"

"We'll just make the round trip. Be home for lunch," he said.

But when they reached the little town they got off for a moment. And beside the station, a meadow rolled down to the sea. It seemed to belong to the sea, although its grass was sprinkled with poppies, and a goat was browsing. But the small trees were wind-blown; there was salt in the air. Children were playing down on the beach.

"Let's stay!" Marco pleaded.

"But your aunts would be worried."

"I can telephone from the station house."

"Well, I'm starving, and I don't see any restaurant!"

"Restaurant!" said Marco scornfully. "We're going to eat in this meadow. You pick the spot."

"*Ecco!*" said Betsy, dropping down. Her green skirts spread out around her. Marco looked at her, nodded judicially, and strode back to the station.

The sea spread a fan of cerulean blue, and Betsy looked off in great content. The steamer whistled two or three times.

"It won't do you any good," she said.

Marco returned, smiling. "The Signora Station House is killing a chicken."

"For us?"

"For us. We're going to eat it on this identical spot. 'Exactly where the signorina is looking so beautiful among the poppies!' That's what I said, and she understood."

He sat down beside her and the steamer with a last reproachful whistle sailed away.

"If they want passengers," said Marco, "why do they build their station house so close to this meadow?"

"Isn't it stupid of them?" Betsy asked. "I feel a thousand miles from Venice."

"So do I. I feel as though you and I were alone in the world."

"Except for a goat."

"Oh, yes! The goat."

"And a station master." For he was approaching with a table. His daughter followed with two chairs. Laying the cloth, she turned her eyes wonderingly from Marco to Betsy.

The children too had come within staring distance. The goat was indifferent for a time. But when the chicken appeared, trailing savory odors, he galloped around on his small hoofs.

"I'm astonished. I thought goats were herbivorous," said Betsy. This one didn't seem to be. Marco brandished a chair. The children jumped and squealed with delight. Betsy laughed until she was weak.

The station master's daughter came out with a stick at last and drove the beast away.

"My family," Betsy said, "writes me that they are always saying, 'I wonder what Betsy is doing now.' Well, if they're saying that this moment they'd have a hard time guessing. They'd never think of me eating lunch with you in a meadow by the Adriatic."

The chicken was served with rice, and peas, and little hard rolls. Marco had the sour red wine Italians are so fond of, and Betsy had very strong coffee. For dessert there were strawberries, and the sun shone down on the little sea meadow.

"This is just about the loveliest time I ever had in my life," Betsy said.

After the table was taken away, Betsy and Marco went down to the point where the rough grass met the sand. There they could look out at the orange-colored sails, dancing over the sea. Betsy was feeling as gay as the waves, but Marco grew serious. He stopped talking. Sprawled on the grass, he pulled out rough blades and chewed them moodily.

"Betta," he said at last, sitting up and turning toward her. "I've been thinking for several days that I'd better have a talk with you."

"What about?" Betsy asked.

"About us. About loving you. I can't go on this way."

"This way? But we're so happy, Marco . . ." Betsy didn't want him to say any more.

But he cut her off short, and went on grimly, "All I want to know is whether I have a chance."

"You couldn't really expect me to be in love with you in three weeks," she answered in a small, weak voice. "I don't believe you're really in love with me."

"I can answer for myself," he said shortly. "As for you, I know you couldn't tell me you love me and promise to marry me so soon. I've not yet had a chance to meet your family. But you must know whether I have a chance or not. You see . . . if I haven't, I'd better go away. If I let myself go much farther, I may never get over it."

At his mention of marriage, Betsy was suddenly

panic-stricken. She didn't know what to do or say. Staring off at the water, she thought of how much she liked him. She had written her family that he was her guardian angel. He had taken her in charge from the very first, and had been so immensely kind and thoughtful.

Perhaps because they were both artists, they were completely congenial. Betsy never tired of him and he never tired of her. He didn't care how she looked, or if she was tired or quiet or had a headache.

"He loves me the same way Tacy does, and Tib and the family," Betsy thought. And yet not exactly that way or he would be content to keep on being friends, and plainly he wasn't.

She had noticed him with his aunts, and knew his affectionate disposition. She loved that about him. It was one of the things that made her so happy with him. It was one thing that had driven her homesickness so far away that it seemed strange now to think she had ever had it. And yet . . .

Something wasn't there. Something she had felt for Joe Willard—and maybe still felt, although she had hardly thought of him since she got to Venice.

She glanced at Marco's strong, handsome profile. He looked more serious now than she had ever seen him. She had to be careful what she said; she had to tell the truth. It seemed to her that her heart would break if he went away, but maybe it would be better for him if he did. She drew a deep breath and squared her chin.

"You know how much I like you," she said. "That's so obvious it isn't worth mentioning, but that's all I feel. Just liking you an awful, awful lot."

He didn't turn. "Do you think that liking will ever change to anything else?"

"I don't think so."

"Why not?"

"I don't know."

They sat in miserable silence and stared out at the Adriatic.

"Is it because I'm not of your nationality?"

"No . . . I don't think so. I love your being an Italian. But . . . I can't imagine you outside of Venice."

"I like the United States. I've lived there. I may go back some day. I would, if you wanted me to, Betta. You could live right next door to that family you're so crazy about. I could practice my profession there. They have architects, don't they, at the Minnehaha Falls?" Which made Betsy smile a little, but there were tears in her eyes.

"Are you in love with anyone else?"

"You asked me that before, Marco, and I told you all there was to tell. That boy I used to go with, Joe Willard. I think I was in love with him, but we don't even correspond any more."

"Is he the reason you can't love me?"

"I don't know," said Betsy wretchedly. "The way I feel now, I don't want to marry you or Joe or anybody else for years and years."

She put her head down on her knees. She had told the truth; but now he would go away. And at the thought, all her homesickness came back. Her tears began to flow.

Marco didn't notice for a minute, because he was still looking at the Adriatic with a frozen face. But when he heard a sniffle he turned, and he changed at once.

"Betta mia! You mustn't cry. I won't have it. I can't stand it." He put his arms around her. He found a wet cheek and kissed it.

"Don't be so sorry for me! I'm not feeling so badly. You have been so sincere in saying no, that I'll know you are sincere when you say yes. And the next time you'll say yes."

"No, I won't," said Betsy, thinking that if it had to end, it might as well end now. She might not be able to be so firm again. "I wish I would. But I know I won't."

"Why do you wish you would?"

"Because I like you so much."

"Is that the only reason?"

"Because . . . I don't want you to go away."

"Do you think you could drive me away?" he asked. He jumped to his feet and pulled her after him, laughing down at her. "You are going to be here for three weeks and a half! In Venice! And, Betta, there's going to be a moon! What kind of a man would I be, not to take advantage of that opportunity to get something I want as much as I want you?"

Betsy dried her eyes. Her hair was loose, her nose

was red, and she knew she looked awful. "I'm going to the station house and ask if I can wash up, and let's take the next boat back to Venice."

"All right," he answered.

"It was a wonderful picnic, Marco."

"Yes, it was. And now, please be happy again, *carissima*. We won't talk about this any more for a while."

He put his arm about her shoulders and kissed her wind-blown hair as they moved off through the waving grass.

When they got home, it was dinner time, and after dinner Betsy went straight to her room. She had stopped crying at Fusina, but she wasn't through crying. She flung herself on the bed and sobbed. She felt guilty. She wanted to talk with her mother. She didn't know if she was doing wrong or right in staying on in Venice, in letting Marco stay.

She heard Marco's whistle, but she didn't answer it. She had not turned on a light; perhaps he would think she had gone for a walk. But after a moment she heard a soft thud on the floor, and then another, and another, and another! Betsy jumped out of bed. Coming through the open window were roses and carnations, roses and carnations. By the time the shower ended there were enough to fill her water pitcher to overflowing.

"He knows how I'm feeling," she thought.

She put on her pink kimono and poked her head out of the window.

"Grazie," she said in a small voice.

"Good night, Betta mia," he answered.

But Betsy could not sleep. The room was full of the scent of flowers, and she was very troubled. After an hour or two, she went to the window again. He was still standing there in the garden, looking at her window.

"An American man would never do anything like that. He couldn't," Betsy thought. "And if he did, he would look silly."

But not Marco, standing down in the garden with folded arms.

Betsy went back to bed and cried some more.

After that they were together even more than before. The aunts understood; Marco had told them. And sometimes he and Betsy still had fun together. Swinging hands, they went through the lanes and over the bridges of Venice. They went to the Rialto and watched the bargaining. They went to St. Mark's Square and ate *casata.* They took the steamboat to the Lido.

But now there was a weight on Betsy's heart. She wasn't so carefree any more. He had told her that if he stayed and fell more in love with her, he would never get over it. Was she doing wrong to keep him with her? She had written her mother all about it, but there wasn't time for an answer that would help.

Sometimes he was very unhappy. When he asked her if she loved him and she had to say no, he flared up: "Oh, you Americans! You can't feel! You're like ice!"

But Betsy did feel. She felt like a murderess.

"I think you ought to go away," she would say. "I really do." But then she would begin to cry, and he would take her in his arms and beg her to forgive him.

The moon came, and poured its golden-silvery light over the pearly buildings and along the canals of Venice, but Betsy didn't change her mind. And the weeks were slipping by fast. They went to the Accademia and looked at the Titians, the Tintorettos, the Bellinis. They went to the Church of San Zaccaria, because her favorite picture was Bellini's "Madonna with Saints."

"You and Ruskin!" he said. Ruskin, it seemed, had called that one of the two most beautiful pictures in Venice.

"Me and Ruskin! I must write that to Tilda."

One morning the King and Queen came to Venice. Betsy was awakened by cannons which announced the arrival of their train. She dressed hurriedly, and after a bite of breakfast ran over to the Santa Maria della Salute with Marco to see their boat go past.

Flags and banners were hung out of the windows of the palaces along the Grand Canal. But it was drizzling and the crowd was so thick that Betsy could hardly see Victor Emmanuel and Elena through the dripping forest of umbrellas.

"Won't they appear again? I want to get a good look at them."

"They'll come out on the balcony of the Palace tomorrow night," Marco answered. "I'll take you, unless it looks as though there is going to be trouble."

"Trouble?"

"I think the monarchy is tottering," he answered. "The Socialists are very strong; there may be riots."

But there were no rumors of riots the next day, and although by nightfall it was raining harder than ever, Betsy and Marco went to the Palace. The square in front was a sea of bobbing umbrellas and filled with a roar of voices.

Betsy doubted that royalty would really appear in such a downpour, but suddenly they were there above her, the little king and the tall, bejeweled queen. They seemed extremely nervous, and bowed hastily to the cheering throngs as though they were anxious to retreat into the room behind them.

The crowd certainly seemed loyal and enthusiastic. A woman beside Betsy almost lost her head with admira tion. She kept tugging at Betsy's arm and shouting, "Ah, signorina! *La regina!*" But there were ominous lines of soldiers and armed police guarding the square.

A few days later, when the sun was shining again, they went to Chioggia. By special request Betsy wore the red jacket. Chioggia, which guarded the entrance to Venice, had been a most important place in the great days of the past, Marco said. Now it was a fishing town, remarkable only for its picturesqueness.

Betsy and Marco took a walk and admired the forests

of rigging. They took pictures, surrounded all the time by an interested, amused, sympathetic, and chattering audience of children.

"Like in Sonneberg," Betsy said. Marco was always ready to listen to her tales of Germany.

They ate dinner in a little café with a view of the sea. Their friends the children stood outside in the twilight and Marco and Betsy tossed them sweets. They were handsome little ragamuffins. All Italians were handsome, Betsy thought, glancing at Marco.

They were happy all day, but on the boat ride home they grew quiet. Up in the stern men were singing strange, fantastic songs. They kept passing quiet groups of fishermen, and by and by the full moon came out.

"My second moon in Venice!" Betsy said.

"Oh, Betta!" Marco answered. "Aren't you going to change your mind? How can I bear it after you go?"

"And how can I bear to go?" thought Betsy, but she didn't say it. She only pressed back tears and shook her head.

It was almost time to leave Venice now. Marco helped her buy her presents—mosaics, laces, leatherwork, beads of Venetian glass. They bought a special print of St. Mark's Square for Betsy.

They went to Thomas Cook's and planned her trip. She was joining the Wilsons in Lucerne. They cashed her father's travel check and shipped her trunk to London. Betsy wondered how she had ever managed to leave Munich without Marco.

He went with her while she said good-bye to Venice. Venezia! She would always remember the varying colors of the sky and water; the time-worn marble palaces with their barred windows and their wave-washed steps and the colored hitching posts in front for gondolas; the little courts and alleys with the swarms of gesticulating people; sunsets in the Giudecca; the Lido with its golden beach and turquoise sea. But, above all, the Square: St. Mark's and the Doge's Palace, the bric-a-brac shops under the colonnades, the streams of people, the little outdoor tables, and the fat glossy pigeons circling down.

On her last afternoon, Betsy got into her kimono, wadded up her hair, and approached her packing. Every other moment Marco knocked and offered to help, but he was refused. He asked her to open the door a crack and handed in some cherries. He threw flowers through the window.

About six o'clock she freshened up and slipped into the white and green dress for dinner. Afterward she took the red blazer and she and Marco went down to the Giudecca.

They had planned to go to the Square again, but somehow they didn't want to. They watched a last sunset over the crazy quilt of water craft, and then he got a gondola. In the darkness on the Grand Canal, people were singing as before, everything from *Il Trovatore* to "Funiculi Funicula." But tonight Marco and Betsy didn't sing. They floated silently, sadly, her hand in his.

In the morning Betsy got up early and finished packing. Then she walked toward Marco's room to meet him. It was misty. The canals were pale, but no paler than Marco, although he smiled his eager, vivid smile when he saw her.

The little aunts gave Betsy a lunch. (They had printed—or Marco had—*Arrivederci* on the eggs.) After breakfast, which neither Marco nor Betsy ate, she said good-bye to the little aunts and a gondola carried them heartlessly through the mist to the station.

Marco helped her buy her ticket. He took her to her compartment. He was behaving cheerfully, but his eyes, Betsy thought, were liked burned holes in a blanket. Yet she didn't think he felt any worse than she did. How could she bear to go out into the world and leave this love, this thoughtfulness, this protection? Loneliness flooded over her and she began to cry.

"Maybe I do love you," she said.

"Don't say it unless you do. I couldn't bear it if you changed your mind."

"Then I won't say it," she answered. "But oh, Marco! I'll never forget you!"

He kissed her, and she clung to him, while whistles blew and bells rang. The train was moving when he jumped off.

It crossed the bridge and reached the mainland. It ran through meadows full of poppies like the ones at Fusina. It ran past white plastered houses with flapping wash-lines, olive orchards, vineyards. Betsy was still crying.

The bad thing about traveling, she thought, was leaving people you got to like—or love. Maida, Mr. O'Farrell, Tilda, Helena—now Marco.

She certainly loved Marco, but not—she still believed, in spite of her tears—the way she ought to love him if she were going to marry him.

Maybe she would have if it weren't for Joe. She didn't know.

19
BETSY WRITES A LETTER

"Onze Rue Scribe," said Betsy, smiling up at the little old driver who was perched jauntily on the seat of his horse-drawn hack. She was standing in front of the Grand Hotel Pension in the Latin Quarter, where she and the Wilsons had lived for the past two weeks, and the address she now gave in her best French was that of the American Express Company office.

"Pardon, mademoiselle, je ne comprends pas," the driver answered politely.

Oh, no, not again! Her next-to-last day in Paris, and she still couldn't make herself understood!

"Onze Rue Scribe," Betsy repeated in a loud voice.

"Mademoiselle?" He threw out his hands in apologetic bewilderment.

Betsy drew a deep breath.

"Onze Rue . . ." But she knew from experience that this could go on for hours. She'd better give up. Pulling from her purse the little notebook she always carried to jot down a bit of description or an idea for a story, she printed the address in large letters and handed it up.

"Ah!" Relief flooded the driver's face. In a torrent of words he begged the mademoiselle's pardon a thousand times for having misunderstood. If she would do him the honor of entering his humble conveyance, they would set forth immediately for *Onze Rue Scribe,* the home of the so-distinguished American Express Company—unless perhaps the mademoiselle would first like a little drive about Paris?

Betsy climbed to the back seat of the hack and vigorously nodded her assent. Patient Miss Wilson wouldn't mind waiting a little longer, and Betsy had wanted to drive through the city and take what might be her last look at it—alone.

But as the sturdy old horse began to move at a gentle clip-clop through the twisted streets of the left bank, she sank into a brown study. The last month had been a disappointment. Ready to leave for London, which would be practically home, she knew she couldn't count Paris as one of the places she had lived in, or Switzerland either.

Of course, in Switzerland she had been bitterly unhappy. The nagging homesickness had returned, mixed with loneliness for Marco. There had been letters and telegrams from him at every stopping place. Sometimes, falling asleep in strange hotels, she had thought again that she was mistaken, that she did love him after all. There was every reason in the world why she should, and it would be so easy to write and tell him so! She had imagined his overflowing happiness on receiving her letter. He would probably join her, she had thought; they would see Paris together, she would give up London and they would go home to be married. But there, somehow, her imagination had always rebelled. Something inside you told you when you didn't love a person, just as . . . something . . . told you when you did, even though he was thousands of miles away and you could hardly bear to think about him because you'd probably lost him.

Betsy and the Wilsons had left Switzerland behind on the twenty-eighth of June. She remembered how, reading in a newspaper about the murder of an Austrian archduke in the Balkan town of Sarajevo, she had amused herself as the train sped through the night by plotting a romantic novel full of titled corpses, spies, and intrigue.

Then, as she tried to sleep in a jiggling upper berth, she had thought about Marco and Joe—or rather, she had suddenly ceased to think about Marco and had begun to think about Joe, with persistent, painful intensity. Venice was fading away—home was coming closer—and how she wished that Joe were waiting for her there!

But it was over a year since she and Joe had written to each other. Betsy wished that night that she had written him about Julia's wedding; she wished that she had written him about her trip to Europe, or from the *Columbic* to explain not having seen him in Boston. Now she had no excuse at all for writing, and she couldn't write without one. She was too proud for that.

The next day, her first in Paris, she had slipped out of the drab little Grand Hotel Pension and had walked out in a soft gray morning to the Pont Neuf, one of the bridges spanning the Seine. She wanted to do something the Wilsons certainly would not understand. Neither of them had read *The Beloved Vagabond* and knew how Paragot, with his world crashing around him, had gone to ask advice of the statue of Henri Quatre on the Pont Neuf . . . or how the king had nodded and pointed to the Gare de Lyon.

Betsy didn't expect Henri Quatre to do the same for her, but she wanted to take a snapshot of him to send to Tacy. And she thought he might, he just might, give her a little hint about how to get in touch with Joe again. He sat on horseback looking out over the Seine, and didn't even seem to know she was there. But just the same she'd been glad she'd gone. And from that day to this, the sixteenth of July, she'd put the problem stubbornly out of her mind and tried to enjoy Paris.

Her hack was approaching the Pont Neuf now, jolting along the cobbled streets, lined with open-air bookstalls presided over by old ladies who sat knitting as implacably as Madame Defarge, or by old men as yellow as their oldest manuscripts. As she crossed over the bridge, she leaned out of the hack impulsively and waved to Henri Quatre. Her only Parisian friend! she thought. No, not quite; she had made others, and equally notable ones.

One was in the Louvre, which they were passing now; her cabby turned to indicate it with a wave of his whip. She would never forget the moment when, down a long avenue of statues, she had glimpsed against a dark velvet background the white gleam of the Venus de Milo.

"I never dreamed she would be so beautiful," she had said to Miss Wilson. "I never expect to like famous things! But I guess they're famous because they give everybody this wonderful feeling."

Victor Hugo was another friend. He had been with her on her first visit to Notre Dame. Gazing up at the great church, she had imagined his little dancing girl among the bells; and inside she had seen the Hunchback lurking in the shadows.

It had been fitting afterward to go to Hugo's tomb in

the domed Pantheon. It was down in a dark, gloomy vault, in a small stone cell behind a grating. She had wished that she had brought him some flowers; it seemed sad for such a lover of life to be shut up in musty obscurity.

Napoleon wasn't a friend, exactly; Betsy had never been an admirer of his. But she had been unexpectedly stirred by the sight of his last resting place. In the silence of the room, awed crowds looked down at the sarcophagus which held the small body of the man who had made all Europe tremble . . . returned from exile as he had wished to be, and buried among the French people.

Fully half the onlookers were Americans, but Betsy had wondered if Germans ever came, particularly when she read the inscription on the fresh wreath prominently displayed: "Let no French soldier rest, while there is a German in Alsace."

The French and Germans really hated each other, Betsy thought, as the hack bounced on past the Tuileries Gardens. Marie Antoinette was there; another friend. And also the Empress Eugenie, who Betsy's grandmother had once seen with her own eyes, sitting on one of these benches.

The hack passed through the Place de la Concorde, spacious and brilliant, with the Obelisk in the center surrounded by fountains, and the eight colossal statues symbolizing the queen cities of France. It swung down the broad, tree-lined Champs Elysées; and the Arc de

Triomphe, the Eiffel Tower, came into full view. The tea gardens and Punch and Judy shows were crowded; the nursemaids and charming French children were out in full force among the strolling crowds.

Betsy felt a lump in her throat. "Paris is so beautiful! A little of it ought to belong to me by now, and it doesn't, any more than it did when I read the *Stoddard Lectures* at home!" She needed someone to share it with, someone who would love the same odd, romantic things that she loved.

Tilda would have understood about Henri Quatre and Victor Hugo. Tib would have wanted to go to the smart restaurants, and shop at Paquin's or Worth's, and see the models parade at Longchamps. Tacy would have liked to picnic in the Bois de Boulogne, and Marco would have appreciated the sidewalk cafés.

She and the Wilsons had never once eaten in a sidewalk café! Dr. Wilson felt sure that none of them would supply his carrots and whole-grain bread, and while Miss Wilson would really have enjoyed going, Betsy felt sure, she had noted Baedeker's warning that unattended ladies didn't eat in such spots.

"French women must think it's all right," Betsy had thought, noticing many of them alone or in twos and threes at the gay little outdoor tables.

It wasn't that she didn't like the Wilsons; on the contrary, she had grown fonder of them every day. The erect little professor with the pointed beard was amusing and often stimulating, and Miss Wilson was wistfully lovable.

Miss Wilson would have liked to have some fun in Paris, Betsy thought now. It was just that she had been brought up so strictly that she didn't know how. Betsy had wished time and again during the past two weeks that she could find a way to give Miss Wilson one good bat. But she had never felt that she should take the initiative in making plans, or urge her chaperones to do anything they hadn't done before.

So she had dutifully gone sightseeing. And she had gone with Miss Wilson to sensible, medium-priced stores like the Bon Marche to buy perfumes and gloves for gifts and to spend her birthday money on a dark blue suit with a soft, wide belt of crimson satin. With a black hat and a crimson veil, it made a stunning outfit.

She was wearing it now, as the hack pulled up in front of the American Express office. She tipped the driver generously, and watched him clip-clop off down the crowded, busy street.

Stopping at a sidewalk kiosk to buy the Paris edition of the *Herald*, Betsy entered the office.

As she saw Miss Wilson standing at the cashier's window, she felt a sudden wave of affection for the kind, reserved little spinster.

"Oh, I wish I could do something nice for her!" she thought again.

Miss Wilson waved. "Here you are, my dear! My, it took you a long time to finish that letter!"

Betsy felt guilty, and she hugged her companion's arm. "I finished the letter half an hour ago, Miss Wilson . . . I let the driver take the long way around. I sort of wanted a last look at the Champs Elysées."

"Of course you did! You have so much imagination, Betsy; you really know how to enjoy things. Let's you and I do something pleasant this afternoon. It's our last. You'll soon be at Mrs. Heaton's boarding house in London, and we'll be off to the Lake Country."

Betsy agreed warmly. They had both exchanged some travelers' checks for shillings and pounds, and were turning away, when Betsy suddenly caught sight of a moving flower garden—purple, yellow, blue, and pink—atop the head of a short, stout woman in a yellow silk suit. She heard a familiar voice raised in animated argument with an American Express attendant.

"Mrs. Main-Whittaker!" Betsy cried, as happy as though she had found a friend from home.

To her astonishment, Mrs. Main-Whittaker not only turned, but bounced over and embraced her. Betsy almost choked on a deep wave of perfume.

"Why, it's little Miss . . . Miss . . . Ray, from the *Columbic*! The one who plans to be a writer!"

"How did you know?" Betsy asked in delight.

"That nice Mr. O'Farrell told me. Well! I suppose you've been to the Ritz? To the Comédie Française? Out to Montmartre where our Bohemian friends are gathering these days? All excellent background for modern fiction."

"I've been concentrating more on background for historical novels," said Betsy, smiling at Miss Wilson.

A flash of understanding crossed Mrs. Main-Whittaker's face. "Well, what are you doing today?"

"We really hadn't made up our minds."

The author chuckled. "You come with me, and we'll do the town together. But first, have you had lunch? How about a sidewalk café?"

In the dazzled silence that followed, Betsy almost prayed that Miss Wilson would say yes.

"Do come!" Mrs. Main-Whittaker urged Miss Wilson. "I've just been wishing I had some good company. And Miss Ray and I can talk shop." She almost seemed lonesome, canary-colored suit, perfumed sophistication, and all.

Miss Wilson's smooth cheeks flushed. "Why, certainly! Betsy and I have never eaten in a sidewalk café."

"I suppose," said Mrs. Main-Whittaker, "you're afraid of the wolves in sheep's clothing. I'd say there were more sheep in wolves' clothing around, at least for an old lady like me!" She laughed exuberantly, and with Betsy on one arm and Miss Wilson on the other, sailed out into the sunny Paris afternoon.

The sidewalk luncheon was the beginning of a perfect day. Mrs. Main-Whittaker, who delighted in spending her money as much as she delighted in talking, ordered the meal, which began with shrimp and ended with *baba-au-rhum*, while Betsy and Miss Wilson beamed at each other and at the occupants of the other tables under the bright awnings.

"Now," said Mrs. Main-Whittaker, after their waiter had bowed to the sidewalk over her tip, "we have just time for two sights no novice writer should miss. We'll go to Longchamps for a look at the models. Then how about dinner at the Ritz?"

Miss Wilson, who had half risen, sat down as though she were suddenly faint. Betsy looked away, and wondered how she could bear it if they didn't go. Miss Wilson adjusted her spectacles and managed a faint whisper.

"Is Longchamps very far away?"

"We won't be walking," Mrs. Main-Whittaker chuckled. "But . . . pardon me for saying so . . . and believe me, I do say so only because I've just had a check for royalties big enough to float a bond issue . . . this is all going to be my treat. Please don't say no."

Miss Wilson, with a common sense and dignity that made Betsy want to hug her, gave a chuckle not unlike Mrs. Main-Whittaker's.

"A teacher's salary," she said, "is definitely no royalty check. But at least I'll pay for the cab."

And the next thing Betsy knew, they were racing through the crowds of fashionable carriages and enormous black automobiles, some of which bore crests, toward the Longchamps promenade in the Bois de Boulogne. There Miss Wilson paid the charge and gave a tip big enough to bring the driver's head down to his very feet.

They made their way down to the benches where spectators were settling themselves for the fashion show, and found front-row seats, Betsy drinking up the sights and sounds of the crowd for repeating to Tacy, Tib, and the family.

Beautiful models began to saunter past with the fashionable limp look.

"And I thought *I* had a debutante slouch!" Betsy whispered to Miss Wilson, whose face was alight. This really was the bat she had wished they could have together, Betsy thought joyfully. Miss Wilson didn't even look shocked, although as the parade progressed the skirts, slit to the knee, revealed long lengths of lavender, yellow, green, and even pink stockings.

"And what heels!" Betsy gasped. They were inches and inches high.

The make-up astonished her, too. She had never seen such make-up, even on the chorus girls of the musical shows that came to Minneapolis. Lips were crimson; eyes were painted with thickly drawn shadows. Hair-dos leaped straight up or spread straight out, and hair was every color of the rainbow.

Capes seemed to be coming in, Betsy noted . . . if you could judge by these fantastic styles. Hats were smaller and the suits had vests and pleated, knee-length overskirts. Looking at one, Betsy heard Miss Wilson gasp, and she could have gasped herself. Beneath the overskirt were trousers! Trousers! On a woman in broad daylight in a public place!

The sun was setting behind the tall trees of the Bois de Boulogne when the parade ended.

"The fashions are really exciting this year, don't you think?" Mrs. Main-Whittaker remarked as she led her charges through the animated, well-dressed crowds. "You'd look stunning in one of those suits, my dear," she added to Betsy.

"With trousers, I suppose!" Betsy thought. She was feeling lightheaded. The ride to the Ritz went like a ride on a roller coaster.

And the dinner opened new vistas of luxury. The attentive waiters she remembered from the *Columbic* were quite outdone by the waiters here who leaped to obey Mrs. Main-Whittaker's waving, sparkling hand. For the party of three there were two waiters, and behind these a captain of waiters hovered, and behind the captain, a maître d'hôtel. He was most attentive of all.

Mrs. Main-Whittaker seemed to know everybody. She waved and called greetings in every direction.

"Cornelia, my dear!" "May, how nice!" "Adele, where have you been?"

Vastly important as she seemed to be, Mrs. Main-Whittaker was really interested in Miss Wilson and Betsy, and in their plans. Over the onion soup, thick with bread and grated cheese, the frogs' legs, the salad which a waiter mixed at their table, they discussed England.

"You must be sure," the author said to Betsy, "not to miss the Agony Column!"

"The Agony Column?" asked Betsy eagerly.

"It's on the front page of the London *Times*. So astonishing that such a paper would give its front page to personals! John asking Mary to write him, Mary warning Eloise to leave John alone, the gentleman who noticed a lady in the bus asking her to let him see her again. There's a plot in every item."

Betsy was enormously flattered that Mrs. Main-Whittaker should talk shop with her!

When they had finished their crêpes suzettes and were lingering over their coffee, Mrs. Main-Whittaker opened a jeweled cigarette case. She extracted a cigarette, beckoned to a hovering waiter to light it for her, and was about to put the case away. But perhaps she noticed that Miss Wilson's gaze had a peculiar intensity.

"Will you join me?" she asked, and passed the case.

Betsy's pride in Miss Wilson's new aplomb soared to the heights.

"No, thank you. I . . . I . . . I was just admiring your cigarette case."

Mrs. Main-Whittaker puffed luxuriously. "It is nice, isn't it?" she said. "But smoking is a terrible habit. Do try not to take it up, my dear," she added to Betsy.

A few minutes later Betsy found courage to open a topic that had been on her mind all day. She mentioned her first sight of Mrs. Main-Whittaker surrounded by reporters on the *Columbic*.

"One of those reporters was an old friend of mine,

Joe Willard. He was covering the story for the *Boston Transcript* . . ."

"Oh-h-h-h!" Mrs. Main-Whittaker interrupted, almost cooing. "The *Transcript* young man! I remember him very well. Extremely handsome!"

"Yes, he is," said Betsy softly.

"And he wrote an excellent story. I received it in my clippings. I subscribe to a clipping bureau. You must do it, too, when you're established, my dear. His story was entertaining, and he got the facts right . . . all my plans and ideas. It was the best story of the lot."

Henri Quatre had helped her at last! Betsy thought, back in her room at the Grand Hotel Pension. She climbed into bed, but she couldn't sleep. She was too full of the promenading models and the bowing waiters and especially of what Mrs. Main-Whittaker had said about Joe.

Here was her chance! It was now or never, if she was going to write to Joe.

Lying there in the darkened room, she thought about Joe, as she hadn't thought about him for months. She thought about the first time she had seen him, a cocky blond boy of fourteen, eating an apple and reading *The Three Musketeers* in Willard's Emporium, in Butternut Center, Minnesota. She remembered him running up and down the sidelines at the high school football games he'd covered so well for the Deep Valley *Sun,* and the evenings they had sat side by side in the library studying for the essay contests.

She remembered the first letter he'd written her, the summer after junior year, and how she had slaved over her replies, copying them onto scented green note paper. She remembered the first time he'd come to see her, in the fall of their senior year, and all the times after that, when they'd made fudge in the kitchen and talked in front of the dining-room fire.

They had had a quarrel in their senior year, but she remembered the beautiful spring when they made up. She remembered when he had first kissed her up on the Big Hill. She remembered the few months they'd had together at the University, and how proud she had been when he went away to Harvard.

She thought about him in quiet adoration. She loved him. She'd loved him for years. He was the finest person she'd ever known—he was bound up with almost her whole past life, and she didn't want to live the rest of her life without him.

Of course that was why she hadn't loved Marco! Deep inside herself, she must have known. She should have drawn the truth out sooner. But at least now she knew what she had to do.

Betsy got up, turned on the light, put on her pink kimono, and got out her fountain pen. But the only letter she wrote that night went to Marco. It told him gently that they must stop corresponding with each other.

Next morning after crescent rolls and *café au lait*, she dressed and went out of doors, taking her fountain pen and box of scented green stationery. She went out to a little square and found a bench, and there at last she wrote to Joe!

It was a carefully casual letter.

"If he's already married to his roommate's sister, he can show it to her without a blush," Betsy thought grimly.

It didn't offer any apologies or excuses, or any explanation other than the desire to tell him about Mrs. Main-Whittaker's compliment.

"I have a t.l. for you, Joe. That charming Mrs. Main-Whittaker from the *Columbic* (I met her in the American Express office today) said that your story was the best one to come out of that interview."

Betsy described her day with the author in sprightly style—the sidewalk café, Longchamps, dinner at the Ritz.

"She really takes an interest in young writers. She gave me all kinds of advice. I'm going to be sure to take a look at the Agony Column in the London *Times* . . . she says it's full of story material."

The letter went on to sketch her trip in three or four well-chosen lines.

"And a story I wrote last summer sold to *Ainslee's* while I was over here. That was how I financed the trip to Sonneberg and Oberammergau."

Betsy wasn't sure whether it was a good letter or not. Maybe it sounded too self-centered, but she didn't want to seem to be prying or hinting for an answer if she asked Joe too much about himself.

She didn't read it over for fear she wouldn't mail it. She put it into an envelope and sealed and stamped and addressed it and found a letter box.

She held the letter between her hands a moment, and prayed . . . then quickly let it go.

That afternoon, rolling toward the English Channel, Betsy remembered that she had not included the address of her London boarding house. Joe could not answer even if he wanted to. It was too bad! But on the other hand, he would know that she wanted to make up. He could write to her in Minneapolis . . . and somehow, she believed that he would.

20
THE ROLL OF DRUMS

*There's a barrel-organ caroling across a golden
        street*
In the City as the sun sinks low;
*And the music's not immortal; but the world has
        made it sweet . . .*
Kneeling beside the window of a small white room in

which her trunk, steamer rug, flag, books, photographs, Goethe's cup, Tacy's doll, and a print of St. Mark's Square were tastefully arranged, Betsy looked down four stories into Taviton Street where a barrel organ was caroling indeed.

She continued saying the Noyes poem to herself after she had thrown some pennies and the Italian had bowed over a velvet cap and trundled his organ away from Mrs. Heaton's boarding house. This overlooked a green square. It was one of a row of attached houses, all tall and thin with neat door plates, bells, and knockers.

> *Come down to Kew in lilac-time,*
> *in lilac-time, in lilac-time;*
> *Come down to Kew in lilac-time*
> *(it isn't far from London)* . . .

This wasn't lilac-time. It was July, 1914. But it was London, and Betsy loved it.

She hadn't expected to love it so much. She had known it would be pleasant to hear English spoken again, and moving to be in the land from which her own country had sprung, a land peopled for her by long-familiar figures of history and fiction. But she hadn't known it would be so . . . heart-warming. The Wilsons had gone on, and although Betsy had been sorry to part from them, she didn't feel lonely. In this vast, ancient city she felt completely at home.

She was happy because she was getting nearer her family. She was happy because she had written to Joe.

She drew satisfaction, too, from the thought that she was *living* in London, not just sightseeing, as in Switzerland and Paris.

She was writing again; she had already finished "The Episodes of Epsie." Search for a shop where she might get it typed had taken her on a legitimate errand to Fleet Street, for generations the stamping ground of publishers and booksellers and anxious young authors like herself.

Of course, while there, she had peeked into old St. Paul's which dominated the region from its little hill. She had browsed down bookish Paternoster Row to Amen Corner and hunted up the Inn of the Cheshire Cheese where Dr. Johnson used to dine while Boswell took worshipful notes. She had only walked up and down in front of that and gazed, for ladies didn't eat there alone.

She attended church every Sunday at Westminster Abbey. "Why not?" she defended herself at the storied portal. "That's what it's meant for." You soaked in more of the dear gray old place, kneeling in the candlelight, than you did walking around with a guidebook.

She did that too, of course. Dick Reed, a law student who lived at Mrs. Heaton's, came along sometimes. He wasn't another Marco, but he was very nice. They wandered about the Poets' Corner, reading inscriptions to Goldsmith, Gray, Shakespeare, Dickens . . .

Afterward they often prowled around the Parliament buildings. Betsy loved the great song of Big Ben because it reminded her of the chime clock at home. And they always walked to Number Ten Downing Street where the Prime Minister lived. Mr. Dick, as the other boarders called him, because his older brother Leonard also lived at Mrs. Heaton's, wanted to be Prime Minister some day.

Number Ten was very dingy. "But it will be fun living there anyway," Betsy consoled him.

When not accompanied by Mr. Dick or her other new friends, Betsy was guided by bobbies. She adored these obliging London policemen. Directing traffic, they would stand as cool as cucumbers, gloved hand in air, to listen to your problems, and advise.

"Take bus Aighty-Aight, Miss."

Betsy consulted them mostly about buses. A top front seat on a bus was a grandstand seat for London.

Of course, you had to scramble down, now and then, to view Hyde Park or Trafalgar Square, or perhaps to watch a sidewalk artist. These amazing people made their living by drawing pictures in colored chalk on the sidewalk and passers-by stopped and dropped tuppence. Naturally you came down from any bus at teatime.

The English were even more devoted to their tea than Germans to their coffee. Tea was served at His Majesty's Theatre where Betsy saw Mrs. Patrick Campbell in *Pygmalion* and became a Shaw devotee. A tray was brought right to her seat for sixpence. It was the same at the movies, or "the pictures" as her friends from Mrs. Heaton's called them. Yesterday, seeing Mary Pickford, they had all had trays of tea.

It was amusing, Betsy thought now, how well you knew when four-thirty came. She glanced at her watch, and simultaneously heard a call.

"Hello up there! Yankee Doodle!"

"Hello!" Betsy ran to the door.

"Tea in the garden!" called Mr. Dick.

"Right-o," answered Betsy, very British. Giving a pat to her hair and brushing a chamois skin over her nose, she skimmed down past the second-floor drawing room to the first-floor dining room and back to the garden.

This was a bit sooty . . . no white, rose-draped walls as in Venice. But there were vines and a snowy tea table, and behind the pot Mrs. Heaton's sweet care-worn face. She mothered everybody, and most of her boarders could use mothering. They were almost all young.

Jean Carver was an actress. When Betsy first arrived Jean had been out of work and her eyes were often red. But now she was engaged for the chorus of *The Arcadians,* and busy with rehearsals.

"Glad to see you home," said Betsy. "Dolly needs your legs!"

Little Dolly Cohen was an artist. Her room was just below Betsy's, wildly untidy, with drawings scattered everywhere, and tubes of paint and brushes about, and an easel in front of her window. She was illustrating a new edition of *Helen's Babies* and everyone in the house had posed for her. Betsy was modeling the lady who listened to Toddy's recitation. Mr. Leonard had posed as Toddy spilling soup. This showed how much everyone liked Dolly, for Mr. Leonard, who was studying to be a doctor, was a most dignified young man, slenderly erect, with eyeglasses. He never went out without a cane.

Mr. Dick was larger and more casual.

"Here's your Agony Column," he said as Betsy dropped down beside him. He clipped it for her every day. It was even better than Mrs. Main-Whittaker had promised. Consuming their tea, Betsy and Mr. Dick read with interest that if I.J. would come home all would be forgotten. Now and then they read an item aloud to the crowd.

This group was really a Crowd, such as Betsy had hoped to start in Munich. Only they called themselves The Crew. And one member was missing today. Claude Heaton, a broker's clerk, was off with his regiment. The Territorial Troops (something like the National Guard at home, Betsy understood) had a period of training over the August Bank Holiday which was impending.

Most of the boarders, like Betsy, were new to London, and The Crew had made a number of expeditions, chaperoned by Miss Dodge, a merry elderly spinster. They had gone to Windsor Castle, but only into the gardens. The palace was closed to the public because of the militant suffragettes who were now starting fires, throwing bombs, and slashing pictures. The suffragettes had closed many places Betsy wished to see.

"Them wild ladies!" a bobby had mourned, turning

her away from the National Gallery. But Betsy was in sympathy with their cause.

And the out-of-door places weren't closed. The Crew had gone to Hampstead Heath; to Stoke Poges, where they saw the country churchyard of Gray's "Elegy"; to Epping Forest. (That had gone into "The Episodes of Epsie.") And they had gone boating on the Thames which was crowded companionably with rowboats, houseboats, punts, canoes. Tied up beneath an overhanging tree, they had eaten apple patties with tea made over an alcohol lamp.

At tea in the garden now, Jean said, "Where are we going to go on Bank Holiday?" And Betsy cried, "Oh, let's go up the Thames again!"

"We could take a boat from Richmond," Mr. Leonard volunteered, "to Kingston-on-Thames."

"I'll provide more apple patties," Mrs. Heaton offered. "I only wish Claude could be with you."

"What is a Bank Holiday anyway?" Betsy asked.

"It's a holiday when the banks close," Mr. Leonard explained. "We have four a year. And one is the first Monday in August."

"Then it's almost here. Today is the twenty-ninth."

"And not a very good day," said Mr. Heaton unexpectedly. He had just come in with a newspaper under his arm. His appearance, like the remark, was unexpected for he worked in the city and seldom came home for tea. He was a large man, fiercely mustachioed but as gentle as a lamb.

"Austria-Hungary," he went on, "has just declared war on Serbia."

"Why? What for?" asked Betsy.

"Oh, it's on account of the murder of that Austrian Archduke last month," said Mr. Dick, helping himself to marmalade. "They'll probably settle things before any shooting starts."

"And it looks as though Germany is going to declare war on Russia," continued Mr. Heaton.

"But why Russia?" Now Betsy was really confused.

"Russia is pledged to help Serbia and Germany is tied up with Austria. France could be drawn in, too. She and Russia are allies."

This was too complicated to follow. And the news was so disquieting that talk of the boating trip died down. But it sprang up again at dinner.

Dinner at Heatons' charmed Betsy. There was a butler (as fascinating as Mrs. Sims' and Mrs. Cheney's ladies' maids). And Mr. Heaton carved with dignity. There were always two kinds of meat and two kinds of dessert.

"Will you have hot or cold, Miss Ray? Hot? A slice off the joint?"

"Miss Cohen, would you prefer cold shape or cherry tart?" Cold shape was gelatin.

English food, Betsy thought, sounded better than it tasted. (The meat pies of which she had read such mouth-watering descriptions in Dickens were cold and clammy.)

But dinner at Mrs. Heaton's was very nice anyway, and it was such fun afterward up in the drawing room. (Betsy rolled that word over her tongue.) They often had music, for Claude had a fine bass voice. Since he wasn't here, they talked about the river trip, making enthusiastic plans.

This holiday expedition was never mentioned again.

The next afternoon Mr. Leonard had no classes, and he and Betsy made a planned visit to the Tower. Within these gloomy walls they were carried from modern perils back to old ones. Betsy could almost hear the ghostly voices of the murdered princeling sons of Edward IV. Mr. Leonard stared at the ax which had struck off Raleigh's head.

"My word!" he said, adjusting his eyeglasses as though they had been a monocle, "Extraordinary!"

"My word!" he said again, over tea and cherry cake, "think of Mary, Queen of Scots, and Anne Boleyn! Their heads chopped off just like snick!" He adjusted his glasses again to frown at Betsy's soft white neck. She closed her hands protectingly about it.

"It couldn't happen today," she said. "I guess the world is really getting better."

"Let's hope it is better enough to keep out of real war."

"Why, of course it is! A war in these civilized days is absolutely unthinkable."

But when they got out into the streets they saw the

big news posters crying out that armies all over Europe were mobilizing. And London was suddenly full of soldiers. Dinner that night was quiet, for it looked pretty certain that the Territorials would not go back to their shops and factories, their offices and universities, when the training period was over. The table missed Claude's deep voice.

"My brother is a Territorial, too," said Dolly.

The newspapers next day, and the next, said that a state of war existed between Germany and Russia. Americans were rushing off the continent like leaves before a storm. They were pouring into London by the thousands, telling of the cold war purpose in Berlin and the fever of excitement in Paris. Crowds there were singing and marching in the streets.

"Oh, I'm lucky to be here!" Betsy cried as each new edition brought more tales. Americans were traveling day and night to get to England. They weren't allowed to leave the railroad stations, even to eat. They were locked into the cars. They couldn't get money. Many who arrived in London had left all their luggage behind and had only the clothes on their backs.

On the eve of the Bank Holiday German troops goosestepped over the French border. The barrel organs began to play the "Marseillaise," but what stunned Mrs. Heaton's even more was Germany's ultimatum to little Belgium demanding permission to send her armed forces unopposed across the Belgian border.

"Why, that's outrageous!" Dolly cried. "Belgium has a guarantee of perpetual neutrality."

"And England has guaranteed the sanctity of Belgium."

"We're as good as in," Mr. Leonard said, but Mrs. Heaton put in briskly, "We may be in, but we'll be out in a jiff. The fighting will be over in a month or so at most."

Everyone looked anxious.

"I'll sign up," said Mr. Dick. "But you ought to finish at medical school, Len."

Mr. Leonard looked thoughtful.

"I don't believe *The Arcadians* will ever open," said Jean.

"I wish I knew what this would do to my brother," Dolly said.

"And your book!" It seemed unlikely that a new edition of *Helen's Babies* would be wanted now.

Betsy, Jean, and Mr. Dick went to vesper services in Westminster Abbey. When they returned, the streets seemed to hold twice as many sailors and soldiers as before. An artillery regiment, complete with cannons, shouted boisterous jokes. A company of Territorials marched by singing.

They were very young and slim, with fresh pink cheeks. The German soldiers had been so big and capable! The memory made Betsy apprehensive, and newsboys were shouting that the last train, the last boat, had come from the continent.

"Perhaps, Betsy," Mrs. Heaton said at tea—it was high tea on Sunday night—"perhaps you ought to be thinking about getting home. Your parents must be worried."

Betsy was sure they were and she was sorry. But she didn't really want to go home. It was partly that she had come to love these people and didn't want to go back to comfort while they were in peril. But it was also because of the great events that seemed to be impending. As a writer, she hated to miss them.

No one at Heaton's slept much that night, and in the morning everyone was down to breakfast early. This was Bank Holiday. Could it really be that they had planned to spend it boating on the Thames?

The crowds on the streets were restless instead of merry. All holiday excursions had been canceled to provide trains for troops. And Germany made her formal declaration of war against France.

Betsy's thoughts went back to the line cut into Napoleon's tomb. It would have to be recarved.

"Let no French soldier rest while there is a German in *France*."

"I can't take it in," Jean stammered. "Thousands of men marching off to be slaughtered. Ruin, terror, misery, sweeping us all. Why?"

No one knew. But Betsy kept remembering the marching soldiers she had seen everywhere in Germany and all the talk of war.

She thought of Tilda. What would this do to her career? She thought of Helena and Hanni. Each loved a soldier who would now be going to war. And how could she ever get Hanni over to the United States?

She thought of Marco. Italy had declared her neutrality, but Italians by the thousands were enlisting in France. Marco might do that.

Down at Buckingham Palace, Mr. Heaton reported, a huge crowd was gathering, singing and cheering. Now and then King George and Queen Mary came out on the balcony.

"Why do the people go to the Palace?" Betsy asked.

"They want to let the King know they're behind him," Mr. Heaton said.

"We talk, eat, drink, and sleep war," Betsy wrote home. It was strange. Belgium had been hardly more to her than a spot on the map, and now she was shaken with pity, excitement, and pride in the human race by the little country's answer to big Germany. The forts at their border were to be defended—to the last man.

On the morning of August fourth the conviction that war would be declared before nightfall was as strong around Mrs. Heaton's breakfast table as it was in the *Times*.

It was strong even in the Agony Column. A penitent Nan begged her Jack—fifth advertisement down—"if you love me, don't enlist until we make up."

In the middle of breakfast Betsy received a cable from home.

"Are you all right? Best return at once. Worried. Love. Dad."

Tears rushed into her eyes. She knew how anxious they must be. She still didn't want to go home, but she knew she would have to if England really did get in.

Shortly it became clear that England would get in. Six German columns crossed the Belgian frontier. The Belgians were waiting for them at the Meuse.

"Good little Belgium!" Mr. Leonard cried.

The Crew went out to roam the streets with the rest of London. Soldiers were everywhere—alone, with sweethearts, with wives hanging to their arms, carrying their children. Some of the boyish Territorials were walking with red-eyed girls. Others went alone, cockily or forlornly.

In front of the German Embassy a long line of people—many tearful—waited for passports. "Some of them have lived here a long time. They've just neglected getting naturalization papers, and now they must go back to fight us," Mr. Dick said.

Peddlers were hawking flags. The sidewalk artists were drawing battleships and the royal family.

By teatime Great Britain had delivered her ultimatum to Germany, and midnight was fixed as the time limit for Germany's answer.

At the Houses of Parliament, crowds cheered as the members came out. At Buckingham Palace was such a throng as Betsy had never seen or imagined.

"I'm so glad I'm with you," Betsy told The Crew. She

was very fond of them, and proud, too, because they made her seem a part of this great spontaneous demonstration.

Dinnertime came and went. The Crew didn't wish to go home without seeing the King and Queen. Both had been coming out frequently, everyone said, but now only Princess Mary appeared briefly, taking snapshots.

"She has her hair up!" Jean cried. "It's the first time."

The young, slim, handsome Prince of Wales, wearing a silk hat, crossed the courtyard to cheers and applause. He disappeared inside.

"But he wiped his feet on the doormat!" Betsy cried. "His mother brought him up well."

Hungrier and hungrier, they waited until almost nine.

"Mrs. Heaton will be worrying," Mr. Leonard said. "I ought to take you girls home. Claude is enough for her to worry about. I'll be back," he added to his brother. They made plans to meet.

"I thought I was tired," Betsy said, when they were raiding Mrs. Heaton's kitchen. "But I'm absolutely wide awake. Let's have a kimono party up in my room, and wait for the news at midnight."

Dolly and Jean agreed enthusiastically and so did Mrs. Heaton. Her husband had returned with Mr. Leonard to the Palace. With a big pot of tea to keep them company, the girls crowded Turkish fashion on the bed, leaving the easy chair to their hostess.

They talked a little, but mainly they listened to the noise outside. Rarely did all of them together look away from the clock.

"And this," Betsy thought, "is what the start of a war is like!"

"A quarter after eleven," Mrs. Heaton said.

A searchlight poked a bright finger into their room, but withdrew as though embarrassed.

"A quarter of midnight," Mrs. Heaton said.

"I'll wager," said Jean, "that if it lasts long enough, they'll enlist girls."

"Tosh!" said Mrs. Heaton. "Never!"

"I'd go," said Dolly. "A girl could be a messenger. She could operate an army telephone."

"Tosh!" said Mrs. Heaton again. "And listen! Just a minute to go! If Britain declares, there'll be a roar that will carry to Ireland."

They all fell silent.

The minute hand of the clock suddenly stood up right, and St. Paul's chimes began to count twelve.

Then Mrs. Heaton's predicted roar came. It could have carried to Ireland. For long minutes it swelled like the sound of the sea. Then it changed. Betsy caught Dolly's arm.

"It's singing!" she cried.

It was singing. First it was singing far off. Then it was singing outside the window in Taviton Street. Then it was singing right in the room. Mrs. Heaton was up from her chair. Jean and Dolly were off the bed. The three of them joined, it seemed to Betsy, with all London.

> *When Britain first at Heaven's command,*
> *Arose from out the azure main,*
> *This was the charter of the land,*
> *And guardian angels sung this strain,*
> *R-u-l-e B-r-i-t-a-n-n-i-a . . .*

That was Betsy's cue. The next two lines, at least, she knew. Her arms went out. Mrs. Heaton's arms, and Dolly's, and Jean's replied. In a weeping, valiant line, the four stood at the window and sang with the crowd below.

> *Rule Britannia! Britannia rule the waves,*
> *Britains never, never, never, shall be slaves.*

Mrs. Heaton broke free, clapped hands to her face, and ran from the room. Dolly followed, and Jean. Betsy continued at the window, fixed there by the magnet of the singing.

But presently, as before, her ears caught a change. The singing became words, two words, intoned over and over. Newsboys were running up and down crying them.

"War declared! War declared!"

Finally it was fused into one word.

"War! War! War!"

Betsy did the only thing she could do at such a moment. She got down on her knees.

21
THE AGONY COLUMN

"What a time," grumbled Betsy, settling herself and her umbrella on top of a bus, "what a time to have to think about money!"

She was going to the American Express Company, but this time not to *Onze Rue Scribe*. It was to Six Haymarket, S.W., in London, to her everlasting thankfulness.

Breakfast had brought a rumor that the invaluable offices were to reopen for the benefit of stranded tourists. The banks had been closed for several days by government moratorium, and money was growing scarce. The boarders at Mrs. Heaton's had been making a great joke of borrowing shillings and pence. But Betsy, needing a ticket home, could not be helped by such small change. Everyone had rejoiced with her over the morning's report.

"You must jolly well go right down!" Mr. Heaton had said. "Get some money and book your passage. Only the early birds among you Americans are likely to get home by Christmas."

"Here goes Early Bird Ray," Betsy murmured. "Jolly well going right down as fast as the bus will take her."

But she was aware that even if she found the Express Company open, the purchase of her passage home was going to take some doing.

Betsy had only one lone American Express Company check, and it was for just fifty dollars. Unless a certain piece of paper in a chamois bag, which she wore carefully pinned to her innermost garments, proved negotiable, she was, she warned herself adventurously, likely to be marooned, far from kith and kin.

Until now Betsy had always had all the money she needed. Her father's monthly remittance had been a modest but dependable mainstay. Extras had been cared for by her American Express checks, now reduced to one. And as a last resource she had always carried, in the chamois bag, a check signed in blank by her father.

"Strictly for an emergency!" Mr. Ray had warned. "But in any real jam, fill it in for whatever you need. Any bank'll cash it if you give 'em time to cable my bank in Minneapolis."

The trouble was that Mr. Ray hadn't reckoned with a war. With the war on, if Betsy gave any bank much time, she was likely to miss out on her ticket home.

"Oh, well!" she thought. "The American Express Company will just have to cash Papa's check for whatever I need!" She refused to worry, but she did object to having to think about anything so mundane as money . . . when the world was in flames, and she should be back at Heaton's, helping the other women. They were going to make shirts for soldiers.

"We'll start this very afternoon," Mrs. Heaton had planned at breakfast where there had been no sugar and no butter. "We women will sew, and one of the young men can read aloud."

That, Betsy realized, was being optimistic. Mr. Claude was already gone; Mr. Dick had enlisted; and Mr. Leonard was only waiting.

"I could certainly be doing something more useful than thinking about money!" Betsy said disgustedly. But alighting from the bus she soon saw that plenty of other people had to do it, too.

An impatient queue already stretched two blocks

from the American Express Company's office. Bobbies were patrolling it; one of them waved her into line.

"You'll save yourself a lot of trouble, Miss, if you just fall in. The door's not even open yet."

His eyes twinkled, and as she took her place, Betsy's eyes began to twinkle, too. Here were all those Americans—or most of them—who had been rushing about Europe so happily with guidebooks and cameras and usually well-filled purses. Here they were, blown by war to England and longing to be blown still farther across the wide Atlantic to their own United States.

"We lost every scrap of our baggage."

"I had my letter of credit, but a lot of good it did me."

"Uncle Sam will get us out of this hole," a booming voice proclaimed. "He looks after his nieces and nephews."

Everyone wanted to talk . . . about past adventures, or the present situation, or the gallant little Belgians, or President Wilson's neutrality proclamation.

"We won't stay neutral long!"

The door did not open and the line grew longer. It started to rain, which struck Betsy and some of the other light-hearted ones as funny. Looking around, under the bobbing umbrellas, she thought she saw Mr. Glenn of the *Columbic*, but he was too far away to be hailed.

"And probably Mrs. Sims and Mrs. Cheney are in this line somewhere. Maybe even Miss Surprise!" But not, Betsy felt sure, Mrs. Main-Whittaker. She would be dashing about Paris scooping up material. And the Wilsons, Betsy knew, were still in Derwent Water. Their last letter had sounded serene, except for concern about her.

"If worse comes to worst," she thought, "Dr. Wilson will cash a check for me." But she was reluctant to burden anyone with her problem. Everyone, it seemed, had problems enough of his own.

These seemed to lessen, however, as the doors of the Express Company opened at last.

"Don't push, laidies," the bobby urged gently. "Remember, laidies and gentlemen, you've got all day."

Some people talked about dropping out.

"But I can't drop out," said the booming voice which had once praised Uncle Sam. "I've got to get at least a thousand dollars."

"But I hear we won't be allowed more than a hundred."

"A fine note!" Uncle Sam's nephew roared. "They sold 'em to us; didn't they?"

A lady standing ahead of Betsy turned around.

"Do you have a passport?" she asked.

"No," Betsy replied, surprised. Very few people bothered with passports for a mere trip to Europe.

"Do you suppose someone might ask us for them?"

"Of course not," Uncle Sam's nephew cut in.

Betsy reached the door at last. The queuers, once inside, were being directed to various windows. Halfway to hers, Betsy stopped short at sight of a familiar figure.

"Oh, Mr. Brown!" she exclaimed.

It was, indeed, her kindly friend from Zurich. He wasn't in any of the lines. Jaunty as ever, even in a raincoat, swinging an umbrella instead of a cane, as thin as ever, too, and no less bald, he was inside an imposing railing, leaning against an imposing desk, talking with the desk's imposing occupant.

"Mr. Brown!" Betsy called again. Except for her own father there was no one, she told herself, she'd rather see.

Mr. Brown turned. His questioning gaze carried along the line from which the call had come, and his thin face broke into the pleasant smile Betsy remembered.

"Miss Ray!" he exclaimed and was alongside her in an instant. "The girl who would to Munich go! How grand that you got out! How are you?"

"I'm fine." Betsy smiled back. She took a step forward in her window line and Mr. Brown followed. "I don't suppose that Munich is very *gemütlich* now."

"I take it," he said, "that you're here for money. But I understand they won't give you much."

"Oh, I only have one fifty-dollar check!"

"Only . . . fifty dollars?" He sounded startled.

"My father's allowance comes monthly, and it hasn't come yet for August," Betsy explained.

"Do you have your passage home?"

"No. And it's sort of complicated." How wonderful, how comforting, to talk it over with Mr. Brown! "I'll have to pay by filling in a blank check my father gave me. He signed it before I left home, and said I was to save it for an emergency. I guess this is an emergency all right."

"Where do you think you can cash it?"

"I thought I'd try here. And in any case I'll cash my fifty dollars."

Mr. Brown in sudden decision drew her out of the line. "Never mind about that fifty dollars!" he said. "Let's think about getting you passage home."

He led her outside. The rain had stopped, and he swung his umbrella thoughtfully.

"The *Arabic* is sailing, I think," Betsy suggested.

"No. Not a British boat. I know. Come along." He took her arm, and they headed for the offices of the United States Lines.

Tourists were besieging it, but Mr. Brown got to an attendant who broke into a broad grin of recognition.

"Mr. Brown!"

"Good afternoon, Joe," Mr. Brown replied. "Tell me where I can find . . ." His voice died away and Betsy could not catch the name he gave. But Joe did. He grinned more broadly and led Mr. Brown, with Betsy trailing, up to a second-floor office and a desk even more imposing than the one at which she had first seen him today.

The desk's occupant looked up, and leaped to his feet in welcome.

"Van!" he shouted. "I thought you sailed a week ago."

"Hi, Petey," said Mr. Brown. "Nope! I didn't sail. And

now how glad I am! Because I can let you be kind to this very good friend of mine. Miss Ray, this is Petey Conant, a man who'll do anything for me because without my help he'd still be a Princeton freshman."

"A slander, Miss Ray," said Petey. "The truth is that I pulled Van through. My coaching got him honors in history when alone he couldn't even have told you that the Civil War was uncivil."

"Look, Petey!" said Mr. Brown. "Can you squeeze Miss Ray into the *Richmond*?"

"Gosh!" Petey said and turned serious, but Mr. Brown cut him short.

" 'Gosh, yes!' you were going to say. Good old Petey! And don't bother about doing anything special. Miss Ray knows there's a war on."

"Gosh, Van!" Petey began soberly once more, but again Mr. Brown broke in.

"Just standing room, sort of, will do in any stateroom. Won't it, Miss Ray?"

Betsy nodded, a little embarrassed, because she didn't, she felt, merit special attention . . . especially when she was in no hurry to go home. She was about to say so, when Petey gave in.

"All right," he said grudgingly. "For Miss Ray I'll do it. But while she's sharing a stateroom with three or four or more, ten thousand disappointed Americans are going to be trying to cut my throat."

"A detail!" said Mr. Brown. "Miss Ray, may I have your check?"

Betsy blushed. She looked around. "I'll have to . . ." For the chamois bag was concealed beneath many layers of undergarments . . . even her corset.

"Of course!" said Mr. Brown consolingly. He too looked around, and so did Petey. Petey beckoned to a pretty clerk and she led Betsy down a corridor and opened a door. There in the necessary privacy Betsy extracted the chamois bag and the check. She also seized the opportunity to powder her burning cheeks.

She trailed the pretty clerk back to the desk where Mr. Brown and Petey waited, smiling.

"Will you have enough, Miss Ray," Mr. Brown asked, "if Petey gives you five hundred?"

"I don't need half that," Betsy gasped. Did the man think her father was made of money? "The fare is under two hundred; isn't it?"

Petey nodded.

"Let's say two fifty then," Mr. Brown suggested. "And Petey will cash your American Express check, too. You must have something extra."

"Thank you so much!" Betsy cried when the tickets and money were safe in her purse and she and Mr. Brown were out on the street again. "My father will never be able to thank you enough. But he'll want to try." She remembered something. "You jumped off that Zurich train so fast that you didn't give me your address. This time you really must."

"Of course," said Mr. Brown, and stopped a hansom cab.

Betsy was shocked. "I don't ride in hansom cabs, for goodness sake! They're awfully nice, of course. But I bus everywhere."

"Not with that ticket in your purse," Mr. Brown replied, helping her in. "We can't have your pocket picked today. We'd never be able to squeeze another ticket even out of Petey." He stepped back to say something to the driver, then returned and held out his hand.

"Good-bye," he said. "And take all your fences boldly, but not too boldly."

"Good-bye," Betsy answered. "Oh, you've been so good!" Then she remembered again. "But you haven't given me your address for Papa."

The driver overhead clucked to his horse.

"To be sure," Mr. Brown said hastily. "Of course." He started fishing in his pockets as he had done before, and just as the cab rolled forward he found a card and thrust it into Betsy's hand.

Rolling off toward Taviton Street, she looked at it. She looked at it again.

"For goodness sake!" she exclaimed aloud. "Just wait until Tib hears of this!"

For the full name of Mr. Brown was as familiar (or even more so) to Betsy and Tib as President Woodrow Wilson's. Just Mr. Brown could be anybody. But this Mr. Brown! They had read about him in society pages for years and years!

"Imagine!" Betsy murmured. "Van Rensselaer Brown!" The eligible bachelor who was angled for by debutantes, and considered suitable for European princesses, even.

Betsy leaned back in the cab. "Tib said it for a joke . . . that I'd meet an American millionaire. But I have. And who would have thought he'd be so plain ordinary nice!"

He was even nicer than she had thought. Arriving at Mrs. Heaton's boarding house, she found he had paid the cab fare.

Her ticket was stamped for September 1, and Betsy was glad that she did not have to hurry away from London. She was grateful to be able to share a little longer in the troubles that had befallen the old city.

She shared the sorrow of the fall of Liège. Betsy and Mrs. Heaton joined the crowds that thronged St. Paul's Church for the Service of the Intercession. They sang "Rock of Ages" and "God Save the King." They sat next to a mother and daughter who held hands and wept. On the other side was an overdressed girl with a round, almost silly face. She cried until her lacy handkerchief was a soggy ball.

Going out, Betsy touched her on the shoulder.

"Good luck!" she said.

"Thanks, ducky!" answered the girl. "And bad luck to the Kaiser! And it will be bad luck for him, all right, if he gets in my Bob's way."

Everywhere in London now there were huge placards saying, "Your King and Country Need You." Sidewalk artists were picturing Earl Kitchener, who had become head of the War Office. As the congregation melted out of St. Paul's, a street organ began to grind out the tune that all the slim young soldiers were marching to these days.

It's a long way to Tipperary,
It's a long way to go . . .

They had played that, Betsy remembered, on the *Columbic* on the first night out. She had been so blue because she was leaving home . . . and because of Joe!

She still hadn't heard from him. Of course, she hadn't given him an address, and not much mail nor many cables were getting through. Still, it wasn't like Joe not to find a way—if he cared to.

Maybe, Betsy thought, he had stopped loving her. Maybe she was going to have to build her life without him. She took brave little Mrs. Heaton's arm.

They had a very special tea that day. Claude was home on leave. Mr. Dick, now in uniform, was coming. And Jean and Dolly would be there, but tomorrow they would both leave for their homes.

Dolly's book had been canceled. Jean's show would not open. Their careers were over for the duration.

"But I've done the best I could for them," Mrs. Heaton whispered to Betsy. "I've baked plum tarts."

Everyone tried to be cheerful. Claude, on the arm of his mother's chair, told some stories about new recruits. Jean and Dolly and Betsy laughed.

Mr. Dick came in, wearing his new ill-fitting uniform. He walked over to Betsy, smiling.

"Still keep up with the Agony Column?"

"Heavens, no!" Betsy answered. "I'm trying to learn to sew."

"Well, it's a good thing I clipped this," he said and reached into his pocket. "Of course," he added, "I know you aren't the only Betsy in London. But do you know anyone named Joe?"

Betsy stared at him for a long unbelieving moment. Without a word she put out her hand.

Joe hadn't forgotten her! And he had found a way! Holding the clipping fast, she ran out of the garden and up to her little white room. She sat down, with tears running down her cheeks.

> *Betsy. The great war is on but I hope ours is over. Please come home. Joe.*

She would cable a reply, Betsy thought, pushing the tears out of her eyes so she could read the wonderful words again. Perhaps she could think of something clever to say? But no, she didn't want to! She was too aware of the worry, the dread, the grief down in the garden . . . the danger hanging over her friends down there, and over London and all of Europe. She was just full of thankfulness and love.

She found a pencil.

> *Joe. Please meet S.S. Richmond, arriving New York September 7. Love. Betsy.*

She hadn't forgotten him! And she hadn't lost him! "Oh, Joe! Joe!" said Betsy.

Here Comes the Bride!

Don't miss the next book in the Betsy-Tacy series

Betsy's Wedding

by Maud Hart Lovelace

When Betsy Ray arrives in New York after a tour of Europe, her old flame Joe Willard is waiting at the dock. Before he even says hello, he asks Betsy to marry him. They've been separated for a year, and they're determined never to be apart again.

But as Betsy discovers, marriage isn't all candlelight, kisses, and roses. There's cooking, ironing, and budgeting as well—not to mention forging her career as a writer! For Betsy, the writing part comes naturally, but cooking is another matter. It's even harder than algebra–and much messier.

Luckily Betsy Ray–make that Betsy Willard—has always thrived on challenge. Her name may have changed, but her life remains as full of love and laughter as it's been since she was a little girl living on Hill Street in the first of the classic Betsy-Tacy books.

High School Hijinks!

*Join the fun with Betsy, Tacy, and the Deep Valley Crowd
in these other books in the Betsy-Tacy series:*

Heaven to Betsy

Betsy and Tacy are growing up! It's Betsy's freshman year, complete with studies aplenty and parties galore. Her dearest friends are all there, and some exciting new ones, too—including boys! Betsy's quite certain she's found heaven at Deep Valley High.

Betsy in Spite of Herself

Betsy Ray is now a sophomore, and she and her crowd are in the thick of things at Deep Valley High. Between studies and socials, the new Miss Betsye Ray is busy juggling her duties as class secretary. But the old Betsy isn't too busy to notice the oh-so-cosmopolitan stranger who has suddenly appeared on the scene. . . .

Betsy Was a Junior

Betsy's junior year promises to be a golden one, especially since one of her best friends from childhood, Tib Muller, has moved back to Deep Valley. Betsy is even inspired to start up a sorority at Deep Valley High—but the consequences are far more disastrous than she dreamed.

Betsy and Joe

Betsy's always had a crush on handsome, elusive, intriguing Joe Willard. And now, in her last year at Deep Valley High, she's determined to go with him. Of course, it's not as easy as it sounds— but when a girl is as determined as Betsy, anything is possible!